John Doe No. 2 and the Dreamland Motel

John Doe No. 2

and the Dreamland Motel

Kenneth Womack

SWITCHGRASS BOOKS   NORTHERN ILLINOIS UNIVERSITY PRESS   DeKalb

This is a work of historical fantasia. The appearance of certain historical figures is inevitable, yet some of their actions are in part motivated by the literary imagination as opposed to any adherence to pure historical accuracy. All other characters are products of the author's imagination, and any resemblance to persons living or dead is entirely coincidental.

Library of Congress Cataloging-in-Publication Data

Womack, Kenneth.
John Doe no. 2 and the Dreamland Motel / Kenneth Womack.
   p.   cm.
ISBN 978-0-87580-640-2 (pbk. : acid-free paper)
I. Title. II. Title: John Doe no. two and the Dreamland Motel.
PS3623.O59735J64 2010
813'.6--dc22
 2010010624

For Dick Caram

It's lovely to live on a raft. We had the sky up there, all speckled with stars, and we used to lay on our backs and look up at them, and discuss about whether they was made or only just happened.

—Mark Twain, *Adventures of Huckleberry Finn*

"I will have no man in my boat," said Starbuck, "who is not afraid of a whale."

—Herman Melville, *Moby-Dick*

Contents

John Doe No. 2 and the Dreamland Motel

1 The Dreamland Motel

Thwack!

Timothy McVeigh is throwing firecrackers at you from across the room.

You are sitting on top of a bedspread in what you would generously describe as a "seedy" motel. The kind of motel that rents rooms by the hour and whose deserted, rectangular swimming pool has a milky sheen to its perpetually unrippled surface. The kind of motel that has a miniature refrigerator next to a narrow, unforgiving bed into which you can feed quarters to experience a halfhearted electrical massage.

You know intuitively that the refrigerator has never seen anything north of a six-pack of beer on the food pyramid, and you are well aware that the bedspread that you are sitting on is exactly the kind of bedspread that your mother has been warning you about all these years. Patterned in a faded, greenish print of garish flowers and ornamental swirls, it is oddly slick and filmy to the touch. You are repulsed by its grotesquerie.

Your mother told you that motels never wash these things, that it's too much trouble, that it's too expensive to buy all that detergent, and, besides, no one stays in these rooms for long, anyway. That's why the TV doesn't get H.B.O., the picture isn't all that good, and the yellowed copy of *TV Guide* on the nightstand is more than two years old. Your mother warned you that whatever you do, you must never—*never*—allow your pristine, naked skin to touch the bedspread directly or you will very likely break out in a rash the next morning. A painful, potentially scarring red rash that lasts for days and days and days on end. But that's not what's bothering you right now.

What's bothering you right now is that your room is located directly next door to the motel's reception office. You could tell from the awkward glances of the burly, droopy-eyed manager with the wide forehead that she was suspicious of you and your roommate from the get-go, that you must be up to no good—that you would have to be, given that you don't look anything like the truckers and the hookers who normally pull off I-70 into her gravelly parking lot.

You know that she is putting you and your companion into Room 25 so that she can keep tabs on you—like this morning when she ran into you next to the ice machine, which is even more danger-ous, with its microbes and its mold, than the bedspread could ever hope to be, and asked what you were doing up so early, this being a weekend and all.

You know that you have already told Timothy McVeigh—you were as explicit and uncompromising as *you* can ever possibly get—that you don't like the way the manager is acting, that you should keep a low profile, that you should check into the Super 8 just off the interstate. You know that the last thing—the very *last* thing—she needs to hear from the manager's desk right next door, through the thinnest of cheap motel walls, is a bunch of firecrackers popping off.

But Timothy McVeigh doesn't listen to you. He never listens to you. Just like he's not listening to you right now when you warn him—in the most direct, most unambiguous tones that you can rea-sonably muster—that he would be very mistaken to throw another firecracker in your direction.

Sporting a blank look on his thin, emotionless face, he sits Indian-style on the twin bed opposite your own with his back resting against the far wall of your dilapidated motel room. You can tell that he is preparing to launch his next fusillade, gingerly removing yet another firecracker from the plastic sandwich baggie that rests in his lap and fidgeting with the Bic lighter in his free hand.

Your mother was very clear when she told you, all those years ago, that you must never play with firecrackers, that they are not a toy, and—here's the really important thing—that they should never discharge anywhere near the vicinity of the head region or serious injury could result. Namely, you could damage your hearing or, worse yet, go blind in one or both eyes. You repeat this to Timothy McVeigh but to no avail. You watch in revulsion as he lights another firecracker and limply tosses it in your direction, where it explodes near the lamp, toppling the *TV Guide* off of the nightstand in the process.

You advise Timothy McVeigh, in the most strident tones possible, that if he throws another firecracker, you will have no choice but to retaliate. Using terms that he could not possibly fail to understand, you tell him that you will be like President Bush taking on Saddam and the Republican Guard back in Desert Storm. You tell him that you are drawing a line in the sand. A metaphorical line, but a line nonetheless. You glare at him a little longer, indicating the gravity of your intent, but the flicker in his eyes tells you that he very seriously doubts your resolve.

"You don't have the stones," says Timothy McVeigh as he prepares to light another firecracker.

But before he can launch another salvo, you are on him with a vengeance—your preternaturally staid demeanor erupting in an unexpected fury. You are punching him about the neck and upper body with all of your might. You feel your knuckles pounding and quickening as they come into contact with the bony chest cavity beneath his faded maroon T-shirt. You surprise yourself at the sudden, involuntary nature of your attack as you begin pummeling him about the face and he extends his arms in a brashly ineffective attempt to deflect your blows down toward his shoulders and torso.

You are taken aback that he doesn't return a single punch, but that doesn't stop you from slugging him a little longer—and a little more forcefully at that. You are caught unawares and a little bothered—*Why lie about it?*—that part of you is enjoying the unfamiliar release that you are getting from beating up another person, especially *this person*, with everything you've got.

You are a little surprised that, for all of your fury and anger, the whole one-sided bout scarcely lasts thirty seconds. It seems like an eternity, and you wish that it could go on a little more, that your euphoria might last just a bit longer before it disappears altogether, returning you to that seedy motel room—Room 25 of the Dreamland Motel in Junction City, Kansas—with Timothy McVeigh.

You struggle to catch your breath as he lowers his arms in defeat, and you return to your corner of the room to regain your senses.

"I thought you people didn't go in for that sort of thing," says Timothy McVeigh, a tiny smile creeping across his narrow face as he shakes the cobwebs out of his head. He looks at you for an answer, but you fix your jaw in exaggerated silence.

"*Whatever,*" he says, his voice dripping with disgust. Timothy McVeigh stands up, dusting himself off with his hands. "Let's roll," he announces, his face and arms still glowing beet-red from your barrage of fisticuffs.

You look around the room, at the rumpled bedspreads and the spent firecrackers scattered about the floor. You realize that you have no choice, really, but to roll.

You roll.

2 Innocents Abroad

You are rolling across the Heartland in Timothy McVeigh's Road Warrior, a silver-colored 1987 Chevy Geo Spectrum with expired New York plates. You are listening to Jefferson Airplane's "White Rabbit" on a withered old cassette tape. It is the only song that Timothy McVeigh really cares for—that and "Bad Company," which you cannot stand.

Go ask Alice—you sing along with the driver, trying to be a good sport for a change—*when she's ten feet tall.*

You glance out of the passenger's seat window in the direction of the side-view mirror. The phrase "objects in mirror are closer than they appear" bisects the face staring back at you in the daylight. You take a moment to examine the quality of your reflection. Some people think you look Hispanic, exotic even, while others swear you are white. Some say you are stocky in build, others that you are scrawny. Some people think that you don't even exist at all.

Sometimes you're not so sure yourself, but it doesn't really matter.

Timothy McVeigh stares intently at the road, singing along with Grace Slick, one hand on the steering wheel, the other fingering the leather flap of the shoulder holster that carries his prized Glock. He always keeps it fully loaded, aching to be discharged. He carries an extra clip in the pouch secured around his belt, while concealing a knife—his weapon of last resort—in an ankle holster. The bullets are Black Talons, he once told you, capable of expanding and multiplying their damage after impacting soft targets.

"'Feed your head!'" Timothy McVeigh sings in his thin, nasally voice. You make a mental note to yourself that he is a terrible vocalist.

You are trying to remember what landed you in the front seat of this car, with this driver, speeding along I-40, thirty-eight miles outside of Amarillo, near Vega, Texas, pop. 840, on a direct, westerly route toward Kingman, Arizona. You have been riding with Timothy McVeigh for some ten months now, traveling from one gun show to another, casing the backwaters of Kansas, Oklahoma, Michigan, and Missouri. Meeting people. Getting into adventures. Losing your mind.

You vividly recall the day you met Timothy McVeigh at a gun show in Topeka. Not just any gun show, mind you, but the International Gun and Knife Trade Spectacular at the Expo Center. The monster of all gun shows. Your gun show of gun shows.

The details of your first encounter are picture-perfect. It's the subtlety of the moment that you seem, irrevocably, to have lost.

Feed your head!

YOU ARE TRAIPSING among the tables of the Expo Center's glitzy Exhibition Hall, where vendors, literally hundreds upon hundreds of them, hawk their wares to anyone who will listen. To anyone with a buck to spare and a thirst for gunmetal.

You are still queasy from your visit to nearby Landon Arena, where the gun show's popular product demonstrations are held. Conducted on a miniature circular stage with flashing strobe lights choreographed to the sounds of Lynyrd Skynyrd's "Saturday Night Special"—What else, really, could it be?—the demos feature bikini-clad models brandishing machine guns in absurdly sexy poses.

You cannot bring yourself to look away as one of the models seductively rubs a vintage German MG 42, its sleek narrow body burnished and ready for action, against her bright orange bikini top. You are revolted by the raw sexuality of her display, but you are also surprisingly titillated. *Your mother would not be proud.* Searching for respite from your weaker angels, you wander into the bowels of the Capitol Plaza Hotel.

Which is where you first lay eyes upon Timothy McVeigh, who is chatting up a mustached man—a man who looks, for all intents and purposes, like a disheveled, unkempt farmer—in the hotel's dimly lit Water's Edge Lounge.

You are sitting on a barstool, staring glumly at your rum and Coke (untouched), preparing to go to the gun show (as of yet, unattended).

A bar and a gun show. For Pete's sake. What's next? A brothel?

You are chiding yourself for taking things too far, for getting yourself into such a perilous situation in the first place. You are disappointed in yourself beyond words. Which is ironic, since you so rarely communicate with the outside world using actual words. You are really disgusted with yourself, your pathetic intemperate self who, if he knew what was good for him, would head back to his dorm room in Wichita at once. You are really something. Yes, you are. And what, pray tell, would you do with a *gun*, much less a mixed drink, anyway?

As you ponder this question—this most significant of questions at what is turning out, more and more, to be one of your life's most defining moments—the voice of Timothy McVeigh interrupts your mind-numbing internal deliberations.

"Well, dog my cats!" he says to the tight-lipped, emotionless, would-be farmer. "We'll empty out that candy store yet. Mark my goddamned words."

Just then you catch his eye. He can tell that you've been eavesdropping, and, rather than look away, he hardens and fixes his stare. Challenging you—no, make that *threatening you*—to look away first.

And you do, of course, shifting your glance back to the unblemished cocktail resting on the bar, the drink's ice melting and diluting the cola and the alcohol in the process.

"That's what I thought," says Timothy McVeigh before turning his attention back to his tousled companion.

After a short while you leave the bar, still restless and unquenched. You gird your courage and return to Exhibition Hall, where you are washed away by a sea of a thousand patrons, almost uniformly male. You are surprised that there aren't more people wearing camouflage. You pace in between the tables, row after row of them, guns of all shapes and sizes for as far as the eye can see. You are staggered by the amount of available firearm accessories, ranging from ammunition and holsters to rifle scopes and reloading equipment. And then there are the knives—scores of them, steely blades of all natures and stripes. A deadly-looking crossbow catches your eye. As does a replica bowie knife. You even spy a vintage Japanese samurai sword.

As you take it all in, a man in a Milwaukee Brewers baseball cap tries to sell you the new TEC-9. "It's molded polymer," he tells you. "You can't go wrong!" As if on cue, you back away from the table and silently lose yourself in the crowd before another vendor corners you into a lengthy pitch about the Walther P88. As he presents the pistol for your inspection, you have to admit, if only to yourself, that it's a heckuva gun.

"Light. Compact. Great action," the vendor exclaims. Like a master car salesman, he coolly unbuttons his smart blue blazer and goes about the business of getting into your head. A gleaming lapel pin announces him as "Tosh Berman, Licensed Firearms Distributor."

What kind of name is Tosh? you wonder. *Tosh Tosh B'gosh,* you think to yourself automatically.

"What do we need to do to seal this weapons deal today?" Berman asks, all confidence and a Crest-flavored smile. "I'm ready, willing, and motivated to dot the i's and cross the t's." He nearly closes the deal, too. If it weren't for the reams of paperwork that he produced—you hadn't counted on such a multilayered paper trail—you would be the proud owner of the slick, double-action pistol.

As if your visit to Topeka couldn't get any more surreal, you spend much of the afternoon in the company of two biker types in Exhibition Hall's snack bar. You sit down innocently enough in the booth next to theirs, only to be drawn, in spite of your reluctance, into the orbit of their conversation. Amazingly, they don't know the first thing about guns.

"We're here for the politics, dude," the older biker reports, a patch of gray hair migrating beyond his black leather cap. "It's about freedom," he adds.

"And it's also about our tapes," his younger companion confides. He's wearing a red bandanna. A pack of cigarettes reveals its distinctive shape beneath the fabric of his short-sleeved white T-shirt. He reminds you of Schneider, the irreverent apartment superintendent a million years ago on TV's *One Day at a Time.*

You must have mistakenly indicated your interest in the merchandise—an arched eyebrow perhaps? too much eye contact?—because no sooner had Bandanna uttered the word *tapes* than he presents a boxful of homemade cassettes for your examination.

"Let me ask you something," he says, glancing back and forth between you and his leather-clad friend, who seems to be grinning uncontrollably at the prospect of finally moving some of the bootleg tapes that he had hauled all the way to Topeka on his chopper. You can't be sure, but you're almost certain that he licks his lips in unrestrained anticipation. You wonder to yourself, Am I this much of a mark?

"What do you know about the life, work, and untimely death of Randy Rhoads?" the younger man asks, adopting the dramatic tones of a hushed whisper. This was serious stuff.

The blankness of your stare tells him everything he needs to know.

"Randy Rhoads," he announces, "was the most talented axeman of his generation. Shit, of every generation. He had a spark, man."

"But that's not all," Leather Cap adds.

"Damn right, that's not all," Bandanna replies. "Quiet Riot. *The Blizzard of Ozz!*"

"Yeah, and shredding. Do you know what *shredding* is?" Leather Cap asks, before launching into an air-guitar solo in order to demonstrate the technique.

Ah, so *that's* shredding. You make a mental note to yourself.

"Randy was shredding long before the metal wannabes who are playing today," says Leather Cap.

"Do you know what Ozzy said the first time he heard Randy tune it up?" Bandanna asks. You cannot conceal your bewilderment. But they hardly seem to care.

"'God has entered my life,'" answers Leather Cap.

"'*God has entered my life!*'" Bandanna repeats—adopting the impassioned rhetoric, improbable as it may seem, of a fire-and-brimstone preacher.

"And do you know why God is no longer here?" Leather Cap inquires.

You don't have the first clue, of course, but nobody's waiting for your answer. Besides, it occurs to you that Leather Cap is broaching a much larger debate than mere mortals such as the biker dudes and you can conclude at the International Gun and Knife Trade Spectacular. And in Topeka, Kansas, no less.

"March nineteenth, nineteen eighty-two," Leather Cap retorts, as if responding to his own question. Which, of course, he is.

"March freakin' nineteenth, nineteen eighty-two," Bandanna echoes, shaking his head from side to side in obvious mourning and disdain. You don't know what to do. You scan the room, searching for a means of escape. Any hasty exit will do.

"It was a plane," Leather Cap decries, looking wistfully into the distance—perhaps at the Sno-Cone machine humming merrily along near the entrance to the snack bar?

"It was a goddamned Beechcraft Bonanza," Bandanna interrupts, "and when that dumb motherfucker buzzed the tour bus—*Who buzzes a tour bus with a private plane?*—the wing clipped the vehicle and caromed into the house—"

"It was a *mansion*, dude," Leather Cap interjects. "The plane catapulted into a mansion."

"And what—*what?*—was Randy doing on that goddamned plane?" Bandanna asks, looking up toward the heavens for spiritual relief that will never arrive.

"Motherfucking pilot was jazzed on cocaine," Leather Cap adds, "but not Randy. Toxicology showed he was clean as a whistle. *No drugs.*"

"No drugs," Bandanna agrees. "All art."

"Over and out at twenty-five years old," says Leather Cap.

"That's all she wrote," Bandanna adds.

"That's *all* she wrote," Leather Cap avers.

"Do you know how we celebrate Randy's memory?" Bandanna asks. You shake your head. You really have no idea whatsoever.

"The music," Leather Cap answers.

"That's right—the music," Bandanna responds. As he brushes his fingers across the box of crudely labeled Maxell cassette tapes, you realize—belatedly, as always—that the tragic story of Randy Rhoads was the pitch. The tapes are the product. Which means that you must be the mark. But you came here, you remind yourself, to see the guns. How is this possible? you wonder. How do you manage to find yourself—time and time again—in these situations?

As if to demonstrate the timeless quality of their wares, Leather Cap stands up and launches into—right there in the snack bar, mind you—an elaborate air-guitar solo.

"'Life's a bitter shame,'" he sings. "'I'm going off the rails on a crazy train!'"

As he gyrates and struts in front of the booth, shredding along with the invisible music in his head, a space opens up in front of your seat as Bandanna rises up to jam with his partner in silent concert.

It's a space that must be reckoned with, and there's no way, by gum, that you're going to ignore such a welcome exit sign.

You thrust yourself forward, as if going through a portal from March 19, 1982, and beyond the Sno-Cone machine into the vast anonymity of Exhibition Hall. You are suddenly, ineffably free. And for all you know, Bandanna and Leather Cap are back there still, performing their air-guitar solos for the ages.

3 The Shooter

In all likelihood, you would have never set eyes on Timothy McVeigh again had it not been for the biker dudes and their despairing tale about the late great Randy Rhoads.

As you make your hurried exit from the snack bar, you find yourself face-to-face, yet again, with the Walther P88 salesman. When he sees you reentering the main floor of Exhibition Hall, he can hardly contain himself. "Let's make a deal!" Berman announces as he models the gun for your inspection. In your usual, bashful way, you duck the issue entirely by making an abrupt about-face—

—an abrupt about-face that plants you firmly in front of Timothy McVeigh's booth at the International Gun and Knife Trade Spectacular. He's staring intently at the book that lies open in front of him. A hardcover. From what you can tell, he's about halfway finished. You strain your eyes in a feeble attempt to decipher the title, but you could never read upside down. You don't have that particular skill.

The first thing you notice is that his table is rife with guns—no surprise there—but his impressive collection of weaponry (a nifty stiletto, a shiny steel revolver, and the contraband components for constructing a homemade silencer) is overwhelmed by, of all things, paper. Mounds of it. Paper in the form of bumper stickers. Paper in the form of brochures and pamphlets. Paper in the form of crude photocopies of something called *The Turner Diaries,* which Timothy McVeigh has generously labeled "For free—yes, free!"—with a faded yellow Post-it note.

You make a mental note that all of his wares are pocked with yellow Post-it notes in various states of discoloration. "Free—take one!" is affixed to a brochure advertising the Michigan Militia. "From Iraq—Operation Desert Storm!" trumpets the Post-it note dangling from the knife. They had stilettos in Desert Storm? You thought it was an air war. "Used by real cops—in the line!" reads yet another faded Post-it note resting lazily next to the revolver. You wonder if he knows that they have other colors besides yellow now.

And then there's Timothy McVeigh himself. He looks up from his book and catches your gaze—and holds it. He doesn't let go, turning his head ever so slightly, but *never ever blinking.* This annoys you on some deeply primal level. You're irritated with Timothy McVeigh after seeing him for only the second time in your entire life. This calls for another mental note.

Staring up at you from his position at the table—his blue eyes glaringly, penetratingly intersecting with your own—Timothy McVeigh cuts an unremarkable physical specimen. He sports a closely cropped head of light brown hair, his thin, angular face descending into a narrow, almost nonexistent chin. His legs, crossed slightly about the calves, extend with some length toward the right side of the table, suggesting that he is a man of considerable height. You are not impressed.

His clothes are equally nondescript. If you spoke of such things—and, let's face it, *you don't*—you would describe his attire as gun-show casual: an orange hooded sweatshirt over a pea-green T-shirt, blue jeans, and a pair of well-worn Nike tennis shoes. You are not dazzled by his choice of ensemble.

"What can I do you for, friend?" says Timothy McVeigh, with a hint of sarcasm in his voice. No blinks. "'Cause there's plenty here to see," he adds, wasting little time as he shifts into gun-show mode. "You've got your silencer," he says, holding up the striated cylinder for your review. "All you need is one-hundred and ninety-five dollars and a dream," he points out, "and that includes the whole kit—and I'll throw in a bumper sticker for free." You have almost $300 in your wallet, you think to yourself, but little in the way of dreams. At least not anymore.

Timothy McVeigh lifts the silencer up to his right eye, posing it like a miniature telescope. "This here'll save a lot of marriages—*if you know what I mean,*" he adds with a hint of conspiracy in his voice. He smiles a little. Still no blinks.

"Then you've got your steel-plated revolver," he observes, extending the handgun in your direction. This must be his favorite, you think to yourself. You are drawn to the shiny weapon.

"This is a cop's gun," he says, fondling the pistol ever so slightly. "Shoot, this ain't no man's gun. It's a gun's gun. A classic. This baby doesn't get the lead out—*it puts the lead in.*" It occurs to you that he must employ the same shtick at all the gun shows. That he's been using the same tired lingo for years. You make another mental note.

Does he ever blink? you wonder to yourself, looking at Timothy McVeigh looking at you from across the table.

"Do you ever talk?" he asks, unblinkingly.

You remain silent. Hunching your shoulders upward, you gesture toward the revolver.

"Excellent choice!" says Timothy McVeigh, standing up from the table and gently placing the weapon in your hands. "This here's a Smith and Wesson AirLite with a .357 Remington Mag. Stainless steel. Rubber grip. Holds five rounds that will explode and penetrate like the lightning punch of Jesus Christ himself."

You cradle the gun in your hands. Jesus Christ himself, huh? Very convincing.

"It may look heavy," he adds. "But that's deceptive. At just over two pounds, the AirLite is an all-terrain weapon. Suitable for any environment. Easy to conceal. Amazingly versatile for its size and power. If it's balls to the wall, there are far worse guns to have on your side."

But when, exactly, would you find yourself balls to the wall? Your twentieth-century Brit. lit. seminar? Biology lab? The dining hall? You briefly imagine yourself practicing tactical maneuvers in the lunch line, diving across the dining tables—cheeseburgers, pizza, and French fries careening in every direction, the other students ducking and hiding as you position yourself, AirLite in hand, for your last, desperate stand in the student mess.

As Timothy McVeigh waits idly by, you trace the contours of the weapon with your hand.

"You can trust me," he says. Still no blinks. "This is a top-grade weapon. And do you know why you can trust me, why my opinion on this particular subject happens to matter?"

You look at him blankly. You really have no idea.

"Because unlike all of these other morons," he says, gesturing around the room, "I'm not just some slick salesman bent on separating you from your money. I'm a shooter, which is to say that I know guns, and—more importantly—that I know what makes a good gun. And this here is not just a fine defensive weapon with surefire accuracy—although it most certainly is. It's a first-strike pistol. Do you know what that means?"

You don't. You really don't.

"It means that when you squeeze the trigger, your man is going down for the count. He's not getting back up, he's not reloading, and he's surely not taking your ass out when you're making your getaway. *Capiche*?"

You nod your head. Got it. *Capiche.*

"But listen up," he says. "This gets even better."

How can it possibly get any better? you wonder.

"I've got seven words for you," says Timothy McVeigh. "No license, no paperwork, no problem."

You count silently to yourself. That's only six words.

You work up the most exaggerated look of incredulity that you can marshal, even tilting your head to one side as if to suggest that he's yanking your chain.

"I know what you're thinking," Timothy McVeigh observes. "The Brady Bill, five-day waiting periods, and all that other blah blah blah. Like I said before, it's no problem. I'm an unlicensed gun salesman. You might even call me a collector. And that means I'm unrestricted—all sales are final. No deposits, no returns. You can take this beauty home with you today. Heck, I'll even gift wrap it for you. I might even be able to round up a to-from card, if you like."

You reach for your wallet. You cannot believe that you're doing this—crimes against humanity and all things decent in broad daylight. Your mother never warned you about purchasing firearms. She never had to. *Would never even thought of having to.*

"Well, all right!" says Timothy McVeigh. "That'll be two bills."

You carefully count out ten $20 bills and hand them over to Timothy McVeigh—straight from the cash machine and into the coffers of the gun show with your wallet serving as the middleman, an unwitting accomplice in the degradation of all that should be right and holy in your world. But no longer. Nevermore. All this iniquity, and you didn't so much as take a sip of the rum and Coke back in the lounge.

"Just let me get you a receipt for that," says Timothy McVeigh as he hands you the weapon, now resting quietly, unobtrusively inside a tattered Adidas shoebox. So much for gift wrapping.

As he rifles through a stack of wrinkled papers, you catch a glimpse of the open book lying prone on his sales table. *Say "No!" to the New World Order,* screams its spine.

You grasp the shoebox with a tantalizing combination of fear and exhilaration. Now that you've finally gone and done it—now that you've actually purchased a handgun—you're not exactly sure how to proceed. You hadn't planned this far in advance. When to leave? Where to go? What to do?

"You be careful now," Timothy McVeigh cautions, leaning forward on the palms of his outstretched hands. "The cons and the scam trade are everywhere." He glances from left to right, at no one in particular, as if to underscore the gravity of his words. He hands you a pair of bumper stickers. Gun-show souvenirs perhaps? Party favors? Consolation prizes?

"These are gratis," he says and smiles. "I can tell you're a patriot."

You carefully run your eyes over the bumper stickers that he helpfully places in your hands. "For peace sake, stop the U.N." What gives with the U.N.? you wonder. "Remember Waco, Remember Ruby Ridge!" Waco and Ruby Ridge. No mystery there—not even for you.

Before you can turn away from Timothy McVeigh's booth, he stops you short, hand outstretched.

"I'm Tim—Tim Tuttle," he says. "Good to meet you."

You accept his hand into your own, gripping it as firmly as you can reasonably muster.

You clear your throat and tell him your name, your voice brimming over with reluctance and uncertainty. You don't really talk all that much—about anything.

"Nice name," Timothy McVeigh responds. "Short and to the point. Kinda rolls off the tongue."

He releases your grip.

"See you around, JD," he remarks, a broad smile unfolding across his face. He blinks. Finally.

"One more thing," says Timothy McVeigh. "I'll need your address for my mailing list."

He hands you a blank address card, and you dutifully oblige, scribbling down your dorm room address. Fat lot of good that'll do him, you think to yourself.

"Wichita, huh?" he says. "I pass through there from time to time on my way out West."

You glance downward at the bumper stickers again, nodding thankfully for his gesture.

You don't have the heart to tell him that you have no place to affix the bumper stickers, that you don't even own a car. That you rode an old Greyhound bus—140 miles of screaming children, lousy fast food, and carbon monoxide-induced nausea—all the way from Wichita just to attend the gun show. You don't have the heart to tell him that you're a firearms novice, that you're really a renegade college student who doesn't have the first clue about much of anything. A renegade college student. You like the sound of that.

And you certainly don't have the heart to tell him that you're not entirely sure that you're a patriot—at least not in the way that he means it. Or that you think he means it.

Clutching the prized shoebox against your chest, you make your way to the exit. Past the snack bar and the humming Sno-Cone machine. Through the double doors of Exhibition Hall. Into the open air.

You'll show them now. They'll never know what hit them.

You are aloft. Into the free and open air.

4 My Platonic Sweetheart

You are watching Gina as she reclines in the chaise lounge in the backyard of her Wichita boardinghouse. You are thinking to yourself that she is immaculate in her white bikini top and periwinkle shorts, the sun splashing down in spangles across her exacting face, her strawberry blonde hair pulled back in a twist behind her head. A pair of oversized sunglasses rests on her face. You gaze at her lips, her dewy, vibrant lips.

You feel that there is something dirty about her—racy even—as she lounges in the sun. The downy hairs above her navel glistening in the daylight, her lithe arms stretching along her sides as she adjusts the line of her shorts with her hands.

You adore them—her pretty pouty lips. You cannot help yourself, but you do.

You think about how different she is from the girl you first met in French class a million years ago during your freshman term. Back then, she dressed impeccably—and prudishly, too. She was more prim. More proper. More demure. She was more—how should you phrase it?—*she was more like you.*

But now you feel that she has become wanton. She is seductive. She even seems a little forbidden. She has become wrong for you. So very, very wrong for you.

You observe as Gina abruptly gets up from the chaise lounge and pulls a pair of black sweatpants over her shorts. You gaze at her as she walks away from you toward the boardinghouse, the word "trouble" stenciled in purple letters across the backside of her tight sweatpants. You know that's right.

YOU HAVE BEEN FAWNING over Gina for more than a year. Trailing her around campus, vying for her attentions in the cafeteria, cramming with her for exams in the library study carrels. You have been doting on her every whim.

Or so you thought.

You remember the first time you laid eyes on Gina. You were at a dormitory mixer. It was movie night. *Joe Versus the Volcano.* You like Tom Hanks and Meg Ryan, but you thought the movie was pretty stupid. Not very realistic either. It was about some guy with a brain cloud.

A brain cloud. You wonder if that kind of condition is covered by medical insurance. Probably not, you think. Probably doesn't even exist.

You fondly recall the after-movie snack. The giant Subway sandwich. Your favorite party food. Six feet of turkey and provolone. And all the fixin's. Yummy.

And then you see her.

Gina Watson.

Quelle surprise! And on movie night, no less.

You sit behind Gina in Madame Wilson's French class. Blonde and cherubic in a staid blue dress with a conservative lace top. Beautiful and appealing. *But not too beautiful, not too appealing.* You are safe here, you think to yourself. Safe as milk.

This girl will never like you. Can't possibly like you. Will never reciprocate. It simply isn't going to happen. You are relieved. You turn your attention back to the giant Subway sandwich. You are safe. Safe as milk and cookies.

You go back to gorging yourself on a wedge of cold-cut nirvana. But then you are suddenly and unexpectedly interrupted—still chewing upon a hefty mouthful of sandwich—by Gina's confident, inquisitive voice.

"You're in French 102, right?" she asks.

How forward. How very forward—you think to yourself—but intriguing. You are impressed with her chutzpah. You wish that you had some chutzpah of your own.

With chunks of sandwich ballooning in your cheeks, you nod your head affirmatively. Yes. French 102. Indeed. You hastily swallow your exquisite bite of turkey and provolone.

Comment allez-vous? you ask, trying to be clever. Trying to use the language of your shared semi-bilingualism.

Oh, my God, you think. Have you already blown it? Should you have used the *tu* form instead? After all, you have been sitting behind her all year long. Surely that merits some kind of familiarity. Right? You urge yourself to feel safe. To feel at ease.

Safe. Safety. Milk and cookies.

Without transition, Gina breaks into a detailed analysis of her academic schedule. There's your French class, of course, with its conjugations and its participles. No problem there, she tells you. She's acing French. Ditto for Statistics, "which is like high school all over again," she laments. No, the real problem, she reports—the greatest obstacle to her unerring happiness and contentment—is her mandatory Foundations of Faith course.

"The Kingdom of God, my ass," she says.

How does such corrosive language emanate from such a divinely beautiful mouth? you wonder.

"I've got a real zealot for a professor," Gina continues. "She vows—*up and down, all the time*—that she only wants to help us enjoy a more intimate life with God, a life of meditation and simplicity. That she'll assist us in experiencing a deeper, more nuanced journey devoted to faith and prayer. But then the exams are a total bitch—"

There's that mouth again, you think.

"—and my professor, Dr. Swearingdon—She's probably a dyke!—is always judging me. *Me.* And all I do is just sit there, with my understated clothing and my overstated politeness, and take it from her. Class after class. Never making eye contact but feeling her wrath as she scolds us—not specifically by our names, but you know what I mean—for bringing shame to the flock. And why should I feel bad anyway if I like listening to Madonna? It's not like I'm wearing a leather bustier to class, is it?"

Madonna. How disheartening. You make a mental note to yourself about your disappointment, your heartbreak, at this awful confession. Perhaps it isn't meant to be? Perhaps you're not her Lucky Star after all?

Gina stares back at you—hopefully, patiently waiting for a response. Without breaking eye contact, she cocks her head to one side, as if to study you from a slightly different perspective, a new angle that might reveal something unusual, something clandestine about you. She nods to herself knowingly, confidently—as if she has discovered what she is looking for in your blankness, your invisibility.

"Damn!" she suddenly exclaims. "My ride's here. Gotta go. Let's meet tomorrow night at Stanley. We can study for the midterm."

You nod approvingly, although you are not entirely certain that you approve. *Who is this girl?* you think to yourself.

YOU NEVER ACTUALLY have a first date with Gina, at least not in the traditional sense. You simply begin meeting up with her regularly to study together at Stanley—the Edmund Stanley Library, with the dull rectangularity of its bland, 1960s-era architecture and its odor of musty unkemptness. Like stale mothballs. Like visiting your grandmother's house.

You decide to bring your roommate, Dakota Fish, along that first night in the library. He's already had French 102, and you figure you can use the intellectual ammunition in case things get out of hand, language-wise. That's the real danger with foreign language courses, you think to yourself. All of that talking. So many talkers, talking all of the time. It never stops.

Besides, you remind yourself, there is always safety in numbers.

You share a dorm room with Dakota Fish in the Academic Village. He is a Native American scholarship student from Oklahoma. Of Shawnee heritage, he is a grand descendant of Tecumseh, the feared and able warrior, bearing his nose ring for all to see as he battled against miscegenation and the unlawful dispersal of tribal lands.

You like Dakota Fish just fine, but there are pluses and minuses— that's for sure—regarding the degree to which you can tolerate him. To which you can tolerate anyone.

Pluses:
- He is exceedingly clean, a regular bather who knows how to use a bar of soap and a comb—although not necessarily in tandem. Good hygiene merits a gold star in your book.
- He doesn't talk too much—certainly more than you do, but not too overly much. This merits an extra gold star.
- He knows his way around a menu. You admire a person who enjoys fine cuisine. Also, his manners are impeccable—keeps his napkin in his lap, knows how to use his salad fork, the whole nine yards.

Minuses:
- He is ridiculously, over-the-top handsome. He wears his long black hair in a headband. Neatly arrayed and not too ostentatious—you have to respect that. But you cannot stand the way the coeds coo over him as if he were a pinup model. It's unseemly in your book. Crass, even.
- He is a tad—just a slight tad—on the arrogant side. And it's not just the looks (although they certainly help). He is significantly overconfident—as if nothing in the world can upset his place in

its delicate balance. You respect a guy who possesses a healthy dose of self-disgust and personal uncertainty. Dakota Fish is not that person. Not in the slightest.

• See items one and two under Minuses. They really get your goat.

YOUR STUDY SESSION with Gina goes off without a hitch. Several other members of your French 102 class are there, too—although you hadn't really expected them to be invited. So much for having a cozy study date with Gina. But no matter.

Dakota Fish performs his role beautifully—but not *too* beautifully. He relaxes on the margins of the study group, pacing back and forth among the library carrels, interrupting now and again to correct a failed conjugation—"that's *j'aime* not *j'ai aimé*"—or to add shades of meaning to your understanding of French vocabulary: "*le dauphin* is both a sea mammal and a successor. *D'accord?*" It is quite a show really, *but not too much of a show.* You are very thankful for that. Or at least you think so at the time.

And then there is Gina—*Gina, Gina, my pretty ballerina!* you think to yourself—sitting next to you in the library. Decked out in a green pastel dress—*but not too decked out,* mind you. She is like a delicate, unobtrusive flower. *La fleur magnifique!* And you are almost certain, or at least as certain as *you* can be, that she is hanging on your every word. As if what you have to say matters. You are unusually confident in her presence, giddily conjugating your way to the very heavens. *Je désire! Tu désires! Il désire! Nous désirons! Vous désirez! Ils désirent!*

AND THAT'S HOW it all began. It's that simple, really. First, you become study buddies, then best friends, then lovers.

Well, not exactly lovers. But certainly companions. *Intimate companions who are not intimate.* It doesn't sound as good when you phrase it that way, you think to yourself. Not very good at all.

But why, for that matter, is our degree of intimacy with one another always such an important barometer for our self-esteem? You have no answer.

Everything is going along swimmingly with Gina. Your relationship really seems to be going places. Good places—places your mother could respect, could feel good about in the morning, could speak proudly and solemnly about in front of her friends and relations back in Ohio. At meetings. At the grocery store. Around the neighborhood.

And the *friendship* with Gina works, you think. The friendship works like a charm. Friendship with a girl. A beautiful, diffident girl. Things are going along just fine, you surmise. That is, until yesterday, when Gina did the most amazing, inexplicable thing.

Without warning, she abruptly quit school.

How could she do it? *How could she quit the life?* A life of simplicity and honesty. A life where everything is sacramental, where every day is holy.

You cannot believe what is happening. You are thunderstruck. You never saw it coming. *Should have seen it coming.*

If everyone else you've ever known can meet together as one—sitting quietly and waiting upon the Lord—then what gives Gina the right to stop?

WITHOUT KNOCKING, Gina bolts into your dorm room in the Academic Village, drops her pink backpack on the floor, and, stretching upon the very tips of her tippy toes, leans into the space above your neckline with her face. Your personal space.

"This is what I want to do. I wanna do this," she says as she presses her lips against your own. They are warm and soft and wet—all at the same time. You want to pull away, but you can't. *You won't.*

"Put your hands on me," she commands.

You stare at her blankly. You weren't ready for this. Not by a long shot.

"Now," she demands. Not rudely nor angrily, but with the confidence of knowing exactly what she wants.

You place your hands limply on her shoulders.

"No. Like this," she says, gripping your hands in her own and placing them upon her lower back while pressing her torso tightly against you in one swift motion.

You suddenly feel like you are developing a brain cloud of your own—but in a good way. You make a mental note.

5 Eff You

"It'll be a cold day in hell before I go back to that fucking place again," Gina announces as you enter her bedroom at the boarding-house.

One lousy day as a dropout and her language continues to devolve. To devolve utterly. You make a mental note to maintain your own language standards even as hers erode into sailordom. At least one of you has to keep from slipping completely into the abyss. From being carried away by the river. By the river of no return.

"Dr. Swearingdon can suck my titties," she continues. You have never even thought about Gina's titties—much less about Dr. Swearingdon sucking on them. You try hard for a moment, but you cannot even begin to conjure up the requisite image in your mind. Would Dr. Swearingdon be sitting or standing during such a proce-dure? you wonder to yourself.

"Dr. Swearingdon can judge me all she wants now. I'm tired of being responsible for the quality of my inner light—whatever that is. If I want to listen to Madonna, I'll listen to Madonna. End of story."

The light is forever, and the light is free, you think to yourself auto-matically.

"And by the way," she adds, "happy birthday!"

It is your birthday, you think to yourself, and you are having a conversation about Gina's titties and Madonna. You could never have seen that coming.

It is your birthday, and Gina has just returned from officially withdrawing from the university. It is your birthday, and it is Gina's spiritual deathday. She is trading in one life for another on the day in which you were given life. It is all a tangle, you think to yourself. A curious and beguiling tangle.

"I got you a gift!" she says, squealing with excitement and planting a kiss on your cheek. This will take some getting used to, you think. This random kissing, these marks of affection. You notice that Gina is wearing red cowgirl boots. Where did these come from? you wonder to yourself. You don't recall these accessories among her prop closet.

For your birthday, Gina presents you with a notepad with the words "Jot It Down" helpfully printed at the top of every page. It's a practical gift, you think to yourself. A practical gift for a practical person.

You are my Gina, Gina, my pretty ballerina, you say gratefully.

"And you are my big stud," she says. Trying to be sassy. Trying to be flirtatious. *Trying too hard.*

And then Gina is on you with a vengeance, with a fury that you have never seen. She is on top of you, pressing down on your limbs, her mouth searching, voraciously, for your own. And before you know it, you and Gina are *doing it.* Which is significant, in and of itself, because *you've never done it before.* Arguably, you've never done *anything* before. But that's beside the point right now as Gina gyrates above you, lost in her erotic bliss.

And then it occurs to you, *belatedly as usual,* that she's done this kind of thing before. And here you are—inexperienced you. Shiny and new. Touched for the very first time.

But before you can consider the issue further—before you can create a taxonomy of the implications—you lose yourself in the sweet oblivion of the moment.

YOU REMEMBER THAT the weirdness began almost immediately, that things started to change almost as soon as you refastened the button fly on your 501 jeans in Gina's bedroom. Your mother warned you that sex changes everything, that you will never be the same again after sharing your body—your temple—with another person. Your mother also warned you that there are few things worse than the green-eyed monster of jealousy. Very few things indeed.

You realize, walking home that night from Gina's boardinghouse, that you will never be Gina's study buddy again. That you cannot possibly be. And while you now know precisely what Gina's titties look like—that they're round and firm with perky pink nipples— you recognize intuitively that something in the calculus of your personal universe has shifted irrevocably, has become imperceptible to you.

But that doesn't stop you from doing it all over again the very next evening.

You and Gina are watching a rerun of *Murder, She Wrote.* Gina is wearing a skimpy pink T-shirt with the letters F.U. emblazoned across the front. And you are in love. Hopelessly, ridiculously in love. Or maybe that's just the sex talking, you think to yourself.

You cannot believe this is happening. Your temple is in ruins, utterly in ruins, and the river is carrying you away—its currents vast and deep.

"Oh my God. You think you're going to hell, don't you?" says Gina.

Of course you do.

"For God's sake, JD. It's just fucking."

And then it hits you—hits you hard. You are Gina's veritable slave. You are her slave of love. And there is a rival, somewhere out there, for her affections.

You feel a sudden, powerful urge to do it again—only this time you are on *her* with a vengeance. Your human bondage becomes your fury. It is quick, intense, and undeniably physical.

"That was terrifying," says Gina as you roll off of her.

You wonder if that is a good thing or a bad thing. You are confused. A look of bewilderment crosses your face.

"Youwannagoagain?" she says, the words tumbling out of her mouth like a manic, babbling brook.

You remain silent. *What was that?*

"Do you want to go again?" she says in exaggerated enunciation. You go again.

YOU REALIZE THAT YOU have become addled in your addiction, in your need to possess Gina. All of her. All of the time.

Your mission has become ineluctably clear.

Early the next morning, you board the Greyhound bus for the International Gun and Knife Trade Spectacular. Your gun show of gun shows.

A FEW DAYS LATER, you return to your dorm room after taking a makeup exam in your biology class. Human sexuality. What a web. A web of a thousand lies.

Dakota Fish is there, of course, with his French language tapes and his textbooks. And his hair.

And so is Gina, presumably waiting for you. Desperate for your return from parts unknown. From the destination of your wanderlust.

So this is how it's going to go down? you think to yourself. You struggle for the words. Words of accusation. Words of recrimination. Words of love, even.

But then it happens—a rap at the door. The most remarkable, unexpected thing. *Deus ex machina.* Perhaps God is in here somewhere?

you think. Your shoulders relax. Your heart rate lessens.

"Well, howdy, folks," says a familiar voice.

You cannot believe it. This doesn't seem possible.

"I'm Tim Tuttle," he says, shaking hands with Dakota Fish, nodding at Gina, winking in your direction.

Timothy McVeigh is clearly struck by the image of Dakota Fish, his jet-black hair done up stylishly in his headband.

"Are you an Injun?" he asks.

"He's a Native American," Gina interrupts. "You need to get with the lingo. It's the 1990s, for God's sake."

"There's no need for political correctness among friends," says Timothy McVeigh. "And we're all friends here, right?"

LATER THAT EVENING, you are eating supper with Timothy McVeigh at Gina's boardinghouse. You are amazed that he is here. Gina is simply amazed that you actually have a friend. Any friend.

"So, JD tells me that you hate the government," says Gina.

"That about sums it up," Timothy McVeigh responds, shifting uncomfortably in Gina's overstuffed chair. You begin shifting uncomfortably on the couch, thinking about how you recently had relations with Gina in that same overstuffed chair.

"How does one go about hating the government?" she responds to Timothy McVeigh, a little too flirty for your taste. "I mean, you can't go and make a career out of something like that, right?"

"Let's put it this way," he answers. "What are you going to do when the government comes—house to house, door to door—and demands that you turn over your guns?"

"I guess I'd just have to bite my tongue and hand over my hot rollers—or, failing that, hit my knees and inveigle the storm troopers the old-fashioned way," she answers with a wink in her voice. Inveigle. Only a fallen English major would say *inveigle*. She's so very precious, you think to yourself.

"It's a serious question," says Timothy McVeigh, "but apparently you're fresh out of serious answers." He smiles.

"Oh, I have a serious answer all right," she responds coquettishly. "I don't own any damn guns. That's my serious answer. But I'm steeped in hot rollers."

You can tell that Timothy McVeigh is nonplussed.

So are you.

AS GINA STRAIGHTENS UP the kitchen, Timothy McVeigh begins nonchalantly going through her mail.

What are you doing? you ask incredulously.

"You can learn a lot about a person from their postal activities. Especially their bills."

Oh my God.

"Like Gina's phone bill, for instance. Check this out," he says, gesturing toward several rows of telephone calls made to your dorm room on campus.

"I guess I might as well go ahead and ask the $64,000 question," he exclaims. "Were these calls to you or the Injun?"

You feel a rush of blood to your head as he hands you the phone bill.

"From the look on your face, I'm banking on the Injun," says Timothy McVeigh.

Can this get any worse? you ask yourself.

ON THE DAY THAT things get worse—considerably worse—you wake up early and walk, briskly, the two miles that separate your dormitory on campus from Gina's boardinghouse.

You knock on the door—loudly, vigorously—three times.

After what seems like an eternity, a groggy Gina, still lost in sleep, answers the door. She smiles at you through her somnambulant haze.

I think you are a female dog, you say to Gina.

"You mean you think I'm a bitch?" she replies.

You don't answer.

"Am I your skanky fucking bitch?" she asks, grinning lasciviously.

You still don't answer, refusing to play along.

Gina giggles to herself, oblivious to your anger, your jealousy.

She is winning. You know that she is winning and that she will win.

She extends a delicate hand in your direction, leading you to her bedroom. To your sweet oblivion. Your sweet, sweet oblivion.

Have you become this predictable, this easy to manipulate? This easy to *own*? In the span of a week—*seven scant days*—your life has gone from an earthly paradise to a living hell. How could this possibly have happened?

But the waiting, alas, is over. And you know—*now*—what you must do.

THAT EVENING, after a late supper in the dining hall, you walk hurriedly through the midwinter dusk, making a detour for the Academic Village basement, where you retrieve the shoebox from its hiding place behind one of the dormitory's gigantic boilers.

You trundle up the back staircase to your room. To the room that you share with Dakota Fish. You glance at your watch. The time is 9:02 p.m. The time is nigh.

You ease your way inside. Dakota Fish turns away from his studies, his French 201 grammar manual lying open on the desk.

"Your mom called while you were out," says Dakota Fish. "You should call her back. She hasn't heard from you in days."

If only she could see me now, you think to yourself.

You stare at each other for a moment. For an eternity in the life of Dakota Fish.

You lift the AirLite out of its box. All stainless steel and plenty of pop. *Like the lightning punch of Jesus Christ himself.*

Dakota Fish's eyes bulge visibly at the sight of the revolver.

"*Attends une minute,*" he mutters nervously. You make a mental note that he is using the *tu* form. Impressive. Particularly during such a stressful instance.

You gingerly aim the gun in his direction.

"*Que diable?*" says Dakota Fish. *Le poseur,* you think to yourself. Doesn't he ever quit?

As you steady the gun in your hand, he removes his headband. He shakes his considerable, immaculate hair loose, inexplicably but oh-so-deliberately turning his head one way—and then the other.

This must be some kind of Jedi mind trick, you think.

And that's when your comedy of errors truly begins.

As you squeeze the trigger, the first shot ricochets off of the bookcase above Dakota Fish's head and burrows itself in his grammar book. *Oh, la . . . le pauvre!*

Your hand is already aching from the AirLite's brutal recoil, the smell of sulfur and oil quickly filling the room.

In a desperate attempt to save himself from your demolition, Dakota Fish leaps over the side of his bed, scattering a whole semester's worth of school supplies about the floor. You squeeze the trigger yet again, and the second bullet lodges in the mattress just above his cowering head.

As you fire another round into the mattress, the door suddenly swings open, revealing the frightened image of the dormitory's resident adviser, a prematurely balding Butch Schwinnicker—his mouth agape—standing in the doorway. Sorry, Butch, you think to yourself. Sorry you had to witness this—*this carnage.*

As you turn to shut the door in Butch's baffled face, your foot slips on one of Dakota Fish's mechanical pencils. Struggling to regain your balance, you fire the fourth shot in Dakota Fish's direction beyond the mattress. You hear a faint cry as your body tumbles floorward.

As you fall on your back in a heap of manila folders, spiral notebooks, and loose-leaf paper, the fifth and final shot discharges into the ceiling.

The cylinder is empty. But the river is already carrying you away. Slowly but surely. *Away from here.*

With your hand still smarting from the AirLite's violent discharge, you climb out of the dorm window and scale down the Dumpster to the streetscape below. You hop into the front seat on the passenger's side of the Road Warrior. As Timothy McVeigh negotiates the campus's narrow streets, you watch the dormitories transition into classroom buildings, and the classroom buildings give way to administration buildings, which eventually surrender to the golf course that flanks the main entrance. There the floodlights cut through the humid evening air and illuminate the stately sign that introduces your would-be, won't-be alma mater: "Friends University."

Won't be.

Timothy McVeigh makes a hard right turn off of the campus proper and, just a little farther off, begins speeding toward the interstate that beckons to the west.

Westward ho.

In a few minutes, you think, Wichita will be nothing but a memory. Dakota Fish, an intermittent ghost that haunts your conscience. Gina, an enigmatic nightmare—a fantasy, even—that can no longer hurt you. Except in your dreams perhaps. If only you had them.

You can already hear the sirens, plaintive and low, as they begin their slow crescendo in the distance. With a sly grin spreading across his face, Timothy McVeigh accelerates into the darkness.

6 The Gun That Won the West

Timothy McVeigh is piloting the Road Warrior into the former territory of Colorado. "Welcome to the Centennial State" reads the sign at the border. Glad to be here, you think. Nice to make your acquaintance.

A white straw dangles from Timothy McVeigh's mouth. He has been chewing on it for the entirety of the three hours since you left the McDonald's drive-thru back in Salina, Kansas, pop. 42,303. With spittle periodically running down his chin, your driver can be a disgusting sight to behold.

Timothy McVeigh finally breaks the silence.

"What are you—a Mormon?" he asks.

You look at him quizzically.

"Back there—at the university. Are you Mormons or Seventh-day Adventists or Jehovah's Witnesses or *what?*"

You've got to be kidding, you think to yourself. Did you see any copies of *The Watchtower* lying around the dorm room?

We're Friends, you say, clearing your throat.

"I know we're friends," he answers. "I don't do midnight getaways for acquaintances, for just anyone. Unless they're hot chicks, that is—"

No, you say, interrupting him. He just doesn't get it. You cannot believe that your personal life requires this much explanation. And for Timothy McVeigh, no less.

We're Friends. Gina and me and Dakota—

"You mean the *late* Dakota Fish?" he interrupts.

You shrug your shoulders. Who can say for sure? You absent-mindedly stroke your right hand. Still aching from the recoil.

We're part of the Society of Friends, you continue. The Religious Society of Friends. *Quakers.* Conversing with anyone is a trial, you think to yourself, but with this guy it can be downright exhausting.

"Why, dog my cats!" Timothy McVeigh responds. "As in Friends University?"

That's right. You extend your index finger like a gun and aim it in his direction to signal that he's on the right track. That he gets it. That he's A-OK.

"A Quaker," he continues. "Like Nixon!"

Oh my God. You cannot believe he is bringing up President Nixon. Why do they always bring up President Nixon? How come nobody ever mentions Daniel Boone? Or Betsy Ross? Or James Dean? It's always Tricky Dick and his sainted mother.

TIMOTHY McVEIGH WHEELS the Road Warrior into the shale parking lot of a thrift store in Colorado Springs. "Snow City Pawns" reads the flickering neon sign above the door.

"I know a guy here," he announces.

You what?

"A guy—one of my suppliers. We need to stock up for Tulsa."

A look of confusion crosses your face.

"You are going to Tulsa—aren't you, *friend?*" asks Timothy McVeigh, sarcastically.

To be honest, you hadn't thought that far in advance.

"If you want, you can ride along with me to Zimmerhaus's Gun and Knife Show. I could use an extra hand with the tables. I'd even pay you a good clean American wage. Tax free," he adds. "Besides, there's nothing for you back in Kansas—that's for certain."

You got that right, you think to yourself. *Friend.*

"Hey, isn't NORAD around here somewhere? Someplace near Colorado Springs?" he asks absentmindedly.

You don't have the first clue.

As he turns off the Road Warrior's ignition, Timothy McVeigh begins—bizarrely—to sing the Kansas state song.

"'Oh, give me a home where the buffalo roam.'"

The sadness overwhelms you—miserable, displaced *you*. But it's clearly time to think forwardly—to be forward-thinking.

"'Where the deer and the antelope play.'"

SNOW CITY PAWNS is an altogether tacky experience. And from the looks of things, it is barely a going concern. An old gumball machine graces the entrance to the store. You habitually finger the metal door to see if there is a stray piece of gum in the dispenser, only to come away with a handful of dust.

The walls are adorned with the cheapest kind of secondhand paraphernalia. Old, beaten-up electric guitars are flanked by world-weary band instruments—a dent-ridden tuba, a mangled flute—and wooden tennis-racket frames, sans strings, that have clearly seen better days.

You follow Timothy McVeigh past display tables covered with rusty toaster ovens, disheveled coffeemakers, and burnt-out television sets. Box after box of faded news magazines are stowed below the tables, along with vacuum cleaners—inoperable in all likelihood—of all makes and models.

"I know what you're thinking," he says. "But this'll get a whole lot better when we get to the manager's private stock."

And what will that be? you wonder to yourself. Decrepit old lawn mowers without the blades? A secret treasure room filled with broken ham radios and busted videocassette players? The mangy remains of taxidermy gone awry? The possibilities boggle the mind.

When he reaches the rear of the store, Timothy McVeigh pauses at a door marked Employees Only and knocks four times in quick succession. He glances confidently in your direction, as if he's just cracked a top-secret nuclear code. "It's not what you know, but who you know, right?"

A buzzer sounds, and the door creaks open. You follow Timothy McVeigh down a flight of rickety wooden stairs into a brightly lit basement. It's a treasure trove all right—but hardly the kind you imagined.

The basement floor is strewn with metal packing cases, nearly every one of which is overflowing with automatic weapons. Hundreds upon hundreds of grenades are piled in a far corner of the basement. Shoulder rocket launchers are stacked neatly, one upon another, against a nearby wall. And unlike the decaying vacuum cleaners upstairs, they seem to be in perfect working condition. At least as far as you can tell.

As you take in the incredible array of weaponry, a voice pierces the basement's eerie silence.

"I thought I heard you knocking!" announces an older man in a red jumpsuit. With his gray hair, his well-tended beer belly, and his wire-rimmed glasses, he looks vaguely like Grandpa Walton. You never cared that much for *The Waltons.* You thought that *Hawaii Five-O* was a far superior show.

Timothy McVeigh helpfully makes the introductions. "This here is Snow," he tells you, gesturing toward the older man.

As in "Snow City Pawns"? you ask jokingly. This cannot possibly be his real name, you think to yourself.

"Hey, we all use aliases in the gun business," says Grandpa Walton. "Ain't that right, *Tim Tuttle?*"

Snow and Timothy McVeigh share a robust laugh together.

"And this here is Daryl Bridges," says Timothy McVeigh, gesturing in your direction. Your new, unexpected identity confounds you. You never thought of yourself as a Daryl. Or a Bridges, for that matter. But you have to admit that it has a pleasing cadence.

Daryl Bridges, you think to yourself. *I am Daryl Bridges.*

Snow grips your right hand. Firmly. A trustworthy handshake. Genuine in spite of the ridiculous pseudonyms.

"Good to meet you, Daryl," says Snow. "Now let's get down to the main event. I believe this is what you're looking for," he announces. Squatting next to one of the metal crates, he gingerly removes a rifle and presents it for Timothy McVeigh's inspection.

But this is not just any rifle. Even a gun-show novice like yourself can tell that it's something different. Something special.

"The Gun That Won the West," says Timothy McVeigh in hushed tones as he holds the weapon aloft. With its original metal fittings intact, the wooden rifle is a sight to behold. "Vintage. Gotta be nineteenth century. The real deal."

"You're sure-shittin'," intones Snow. "This one here's from 1866. Post–Civil War. Practically a prototype. Pure cherry."

Somehow, when Grandpa Walton says *pure cherry* it sounds offensive. At least to your ears.

"You got a buyer?" he asks.

"Oh, I got a buyer all right," Timothy McVeigh answers. "He's a top-dog collector. All's I gotta do is reel him in nice-and-easy-like." You blanch at how effortlessly your partner adopts a folksy, down-home demeanor. As if he's just one of the boys. One of the good ol' boys.

Timothy McVeigh hands Snow a bankroll the size of your fists—both of them.

"This ought to do her," he says.

"It ought to do just about anything," answers Snow, his eyes aglow at the wad of money before him.

BACK IN THE ROAD WARRIOR, Timothy McVeigh can scarcely contain his glee. "We're set up now!" he announces. "We are going to rock Tulsa to its very foundations! Yeah, daddy!"

Yeah, daddy? What gives?

Timothy McVeigh's awful singing resumes as he motors away from Snow City Pawns.

"'Where seldom is heard a discouraging word.'"

It must be stuck in his head, you think.

"'And the skies are not cloudy all day.'"

You watch the cityscape glide by as Timothy McVeigh negotiates the peaks and valleys of Colorado Springs. Storefronts and filling stations. Stately churches nestled among tony neighborhoods.

Demure and understated, a quaint meetinghouse proclaims its ministry: "We Are a Fellowship of Seekers" the sign in front announces. "Heed the Call of Concern."

Heady stuff, you think to yourself. You make a note on your "Jot It Down" pad.

Timothy McVeigh suddenly stops singing and begins staring, blankly, in your direction. Clearly, something is on his mind.

What now?

"Why don't you ever talk?" Timothy McVeigh inquires. A thoughtful question, you think to yourself—especially from a man who seemingly *never stops talking.*

You will speak when you are moved to speak, you reply. Like any good Quaker.

The sly wink in his eye indicates that he remains unsatisfied with your answer.

You could tell him that you will speak when your sleeping soul awakens, when you are driven to explode the quietude of your inner light. You could tell him *that*—you most certainly could. You could tell him that your inner light kindles and grows, that you are a tiny spark among many thousands, millions of emergent flames. Many thousands of millions.

But you remain silent. What more, really, is there to say?

The light is forever, and the light is free.

TIMOTHY McVEIGH STEERS the Road Warrior into the Tulsa State Fairgrounds. A crowded, noisy amusement park rises up on the left, with the massive Pavilion towering in front of you. "Zimmerhaus's—World's Largest Gun and Knife Show," the Pavilion's brightly lit marquee reads. "Accept No Substitutes."

"First things first," says Timothy McVeigh as he removes the precious cargo from the trunk. "We have a delivery to make."

While your partner pays your registration fees at the entrance to the Pavilion, you glance at the newspaper racks for signs of your recent mischief back in Kansas. You can only imagine the headlines screaming across the Heartland: "Desperate Quaker on the Loose." Or, worse yet, "Pacifist on the Prowl: Armed, Dangerous, and Defiantly Timid." Oh, the inhumanity of it all, you think to yourself.

You enter the gun showroom with Timothy McVeigh.

"Damn. There's a lot of camo in here today," he says.

You ask him why he never wears camouflage clothing.

"'Cause I'm the real thing. I'm not a wannabe," he responds. "I'm a shooter. Remember?"

You ask yourself why you continue to engage him in conversation.

The Pavilion is bustling with vendors—nearly four thousand of them crowded amidst the arena's expansive showroom floor. The Tulsa gun show makes Topeka seem like a quiet rural fair.

From the looks of the salesmen and their wares, you can tell that Zimmerhaus's caters to a much edgier crowd. And it's not just the overabundance of camo either. You are flabbergasted by the massive Hitler Youth poster that greets visitors as they enter the Pavilion. The image of a German teen transforms into a Nazi storm trooper beneath the motto *Jugend dient dem Führer!*

Sieg Heil, you think to yourself.

As you maneuver through the throng with Timothy McVeigh, you are overwhelmed by the sheer number of anti-Clinton bumper stickers on display. Perhaps the President's rumored assault-weapons ban isn't going over so well? you think.

And then you find yourself in front of the largest booth in the arena. The National Rifle Association's glitzy public information and awareness center. As you leaf through one of the N.R.A.'s glossy brochures, Timothy McVeigh begins to pout, sighing loudly. Visibly irritated. You have never seen this side of him before. It is decidedly unimpressive.

"The N.R.A. is weak-ass," he tells you, adopting a voice that is just loud enough to attract the attention of the booth's other patrons. "They act like they wanna save the Second Amendment, but they're pansy-ass politicians like everyone else in Washington. Don't be fooled by their hard-line rhetoric," he adds curtly. People are now openly glaring at your partner. You receive a few disapproving glances of your own. You like the idea of being notorious. Of being slightly bad.

Well, all right then, you think. Timothy McVeigh—1, National Rifle Association—0. Your partner is in fine fettle. And the day is still young.

7 The Mysterious Stranger

As you leave the N.R.A. booth, a bizarre cuckoo clock catches your attention. An attractive timepiece with a replica wooden chateau from the Bavarian Alps as its face, the clock signals every quarter hour by producing a miniature Adolf Hitler—his right arm extended upward in his iconic, eerie salute—from an elegant alpine doorway. What could possibly be next? you think to yourself. A Mussolini action figure? A Hirohito lunchbox? The Axis powers have never had it so good.

"Well, if it isn't Bob Miller!" Timothy McVeigh suddenly exclaims. He is vigorously shaking hands with an older, immaculately dressed gentleman. Wearing a white vest, a silky white scarf for a tie, and a long white overcoat, he cuts a remarkable figure—especially at a gun show, where the chosen attire tends to run in the tan, green, and brown families. In addition to his shaggy coif of white hair, he has an exaggerated neck, like a turkey's wattle. You can barely suppress the laughter that is gathering in your throat.

Your partner introduces you to the gentleman as Daryl Bridges. "Please, Timothy, let's dispense with noms de plume among old friends." Cradling a white top hat in his left hand, he shifts his weight in your direction. "I am Roger Moore from the great state of Arkansas," he announces, "and I am so very pleased to meet you." Moore gives your hand a healthy shake, his turkey wattle jiggling in tune with his unvarnished delight at making your acquaintance.

In spite of your more well-mannered instincts, you are gawking rather obviously at his attire. "I can see that you are stirred by my ensemble," he observes. "There is nothing more somber, my boy, than a man who wears black for any and all occasions. It reminds me of one of my favorite apothegms: 'A group of men in evening clothes looks like a flock of crows—and is just about as inspiring.'"

Moore laughs heartily at his own joke as Timothy McVeigh carefully presents him with the prized weapon from Snow City Pawns.

"Ah, there it is!" says Moore admiringly. "The Winchester repeating rifle." He lapses into a protracted silence, caressing the smooth wood of the barrel, getting a feel for its pristine metalwork. You cannot be certain, but the regal gentleman from Arkansas seems to have begun weeping quietly to himself.

"This is the very gun that spelt so much doom for the Indians," says Moore. "The technological shift that gave the white man the upper hand—once and for all—in the Indian Wars of the 1870s. This is the weapon that won the frontier. That vanquished the red man. That wiped out the buffalo."

You cannot be sure if he's merely pontificating or genuinely moved. Either way, you are impressed with Roger Moore's imitation of the perfect Southern gentleman. Right down to the faux English accent—like some kind of contemporary Robert E. Lee.

"Our modern America lives and breathes in this rifle," continues Moore. "It is everything we are—and everything we ever hope to be. It is domination. Subjugation. It is the overwhelming sense of supremacy that we covet in our most secret thoughts. It is what winning feels like—winning against fearsome odds. It is, in a word, devastation. Our primal need to devastate and to overawe at the very same time."

Devastation. You make a mental note.

His performance seemingly having ended, Moore turns to Timothy McVeigh and hands him a well-worn Nike shoebox.

"Your money, good sir," says Moore. Apparently, shoeboxes are the depositories of choice in the gun-show trade. "It is all there—to the penny," he adds, his turkey wattle galloping up and down with his every breath. "You have my eternal gratitude," says Moore. You could swear that at this point he actually bows slightly to Timothy McVeigh. As if he were on some field of honor and not standing in the middle of the world's largest gun showroom.

REVELING IN YOUR NEW, tax-free employment, you assist Timothy McVeigh in setting up his sales tables for the gun show. Back are the yellow Post-it notes, the bumper stickers, and the homemade silencer kits. He's even managed to round up some VHS copies of *Waco: The Big Lie*, as well as some rare back issues of *American Rifleman*. And then there are the requisite photocopies of *The Turner Diaries*.

"We're gonna knock this show on its ass!" announces your partner. "We've got the usual bullshit available—naturally. But I've added some hot items that are going to rock this show. Just rock it."

Timothy McVeigh opens up a green, army-issue duffel bag and presents you with a trio of bumper stickers. "And these are just the appetizers, my friend," he says. "To whet the palate." You collect the stacks of bumper stickers and arrange them tastefully along the front of the sales tables. You can't help assessing the new wares. Like some kind of beauty-pageant judge. A very quiet and circumspect beauty-pageant judge, that is.

"Fear the government that fears your gun." That's a good one, you think. Short and pithy, but also imperative and to the point.

"A man with a gun is a citizen. A man without a gun is a subject." Very effective, you think to yourself. Makes you think of the American Colonies *vis-à-vis* Great Britain. Nice connotation.

"When guns are outlawed, I will become an outlaw." Your personal favorite among the new line. Threatening? Most certainly. But brimming with reality. Real patriot kind of stuff.

"And now for the main course," announces Timothy McVeigh. "Survivalist gear. It's the next big thing—especially after Ruby Ridge and all that gun-control malarkey a few years back. It's primo stuff. Besides," he surmises, "survival gear will be a necessity for living under the New World Order."

You think that Timothy McVeigh's latest product line is nothing more than a ragtag assemblage of canteens, T-shirts, sleeping bags, and camouflage pants. He's managed to round up a couple of jagged knives for gutting fish, but beyond the water-purifier tablets and the snake-venom kits, all of the gear is available at any respectable Boy Scout retail outlet.

"And then you've got your dessert course!" says Timothy McVeigh, beaming with pride. "And people are gonna be talking about dessert around here for a long, long time! Like Fudge-Ripple Delight—or, better yet, Strawberry Shortcake!"

You have never seen Timothy McVeigh acting this giddy.

He can hardly contain himself, devoting an entire table to the 37mm flare-launcher kit. He unwraps a slick black rifle with an unusually wide barrel for your inspection. The flare launcher, you presume. He positions a trio of silver cylinders alongside the weapon. Your partner clears his throat and begins reciting aloud from a typewritten index card: "The 37 millimeter flare-launcher kit. With or without optional collapsible folding stock, the 37mm flare-launcher kit can transform any AR-15 type rifle to fire 37mm, 26.5mm, and 12-gauge flares! Purchase a 37mm flare-launcher kit today for the bargain price of just $295, and we'll throw in the optional duplex adapter—a $195 value—for free. That's right, free—if you act today!"

Not bad, you think to yourself. A little short on detail perhaps, but well-written and plainly delivered.

"Now, that's a sales pitch that's made in heaven!" declares a self-congratulatory Timothy McVeigh. "And the real beauty of it all," he adds slyly, "is what everyone in here already knows—shit, even the camo-clad infants sucking at the titties of their camo-wearing mothers—*my flare-launcher kit can be used to modify any AR-15 to project hand grenades.* Don't you get it? To launch hand grenades instead of flares! And as every good patriot recognizes, hand grenades are a whole lot more persuasive than your garden-variety signal flares. And do you know why that is, JD?"

Because they go boom? you think to yourself.

"Because they go boom!" Timothy McVeigh echoes. "And that's what I call *devastating* your enemy. Damn straight, it is."

LATER THAT EVENING, you join Timothy McVeigh for a celebratory drink in the hotel bar across from the state fairgrounds. He is drinking a screwdriver. You are nursing a Shirley Temple. No rum and Cokes for you this time. No sirree. You are bound and determined not to stray again. You are hoping—hope against hope—that the incident back in the Academic Village was anomalous. That the real you—*the ethical you*—is now in evidence. In full bloom.

You are encouraged for the first time in weeks. Your life has possibility.

Perhaps you can be holy again. You could even be whole.

You could rediscover the light.

YOU AND YOUR PARTNER are in fine spirits. You sold five flare-launcher kits this afternoon, and Timothy McVeigh picked up a new T-shirt to boot. "At fourteen bucks," he announces, "this shirt is a freakin' steal!" The front features a picture of Abraham Lincoln embossed with the words "*Sic Semper Tyrannis,* Thus Ever to Tyrants," while the back of the T-shirt depicts the Liberty Tree spilling droplets of blood over the words of Thomas Jefferson: "The tree of liberty must be refreshed from time to time with the blood of patriots and tyrants."

Since when did blood become a cleansing agent? you ask your partner.

"Sometimes you are so naive, JD," he replies. "Blood has always been democracy's disinfectant. Always has been. Always will be."

As Timothy McVeigh downs one convivial screwdriver after another, you are joined in the hotel bar by a diminutive, balding man in a conservative, double-breasted suit.

"Andy the German!" announces Timothy McVeigh. "How the heck are you?"

The smiling little man seems genuinely pleased to meet you. "Any friend of Timothy McVeigh's is a friend of mine!" he declares jovially in his heavy European accent.

A former military intelligence officer, Andy the German tells you that he first came to the United States to halt the exportation of Nazi paraphernalia from America to Germany, where it is illegal to possess any materials that venerate the Third Reich. "It is my calling," he admits, with a sigh in his voice, "to stave off the progress of evil in our world. But alas, there is only so much that one man can do in the moral wilderness that is our age." There is something endearing about Andy the German. Something endearing in his earnestness and his nostalgia.

"But now I am head of security at Elohim City," he continues. "And I try to fight the good fight here in my adopted homeland of Oklahoma." He stares into his cocktail for a moment. "I no longer dream of saving the world when all I can possibly save is myself." You recognize a hint of sadness in his voice. A sense of overwhelming despair.

"Elohim City?" says Timothy McVeigh. "I heard that it isn't even real. That it's a mirage—or a dream. Like Shangri-La or Brigadoon or Camelot or some such thing."

"Oh, it exists all right," says Andy the German, perking up a bit. "It is the only place left for a freethinking man in this hemisphere. Where a free person can roam the land and think for himself. And live rightly and deeply. Without, shall we say, any governmental interdiction." He smiles slightly to himself.

As the evening continues, Timothy McVeigh begins to hold court in the hotel bar over the ills of the New World Order. You notice that he has developed a buzz. That he is slurring his words.

"Don't get me started on the New World Order," says Timothy McVeigh. "Now there's a crock of shit for you. It means bleeding away everything that's real, that's valuable about being an American."

As you might expect, Andy the German provides a more thoughtful, nuanced answer. "People need to understand that the New World Order is a metaphor, not merely a paranoid belief," he says. "In essence, it means that one superpower is going to presume to lead the world morally into a new and vastly different age. It will be the force of subjugated, undemocratic will." You make a mental note that he pronounces *will* as *vill*. Like German characters in the movies do.

"You will agree with our way of living," Andy the German continues, "or we're going to bomb you into submission. That is what the New World Order would have us all believe." He pronounces *what* as *vhat*. *Would* as *vood*. It's uncanny, you think to yourself. Absolutely uncanny.

As Timothy McVeigh nods his head in agreement, you are suddenly interrupted by the appearance of a familiar face. And by the effete elegance of his unforgettable voice.

"Ah, the New World Order," observes Roger Moore. "*Novus Ordo Mundi.*" He is still immaculately dressed in his white ensemble, but his face has been reduced to a bleary-eyed, drunken mess, his voice audibly slowed by drink.

And then the darkness enters the room. It is a palpable, unmistakable presence. You could see it, quite literally, in Roger Moore's eyes. The venom that he brought from the gun show.

"Tell me, Timothy, why do you insist on parading my flare-launcher design at your table?"

The color quickly drains from your partner's bewildered face.

"You know precisely what I mean—the design that I demonstrated for you last year at my ranch back in Arkansas." He clumsily sets his snifter of Courvoisier on the table in front of Andy the German, who looks away in embarrassment. "You certainly couldn't have learnt it anywhere else. Or from anyone else, for that matter. And now I am loath to discover that it's all the rage around the showroom." There is a strange, ominous tone to Moore's voice, acidic even, as he flays and dissects your partner.

"Look, dude, it's not like you hold a patent on the thing," responds Timothy McVeigh defensively. You sense that this conversation is taking a nasty turn. And very quickly, at that. You are amazed at how rapidly Roger Moore's Southern gentleman act can shift into bloodthirsty overdrive. It would really be something to see—you think perversely to yourself—if he were to let himself go and eviscerate the world. If you weren't afraid for yourself, that is. And for Timothy McVeigh.

As if things couldn't get any worse, Roger Moore begins to wax nostalgic. "The first time I saw you," he says to your partner, "you were wearing your sand-colored Desert Storm regalia, spit-polished boots, all military precision and a no-nonsense mien. A fantastic sight to behold. I cannot tell you how proud I was to call you my friend. But now look at you—you are a thug in a sweatshirt and black jeans," Moore continues, with his turkey wattle galloping at full tilt. "I'd ask what happened, but I am not sure that I really want to know. What's next—combat boots? The skinheads? The Knights of the Ku Klux Klan?" He shoots a suspicious glance in Andy the German's direction.

Timothy McVeigh is turning as red as a beet, his eyes unblinking, his expression unchanging. You observe him clenching and unclenching his fists.

"This reminds me of another apothegm," Moore continues. "'Inside of the dullest exterior there is a drama, a comedy, and a tragedy.' And you, dear Timothy, are briskly becoming duller by the minute."

Apparently, Roger Moore's gratitude isn't that eternal after all. So much for the field of honor. He awkwardly attempts to stand up, delicately placing his white top hat upon his head.

"I'm sorry to say that this isn't over, Timothy," says Moore. "When you cross me, you'd better be prepared, quite fully, for the blowback. Which will be considerable, I fear, in your case."

And with that, the older man ambles out of the hotel bar, leaving the three of you—a distraught Timothy McVeigh, a befuddled Andy the German, and a fallen, teetotaling Quaker—to negotiate your path through the morass. To find your way in a darkling world. A darkling new world order.

WHEN YOU PREPARE TO LEAVE the Tulsa fairgrounds the next morning, your driver—eyes red and acutely hungover—hands you the Nike shoebox. "Should be twenty-seven grand in there. Count it," instructs Timothy McVeigh as you climb into the Road Warrior. "Shit. Count it twice for good measure."

You can tell that Timothy McVeigh is still slightly rattled—shaken, even—after the encounter with Roger Moore back in the hotel bar. That his usual confidence and certainty about the world has been shattered. That he has become lost. Like you.

"No one, by gum—no one will ever make me feel that way again," says a determined Timothy McVeigh. "That small. That weak. That much"—he pauses in his self-disgust, in his unquenchable anger—"that much of a waste." His resolve has clearly been piqued. But so has his shame. His disgrace. His dishonor.

You are thunderstruck by Timothy McVeigh's predicament. You find yourself—impossible as it may seem—actually feeling sorry for him. For Timothy McVeigh.

And you realize—right then and there—that you have been called. That you will heed your calling. You will atone for your sins—*you will reclaim the light*—by cleaving to Timothy McVeigh in his time of need, by remaining at his side. Just as he has been there for you during your own crisis of great despair and uncertainty.

There is that of God in every man.

You will answer God's call of concern by acceding to his ministry. By becoming Timothy McVeigh's earthly minister.

You will hold him in the light.

8 Life on the Mississippi

Timothy McVeigh is gone.

You shake yourself out of a deep sleep. You are sitting in the passenger's side of the Road Warrior. The bright light of morning is shining on your face through the prism of the vehicle's windshield.

There is no Timothy McVeigh in evidence. He is nowhere to be found. Disappeared. Just like that.

You glance around the interior of the car. The doors are locked. The key is in the ignition. The heat is blowing at a comfortable level. How thoughtful, you think to yourself. How thoughtful of your partner to consider your creature comforts. Before utterly vanishing into thin air.

You open your wallet. You have $11 to your name. A five-dollar bill and six singles. Your dorm-room key still rests in your pocket. Not much use there, you think. No credit cards either—not even a phone card to call your own. For all intents and purposes, you are off the grid. A nonperson, a nonentity. Like Timothy McVeigh—wherever he is. *Whomever he is.*

You glance at the Road Warrior's spotless floorboard, where the Nike shoebox lies undisturbed. Timothy McVeigh really keeps this thing clean, you think to yourself. It's downright immaculate.

You pick up the shoebox. It would be a mistake to leave $27,000 lying around, you think to yourself. Removing the key from the ignition, you climb out of the Road Warrior and lock the doors.

You are standing in the light. In the stark light of day.

You check the trunk, which is chock-full of gun-show paraphernalia. The Adidas shoebox is intact, with the AirLite still tucked away safely inside. Boxes of flare launchers lie untouched near the wheel well. Sheaves of bumper stickers line the trunk's perimeter.

The Road Warrior has been parked near the middle of a town square. Somewhere, you can only presume, in small-town America. Anyplace, U.S.A. There are a variety of storefronts in every direction. A mom-and-pop grocery, a five-and-dime store, a diner. Nothing seems to be open yet. It must be too early in the morning, you think—although it has to be a Friday. Or Saturday, at the latest.

By force of habit, you cast your eye on a nearby newsstand, where copies of the *Quad-City Times* are on display. "Terrorists Convicted in World Trade Center Bombing," reads the headline.

Where am I? you ask an older man in blue overalls walking in your direction. He is carrying a bamboo fishing rod and a fire-engine red tackle box.

He looks at you in utter disbelief.

"You're in Princeton," he finally answers gruffly.

This simply cannot be possible, you think to yourself. You surely haven't traveled all the way to New Jersey. The Road Warrior is fast all right, *but not that fast.*

"Princeton, Iowa," Blue Overalls grumbles before loping away. You have nothing to lose, you figure, so you follow him. Semi-discreetly, several yards back.

Hiking from the town square past several quiet, well-kept clapboard homes, you trail him from the main road onto a dirt path—and beyond that to a riverbank. The sky is becoming a hazy shade of gray. As if it were about to rain.

The farther you get from the town square, the more Princeton's fortunes seem to wane. As you make your way toward the water's edge, several vacant storefronts come into view. The town's library, neglected and forlorn, nestles beside the river. An abandoned, rusted-out bookmobile sits out front, waiting for a decaying populace seemingly never to return.

Up ahead, you observe Blue Overalls preparing to fish from the riverbank. Scanning your eyes across the horizon, you see another man sitting a few hundred feet away, casting his line into the silty brown water.

Timothy McVeigh. It's just gotta be.

You lumber in his direction, where the river narrows and comes to a slight fork across from a pair of pine-covered islands.

Timothy McVeigh doesn't seem all that surprised to see you. Nonchalant, even.

You ask him where he found the fishing pole. He nods toward a nearby cottage. A large tear in its screened-in front porch catches your attention.

So we're stealing now? you think to yourself. We've become petty thieves. And possibly murderers. Or attempted murderers—who the devil knows?

You sit next to your partner on the riverbank, the Nike shoebox resting in your lap.

"The Mighty Mississippi," says Timothy McVeigh. Without emotion. Without any verve whatsoever.

M-i-s-s-i-s-s-i-p-p-i, you think to yourself automatically.

You sit silently by his side for quite some time, the wind whipping up from the river as it begins to sprinkle. The rain hissing and spitting in your faces.

Timothy McVeigh finally speaks.

"Listen, JD," he says. "I've been thinking—I've been thinking of getting off of the road for a while. Don't get me wrong—you're welcome to come with."

You nod quietly to yourself. And to your friend.

"I just can't do it much longer. Going from gun show to gun show. I mean, shit, I've only got, like, three shirts. I don't live out of a suitcase—*I live out of a trunk.*"

He pauses for another stretch. "I've been living this way for two freakin' years, and here's what I propose," he continues. "I propose that we meet up with some guys I know in Michigan. They got a place up there. You'll totally dig them. I may be a shooter, but they're patriots. Tried and true. And you—you've become a regular gunrunner!"

A gunrunner. You like the sound of that.

You nod in his direction. He seems pleased by your acquiescence. By your seeming acceptance of his plan.

Timothy McVeigh reels in his line.

"A whole lot of nothing," he says dejectedly. "I guess it'll be Filet-O-Fish for us tonight."

He sets the fishing rod next to the cottage. "No worse for wear," he says, wrapping a crisp $100 bill around the pole's bamboo handle.

Timothy McVeigh is clearly beginning to perk up a bit, you think to yourself.

With your partner in tow, you walk past Blue Overalls, perched precariously on the riverbank below, and follow the dirt path back into town.

And then Timothy McVeigh stops dead in his tracks.

"This cannot be possible," he says. "The Road Warrior has been moved. Only a matter of a couple of parking spaces," he continues, "but it's definitely been moved."

It simply cannot be, you think. Were you so overwhelmed in your delirium this morning that you don't even remember where the car was parked? What space it was in?

Is it merely a matter of physical space and time, you wonder to yourself, a set of circumstances defined by where you exist from one moment to the next? Or are there larger forces at work here—forces well beyond your ken?

Timothy McVeigh looks around the square. Gazing from one storefront to the next as if he were attempting to catch a glimpse of the culprit.

But there's nobody around. *Except you.*

Taking the keys from your hand, Timothy McVeigh hops into the Road Warrior. He shrugs his shoulders to himself. He's suddenly unfettered. Unworried. He acts as if he doesn't have a care in the world.

What gives?

"Let's roll," he announces as you settle into the passenger's seat. Your uncertainty is now at full throttle even as your partner's paranoia quickly ebbs and dissipates altogether.

"To the Thumb," says Timothy McVeigh as he revs up the Road Warrior.

The what? you ask.

"The Thumb," he repeats. "The Michigan peninsula. Bounded by Saginaw Bay and Lake Huron. Looks like a giant thumb on a big-ass mitten. Geographically speaking, that is."

You roll. On into Illinois. From the Land of Lincoln into upper Hoosierdom before crossing into Michigan. Or, as Timothy McVeigh likes to call it, *Militiagan.*

IN ALMA, MICHIGAN, pop. 9,034, Timothy McVeigh pulls over to make a telephone call in the back of a gas station.

You are impressed with the city's quaint Midwestern charm. In dramatic contrast to Princeton, Alma is clearly a going concern. Vintage gaslights line the streetscape, along with a series of neatly manicured American elms.

You glance back at your partner, who is busying himself with the gas station's pay phone.

"I'd like to make a person-to-person call in the name of Kling— Robert Kling," he tells the operator.

Another alias, you think to yourself. How many different identities does one guy need?

"Hey, *muchacho*," he says into the receiver. "It's code green. We're only a couple of hours away. If that. You be ready now, you hear?"

As Timothy McVeigh wheels the Road Warrior back into traffic, you can feel the rush of his excitement. His giddiness at the prospect of seeing his old friends again.

"You'll like Terry," he tells you. "He refuses to cuss—*sound familiar?*—and you can scarcely get a word out of him edgewise."

You stare daggers in Timothy McVeigh's direction.

"It'll be like *déjà vu* all over again!" he remarks, laughing to himself.

IT'S WELL AFTER DARK when you arrive in Decker, Michigan. In the heart of the Thumb. Timothy McVeigh pulls the Road Warrior into the gravelly driveway of an old farmhouse. Behind it, in the distance, you can make out a barn and, a little farther beyond, a silver-colored silo.

What do they grow here? you ask your partner. Corn? Wheat? Soy? Do they raise livestock?

"Tofu," he responds blankly. "They raise tofu." That's clever, you think. Very funny.

As Timothy McVeigh climbs out of the Road Warrior, a voice calls from the darkness. "Who goes there?" the voice asks in a menacing tone. "I'm training an AK-47 on your privates right now," the voice continues. "One false move, and it's curtains." You didn't think that anybody used *curtains* in that context anymore. How archaic, you think to yourself.

Timothy McVeigh slowly lifts his hands in the air. "James, it's me. It's Tim. Don't shoot. OK, pal?"

"That's James Nichols," Timothy McVeigh mutters under his breath. "He's mostly harmless. Just a little crazy. A little touched in the head sometimes."

A wide-eyed, middle-aged man steps out of the darkness. Balding, with a neatly trimmed mustache and beard, James Nichols smiles at the sight of your partner.

"Sorry about that, Tim. There's wackos out there," cautions James, glancing toward the main road. You've just driven through the heart of Decker, Michigan, you think to yourself, and there's nobody out there. *Nobody at all.*

"Where's the AK, Jimmy?" asks Timothy McVeigh hesitantly.

"Oh, *that*—that's just talk," James answers, glancing back and forth at you and your partner. "You know me—I've got a couple of shotties in the kitchen. Some rifles scattered around the barn. And then there's the .44 Magnum that I keep under my pillow. But that's just for protection. Not for idle threats." You notice that he laughs nervously to himself. Frequently—like a mannerism. Like a nervous tic.

"And then there's the pipe bombs in the barn," he continues, "but that's only in the case of a siege. Or a standoff. Something along those lines. Something more serious." You notice that he's beginning to laugh even more nervously now.

"Let's get on into the house," says James. "I don't like to stay outside any more than necessary. Just a precaution is all." He's glancing around feverishly at this point. As if something—*or someone*—might leap out of the night at any moment.

YOU WAKE UP THE NEXT MORNING to an exquisite country breakfast in James Nichols's kitchen. It occurs to you that this is the most absurdly normal experience that you have had in years. The breakfast consists of scrambled eggs, bacon, and flapjacks. All of which are expertly made. For all of his nervous tics and paranoia, James Nichols is a magnificent cook. And the kitchen itself is a masterpiece of down-home Americana. With its Midwestern craftsmanship, white-painted cabinetry, and its maroon trim, the kitchen makes you feel like you are dining inside a gingerbread house.

Your host finally breaks the silence while you and Timothy McVeigh indulge yourselves in second helpings.

"Man, that dude sure does talk a lot," says James Nichols, gesturing in your direction.

"Yeah, he never shuts up," responds Timothy McVeigh.

Your culinary bliss is interrupted by the appearance of James's rumpled, disheveled brother. You feel a shiver run down your spine as you realize that you've seen him somewhere before.

And suddenly you've got it. He's the mystery man from the Water's Edge Lounge. A million years ago in Topeka.

"I'm heading down to Flint to pick up Josh and Marife at the bus station," announces Terry Nichols. It occurs to you that he may be the most staid, emotionless person you've ever encountered. Perhaps even more staid and emotionless than yourself—which is saying a lot.

Terry Nichols seems lifeless—robotic, even—as he stares, blankly, off into the vast, empty space of the kitchen. It's as if something is missing deep inside him. As if he's not entirely there.

9 The Royal Nonesuch

You are hiking with Timothy McVeigh around the far-flung reaches of the Nicholses' farm. Off in the distance, you can see the farmhouse and the barn, the silo looming like a silvery monument above the fields. The sun flashes and glints upon its smooth, rounded steeple.

You follow your partner along a dusty trail and into a copse of trees. He's cradling one of James Nichols's rifles in his arms. The smell of dank grass and pine fills the air. At the far end of a clearing, you can make out a berm with rusty soup cans resting upon its ledge. In the foreground, a man in a woolen coat carefully aims a rifle. The words "Michigan Soldiers of Christ" are embroidered on the back of his coat. Squatting behind him is his son, a rifle propped against one knee.

A shot rings out. One of the soup cans disappears beyond the berm.

"Welcome to the world of the citizen-soldier!" says Timothy McVeigh.

Glad to be here, you think to yourself. Much obliged.

"It's about time you learned how to handle yourself around guns," your partner announces. "First things first: when you're carrying a gun on the road, the ammunition is always in your back pocket." As if to demonstrate, he pulls some shells out of his own back pocket. "The barrel is not pointed at traffic—or at another person. When you're shooting, you make sure you have a backstop"—he gestures toward the berm off in the distance—"and you must always consider the possibility of a bullet ricocheting." You've seen that happen already, you think to yourself, recalling the collateral damage to Dakota Fish's French grammar book.

"That's what my dad taught me about shooting," Timothy McVeigh continues. It's the first time you have ever heard him speak about his family. You are surprisingly moved. It is almost loving. *Almost.*

"Show me what you've got," he says, handing you the rifle.

"And watch out for the recoil," he adds. "It can be fierce. Hold the rifle comfortably. Don't get stiff—that only makes things worse."

You lift the weapon, resting the butt in the crook underneath your right shoulder. Tilting your head to one side, you train your eye on the rear sight.

"Don't forget to breathe," Timothy McVeigh interjects. "Breathe in and out a couple of times slowly. Then hold your breath to steady your aim and fire."

You squeeze the trigger. Your shot misses the can entirely, ricocheting off among the trees.

"And even after all that," your partner jokes, "some people still can't hit the broad side of a barn. Or a soup can."

You can already feel the throb of the recoil as it begins traveling up and down your arm.

YOU ARE HIKING BACK to the Nicholses' farmhouse with Timothy McVeigh. He is carrying the rifle by his side while you massage your aching arm with your left hand.

"Some people say that the Michigan Militia trains around these parts," he says.

Are they patriots, you ask, or gun nuts and lawbreakers? You know, like you read about in the newspapers and such.

"There's a mighty fine line," answers Timothy McVeigh, "between being a renegade and being civic-minded. I reckon that it all comes down to a person's ethics. What's a body going to do—*how far will he go?*—when the chips are down?"

Are you a patriot? you ask your partner.

"Well, that depends upon whom you ask," Timothy McVeigh coolly informs you. "But here's the thing—the only thing that really matters to me: I live by a code."

Oh really. And what, pray tell, is your code? you ask suspiciously. Your arm has stopped throbbing, the pain now displaced by a steady burning sensation.

"Rule number one," he says. "Speak the truth and be an honorable man." OK, fair enough, you think to yourself. We'll conveniently sidestep the matter of the $100 fishing pole back in Iowa.

"Be a John Wayne type of guy," he continues. *Red River*–era John Wayne or *Big Jake*–era John Wayne? To your mind, they are not even remotely the same.

"And, most importantly, don't bullshit people," he adds. Now there's some common ground, you think. An area of shared concern. Of like-mindedness.

"WE'RE GOING OUT TONIGHT, gents!" declares James Nichols upon your return to the farmhouse. You are visibly disappointed, having come to expect a fanciful dinner in the tradition of the morning's opulent breakfast. But you are the guest, and, as your mother always told you, you must graciously respect the wishes of the host. You console yourself, recognizing that your mother surely never had a host quite like James Nichols. That she had never sampled the exotic possibilities of the Thumb.

"Enough of the mystery, Jimmy," Timothy McVeigh remarks

as you troll the quiet, nondescript streets of Decker in James Nichols's vintage Cadillac DeVille station wagon, complete with imitation wood-grained siding. "Let's get some eats!" he implores your host. You make a mental note that your partner has taken to adopting his down-home persona yet again. And in upper Michigan, no less.

James Nichols brings the station wagon to a sudden, sputtering stop in front of an old clapboard house. Your eyes are drawn to the battered marquee: "Sanilac Gentlemen's Club. Cocktails and Adult Entertainment."

You experience a sudden inkling about what it means to be *going out* in the world of James Nichols.

"I'm no expert," intones Timothy McVeigh, laughing nervously, "but this doesn't look like a restaurant." No, it most certainly does not, you lament to yourself. It surely doesn't.

A heavily tarnished brass spittoon guards the Sanilac's entrance. Inside the club, James orders the first of several rounds of drinks. You stick to ginger ale, while your partner orders his requisite screwdriver. As James Nichols drains his first Long Island Iced Tea, the lights begin to dim.

The PA system crackles to life. "Welcome to the Sanilac Gentlemen's Club," trumpets a husky male voice. "Let's show our appreciation for Lady Godiva!"

Lady Godiva, you think to yourself. Now, there's an original stage name.

With the *thump-thump-thump* of a tribal drumbeat, the music begins. Lady Godiva struts her way to the center of the stage. With her deep, ebony-toned skin, she cuts a sensual figure under the hot lights of the Sanilac Gentlemen's Club. You can barely make out a butterfly tattoo on her lower abdomen.

"Now, that's what I call local color!" says Timothy McVeigh, staring at the black stripper, his mouth agape. You seriously doubt that the Duke ever said anything like that.

As Lady Godiva thrusts and gyrates about her silver pole, James Nichols leans forward and tucks a dollar bill into her G-string. He has crazy eyes, you think to yourself. Like he did outside the farmhouse last night. The crazy eyes of a genuine paranoiac.

"I heard that she gives the best head in five counties," says James Nichols, nodding in the stripper's direction. Good to know, you think to yourself. You make a note on your "Jot It Down" pad.

As Lady Godiva's striptease comes to its explosive, erotic end, the stripper descends into the waiting throng for lap dances. You observe as James Nichols begins anxiously counting the remaining dollar bills in his wallet. Meanwhile, Timothy McVeigh sidles up to a comely female patron at the bar.

"Hey, don't you need some kind of special license to wear an outfit like that?" he asks, smiling confidently to himself.

Oh my God. You've just witnessed Timothy McVeigh on the make. And it's not a pretty sight. Not by a long shot.

And then things get worse. Decidedly worse.

With a quizzical smile on his face, James Nichols produces a Visa credit card to settle the bar tab. Moments later, the club's cashier informs him that the card has been rejected.

"I forgot to tell you about the common-law movement I recently joined," James Nichols groggily explains to your partner. "We've dedicated ourselves to proving that the American banking system is fraudulent," he adds. "That it doesn't really exist."

"*You what?*" exclaims Timothy McVeigh.

"Under common law, I cannot be responsible for accruing any debt," James responds. "I am naturally exonerated from paying interest to invisible banking entities that issue plastic currency to people they don't even know."

Those Long Island Iced Teas must really be taking their toll, you think.

"Under whose common law could this even possibly be true?" asks an exasperated Timothy McVeigh.

"The natural, common law of the people," James answers, his sluggishness slowly transforming itself into anger. "Not the bullshit governmental laws that we endure under threat and duress."

Timothy McVeigh violently stands up from the table, thrusting the entire club into an abrupt and unexpected silence. Even Lady Godiva brings her lap dance to a halt, pausing midgrind above her eager customer.

You observe that your partner has become furious beyond all reason. You have never seen him like this. You have never seen *anyone* like this.

Staring intensely at James Nichols, he peels off a series of $100 bills to cover the tab and curtly exits the bar.

YOU ARE JOINED, THE NEXT MORNING, by Terry Nichols and his newlywed Filipina wife, Marife, for breakfast. James Nichols is still asleep. He must be hungover, you can only presume, from your evening of fun and frivolity back at the Sanilac Gentlemen's Club. Timothy McVeigh is nowhere to be found.

A cup of coffee and a bowl of Cheerios sit before you on the kitchen table. How disappointing, you think to yourself. How very disappointing.

In a desperate attempt to make conversation, you ask Terry Nichols if he and Marife plan to settle in the Thumb. If they intend to buy a place of their own.

"That would be impossible," answers Terry Nichols quietly. "I have renounced my American citizenship. I am a nonresident alien and a nonforeigner."

A what?

"And Marife has no standing in this country," he continues robotically. "We are, in effect, nonpeople." You are perplexed by Terry Nichols. His perpetual numbness leaves you feeling numb.

You ask Marife if she likes living in Michigan.

"Dis place is haunted," she replies in her thick Filipina accent.

Decker? you ask incredulously. The whole town?

"No, dis house," she answers. "Dis is a haunted house. Dese are haunted people."

Your partner arrives in the kitchen in just the nick of time. Smiling, as if nothing untoward has ever happened. Following closely on his heels is James Nichols. Still bleary-eyed from the previous evening's exploits, he easily returns to the anti-government tirade that he had begun in the club.

"Don't kid yourself about what happened back at the Sanilac. This country is in a freakin' crisis situation, my friend. Whether it's the banks or the Justice Department or Congress or whatever. We have become a nation of sheeple."

Sheeple? you think to yourself. What the heck are sheeple?

"Even young Timothy here is among our nation's great stable of sheeple, its army of mindless followers. And do you know why?" James Nichols asks. You are genuinely afraid to ask.

"Because when he was serving our country in Desert Storm— risking his very life and limb—they implanted a computer chip in his buttocks," continues James Nichols. "A tiny computer chip." His eyes are glazed over, as if he were in a trance. "That means that they can track his location from satellites way up in the earth's orbit. Whenever and wherever they want. They can find him."

You look at James Nichols in utter disbelief.

"I'm not shittin' you, JD. When you join the army, they got you for life."

"Well, they sure as heck don't have me for life," interjects Terry Nichols. "I don't have any computer chip implanted in my posterior. When I was in the army, I rarely slept. I refused to go under anesthesia of any kind. I wouldn't even take laughing gas from a dentist—I still won't," he adds, quietly as usual.

"Shit," says James Nichols, "if anyone has a computer chip in their ass, it's Terry here. Just look at him." You observe Terry

Nichols staring off into the distance.

"Well, what do we do, then, Jimmy?" interrupts Timothy McVeigh, winking at you slyly. "How do we fight such tyranny from the same federal government that we count on to uphold our laws, to protect our vital interests?"

"Personally, I fight back by using the pen," announces James proudly, "'cause the pen is mightier than the sword. But you must always keep a sword handy for when the pen fails." Visions of Cardinal Richelieu begin dancing in your head.

"That's swell," remarks Timothy McVeigh, "but don't try selling no pens at a gun show. Or a flimsy old sword, for that matter." Your partner is getting folksy again, you think to yourself disgustedly. This is really getting out of hand.

"My customers want to feel the cold steel of gunmetal on their fingers," he continues. "They're not interested in getting civic—in signing a bunch of petitions. They're men of action. Like me." ·

AFTER BREAKFAST, Timothy McVeigh abruptly announces your imminent departure from Michigan. "We're gonna run the table for a couple of days down at a gun show I know in Missouri," he says. "We need to make up some of the money we've lost out here—especially after Jimmy's nocturnal visit with Lady Godiva."

But what about the profit that we earned from selling the Winchester to Roger Moore? you ask. The cash from that sale alone could last us for months, you think to yourself.

"I have other plans for that money," Timothy McVeigh remarks with perceptible annoyance in his voice. "And besides, the gun show will give us a chance to unload the last few flare-launcher kits."

You nod affirmatively to your partner. What else, really, can you do? You have abdicated all sense of free will—*everything you were and everything you are*—in order to heed the call.

YOU ARE SITTING at the kitchen table, observing Marife as she begins stirring up a batch of chocolate-chip cookies, the cupboards hanging open, the ingredients strewn about James Nichols's formerly tidy kitchen.

You love brown sugar, you tell Timothy McVeigh.

"You mean you like the black girls?" he responds. "Or do you mean that you like this one here?" he says, gesturing toward Marife. Wearing a green sundress embroidered with yellow daisies, she looks away bashfully.

You ignore Timothy McVeigh's irreverence and play cards with Josh, who looks to be in the vicinity of twelve years old. Josh is teaching you how to play a game called War in which you try to capture all of the other guy's cards before he captures yours. Or something to that effect. Terry Nichols sits nearby, seemingly oblivious to everyone—and everything—in his orbit. That guy must have a brain cloud, you think to yourself.

Is Josh your son? you ask Marife Nichols, making conversation yet again.

"Nah, dat's de udder bitch's kid," she answers.

The other bitch?

"Terry's first wife, Lana," interjects an amused Timothy McVeigh. "She lives back in Vegas. She'd be the *udder bitch*," he says, mimicking Marife's accent.

You decide—right then and there—that you will no longer be making conversation in the Nichols household. Or with Timothy McVeigh, for that matter. You prefer to remain mute. It's safer that way.

It makes it easier—considerably easier—to see the light.

YOU ARE PACKING YOUR belongings—what scant belongings you have, that is—into one of Timothy McVeigh's army-green duffel bags. You find yourself startled by the hushed sounds of human voices emanating through the wicker door that separates you from the second floor's lengthy hallway. A wicker door that you can see through rather easily.

And what you observe through that wicker door sends a veritable tremor through your body.

Timothy McVeigh and Marife. Hand in hand. And heading directly your way.

You rush into the dusty bedroom closet, where yet another wicker door separates you from the bedroom proper. You secret yourself amidst a slew of old bowling balls, hunting regalia, and other assorted mothballed clothing. It takes everything you can reasonably muster to stifle the sneeze that is building in your lungs.

As you peer through the wicker slats, Timothy McVeigh secures the latch on the bedroom door. And before you can say *infidelity,* Marife shakes her sundress loose from her body. The green outfit falls—placidly, daisies and all—onto the wooden floorboards.

Timothy McVeigh places his arms around Marife's tiny Filipina waist and brusquely turns her body away from his own. Arching her sepia-colored back, she descends on all fours and presents herself. This cannot possibly be their first time, you think to yourself.

As your partner—correct that: *Marife's partner*—begins to unzip the fly on his black jeans, you look away in horror.

You are trapped—trapped inside your claustrophobia. Trapped inside this closet. Trapped in wicker.

You cannot bear to look.

But you look anyway. And you keep on looking in spite of yourself.

In spite of the better angels who have seemingly abandoned you.

10 Buffalo Bill's Defunct

You are convinced that Timothy McVeigh is a pervert. That he has become a sexual deviant. A man who is dangerous to all things good and holy.

That he cannot possibly be a John Wayne type of guy.

Timothy McVeigh is driving the Road Warrior across the southern Michigan border into Indiana. You have been traveling wordlessly since you left Decker. Not surprisingly, your driver has taken to mocking your quietude, the silent treatment that you are giving him. The silent treatment that he so richly deserves.

Timothy McVeigh adopts a Tarzan voice for his own amusement. "Me TM. You JD," he says in a blunt, neo-native accent. He knows how much this pisses you off.

You ignore his efforts to make conversation, concentrating instead on the bland Indiana scenery—farmland, mostly—as it passes through your purview.

A massive dairy farm with dozens of burnished red barns and countless outbuildings pocking its grounds emerges on the Road Warrior's passenger side. Tour buses line the highway, with their riders, mostly elderly, waiting to sample the establishment's wares.

An enormous billboard frames the farm's magisterial entrance: "30,000 Cows—No Waiting!" it reads.

Waiting for what? you wonder to yourself.

Timothy McVeigh turns on the car radio, interrupting the silence. "The Sign" by Ace of Base is playing.

Eurotrash, you think disgustedly.

Life is demanding, you sing along in spite of yourself, *without understanding.*

You drive really fast, you inform Timothy McVeigh, who is traveling some 30 miles above the speed limit.

"The Road Warrior is turbocharged," he replies proudly. "Besides, I've got a friend," he says, tapping on the radar detector resting on the dashboard.

"By the way, I made that shit up," Timothy McVeigh confesses.

What shit?

"That shit about the computer chip."

You thought he didn't BS people. That it was part of his almighty code. *What gives?*

"I just wanted to get a rise out of those guys," he remarks. "And what do you know? They bought it—hook, line, and sinker. It kinda fits with their worldview, I guess."

You are still puzzling over his fishing metaphor.

"James and Terry live in a context in which the government is actively attempting to infiltrate their lives," he continues. "It works for them to see life that way. As a kind of us-versus-them situation."

But what about you? you inquire. How do you see the world? *Especially now that you're having relations with one of your best friends' wives,* you think to yourself.

"From my perspective, I realize that it's much, much worse than they'll ever know. That the government is too big, too inhuman to care much about the little people up in the Thumb," he responds. It occurs to you that some people really like the sound of their own voices.

"That it's a massive, lumbering, thoughtless giant of a thing that doesn't know any better," Timothy McVeigh continues. "That it couldn't possibly know any better. It's like a big ol' rabid dog. Like Old Yeller. And sometimes, that big ol' dog needs to be put out of its misery."

Are you the rifleman who can put that dog down? you ask, condescension dripping from your voice.

Your partner shrugs his shoulders. "Could be," he says. "It could even be you. *Gunrunner.*"

TIMOTHY McVEIGH PILOTS the Road Warrior off of the interstate near Angola, Indiana, pop. 5,824. Dusk is falling as he wheels the car into the empty parking lot of a convenience store.

"I want to grab a Slurpee," he announces. "It'll take five minutes—tops."

You have got to be kidding, you think to yourself. A Slurpee is produced almost entirely out of air. Which means that the food value from a Slurpee is virtually nil.

You follow Timothy McVeigh into the store. There are no other customers around, and the building is eerily quiet. The only sound is a box fan purring near the entrance. Exhaling the cool night air of early spring throughout the store.

Your partner makes a beeline for the Slurpee machine. If you were a betting man, you'd wager that he opts for cherry. Your personal favorite is cola.

You glance at the headlines on the newsstand. "Loch Ness Monster Photo Hoax Revealed!" screams the Fort Wayne *Journal Gazette.* "Nixon Ailing in N.Y.C. Hospital," reports the *South Bend Tribune.* No mention of your troubles back in Kansas. You're still safe—safe as milk and cookies.

You are startled to hear Timothy McVeigh shrieking your name from across the store. "JD," he barks. "Get over here. Pronto!"

That's a voice that could wake the dead, you think to yourself.

Rounding the corner from the newsstand and the brightly colored potato-chip display, you come face-to-face with Timothy McVeigh, who is standing, Slurpee in hand, next to the row of coolers in the back of the store.

And at his feet lies the very dead body of a twentysomething woman with a serrated knife stuck in the side of her head. A puddle of blood, still glossy and fresh, has pooled around her face. The name tag on her left breast pocket identifies her as Betty. She is remarkably attractive, you think—for a dead person. A redhead with a delicate oval face, her green eyes stare blankly in front of her. As though Betty were still in the act of being startled by the intruder, by the trauma that ended her life only moments before.

Timothy McVeigh squats on his haunches next to the woman. Staring intently at her. Fascinated, as if he were trying to decipher the events that led to her demise. He carefully removes the clear red straw from his Slurpee and runs it lightly across Betty's face. Finding her unresponsive, he pokes her arm with the straw as if to confirm the verdict. She's dead all right.

"Who, in fuck's name, would destroy an innocent person in such a heinous fashion?" he asks. "She's toiling away—making what? four dollars an hour?—and some guy comes in here and offs her out of thin air."

You agree. It's despicable. How could you argue otherwise? *How could anyone?*

Timothy McVeigh is clearly shaken. Worse yet, he's frozen in his tracks. Still staring intently at Betty's lifeless body.

With the heart of a fugitive pounding briskly in your chest, you find yourself listening for sirens. For evidence that the outside world has been alerted to the homicide lying at your feet.

You lean down and gently tug at your partner's arm, slowly lifting him back onto his feet in the process. Pushing him toward the exit at the front of the store, you reach around the counter and pick up the telephone next to the empty, open cash register. You dial 9-1-1 and place the receiver on the counter without returning it to its cradle.

You glance upward and find yourself staring directly into the security camera that is trained above the cash register. You gaze into the lens for a moment—and then for a moment more—before turning on your heels and walking quietly out of the convenience store.

Surprise! You're on Candid Camera, you think to yourself automatically.

You resume your seat in the Road Warrior, and Timothy McVeigh—still shaken over discovering Betty's corpse back in the store—slowly exits the parking lot. You strain your ears—but to no avail. There are still no sirens to be heard.

As Timothy McVeigh merges into the southbound traffic on the interstate, he hands you a cap with white-and-blue trim. The insignia in the center features the image of a panther bearing its grisly teeth. "I grabbed it for you on the way out of the store," he says.

You don't know what to say. You really have no idea. You are stunned. Absolutely stunned.

"I thought you'd enjoy a souvenir," he says. "I bet you don't even know what sport the Carolina Panthers play, do you?" he adds, sardonically.

Again, you really have no idea. None whatsoever.

"Football," he says, answering his own question. "They play professional football."

You glance at Timothy McVeigh's Slurpee. It's cherry.

You win.

AS TIMOTHY McVEIGH WHEELS the Road Warrior into St. Charles, Missouri, pop. 54,555, the sun is shining brightly in the sky. There is nary a cloud in sight.

"Do you ever get the feeling somebody's following us?" he asks.

Without thinking, you turn around in the passenger's seat and look out the rear windshield. For good measure, you shoot a glance at the side-view mirror as well. Nope, nothing there, save for the city's quaint Midwestern homesteads nestled among the sycamores.

"I just can't shake the notion that we're being shadowed. That somebody is on to us," he adds.

On to us for what? you think to yourself. By this point, it could be a whole myriad of things. Are we being tracked from outer space? you wonder. Perhaps there is a chip in Timothy McVeigh's buttocks after all.

YOU FOLLOW TIMOTHY McVEIGH into the St. Charles Convention Center. "Welcome to the Midwest Civil Liberties Association's Annual Gun Extravaganza!" announces the banner above the entrance. "The Second Amendment Is Alive and Well in the Show-Me State," reads another.

As your partner visits the registration booth, you study a vintage poster that is on display from a turn-of-the-century Wild West show. With a lasso in one hand and a Colt Peacemaker in the other, Buffalo Bill Cody, sitting astride a horse, performs his acts of derring-do for the ages.

Buffalo Bill's defunct, you think to yourself automatically.

"They won't give us a table," Timothy McVeigh blurts out, interrupting your reverie. "We're screwed."

How is that possible?

"Bob's been blackballing me," he laments.

Bob? *Bob who?*

"Bob—Bob Miller. Goddamned Roger Moore, that's who. He's gotten my registration revoked at the gun show. The son of a bitch is out for me. *For us.* Over the goddamned flare launchers."

Timothy McVeigh is beside himself. His face is drained of all its color.

"I didn't think the motherfucker had that much juice," he continues.

It must be Roger Moore's all-white outfit that does the trick, you think to yourself. Who could resist such a delectable ensemble?

"I thought we could slowly wean ourselves off of the gun-show circuit, but I reckon we're gonna have to expedite things," Timothy McVeigh continues. "We're gonna have to lay low for a while. And I know just the place."

TIMOTHY McVEIGH DRIVES all day and all night. Stopping only to refuel the Road Warrior or to replenish himself with another Slurpee. From the rolling hills of Missouri across the flatlands of Oklahoma and the Texas panhandle to the desert terrain of New Mexico. To the desolate, rugged topography of western Arizona. To Kingman, pop. 12,722, with its outlaw culture and its storied, folkloric place on Route 66. The last-chance, last-hope destination for America's lost, troubled souls.

With two troubled souls of its own on board, the Road Warrior coasts past a wind-burned sign marking the entrance to the "Canyon West Mobile & RV Trailer Park."

Timothy McVeigh brings the vehicle to halt in front of a faded blue-and-white trailer. "Behold the home of Mike and Lori Fortier," he says. A rusted-out barbeque pit sits in front of the trailer. An aluminum flagpole is planted nearby, with a pair of banners on display—the requisite Stars and Stripes, as well as the familiar yellow flag with its coiled snake and the immortal words "Don't Tread on Me." Patriots clearly live here, you think to yourself.

The Fortiers' dented black mailbox, adorned with a hand-painted red rose on its flap, is missing a letter. "Fort er," it reads.

Your partner can't resist mocking its absence. "Welcome to Fort Er," he says derisively, "where the West was lost. Where the men are unemployed dopeheads and the women are brainless bimbettes."

A tallish man with long black greasy hair and a goatee is painting a white picket fence in front of the trailer next door, an old-fashioned silver-colored mobile home with newish-looking rattan patio furniture on display. He smiles broadly as you and Timothy McVeigh hop out of the Road Warrior.

"Howdy, Sarge!" he says as he embraces your partner in a robust bear hug. "Damned glad to see you!" Mike is wearing a sleeveless T-shirt and blue-jean shorts. A pair of granny glasses rests precariously on his nose. They jiggle slightly whenever he laughs.

"JD!" he cries out, shaking your hand vigorously. "I've heard all about you!"

Really? How is that even possible? you think. Is your partner leading a double life? He must be burning through the minutes on that calling card.

"Take over for me, bud," he says, handing you the paintbrush. You stare at it for a moment blankly before dipping the brush into the gallon can of white latex paint and resuming the job. What else can you do?

As you begin painting the picket fence, Mike ducks inside the blue-and-white mobile home. He quickly returns, accompanied by a woman cradling her infant daughter in her right arm and holding a can of Pabst Blue Ribbon in her free hand.

"This is my girlfriend, Lori," says Mike. With her stringy brown hair done up loosely in a bun, stylish horned-rimmed glasses, and her too-tight black shorts and halter top, she cuts a rather incongruous figure. She may be trailer trash, you think to yourself, but at least she's sophisticated-looking trailer trash.

"I'm your *fiancée*, silly!" says Lori, giggling, as Mike frowns to himself.

Mike joins Lori and your partner on their neighbors' patio, where Mike leans back in a chaise lounge and drains a can of Pabst Blue Ribbon of his own. "It's OK if we kick back here," he announces. "They're out of town, and, besides, I look after their trailer for extra money. I do some painting and odd jobs and stuff for them," Mike remarks.

As your host reclines in the Arizona sun, you whitewash the picket fence. Dipping your brush into the paint, you make broad, deliberate strokes—up and down—across the dilapidated wooden strips.

At least it's a dry heat, you think to yourself.

11 Aliens—and More!

Timothy McVeigh is doing the dishes in the Fortiers' tiny eat-in kitchen. With its lingering stench of stale food, alcohol, and cigarettes, the trailer is a filthy mess. Your partner begins tidying the place up almost immediately. Sweeping. Vacuuming. Gathering up old pizza boxes, dirty clothes, and beer bottles. Emptying one Lysol can after another into the tiny, claustrophobic atmosphere of the trailer.

"You two are fucking pigs," says Timothy McVeigh. "What kind of example are you setting for baby Kayla—or JD here?

"I'm gonna need a sandblaster for the shower," he continues. "And I'm not even talkin' about that toilet." You had no idea that he was such a neat freak. That he was so obsessed with cleanliness. With establishing order out of chaos.

LORI REMOVES A BOARD GAME from the closet. You cannot even begin to imagine the housekeeping horrors that lurk in its dank, dark recesses.

It's Trivial Pursuit. Finally, something worth being excited about—enthusiastic, even, you think to yourself. You once finished third in a Trivial Pursuit tournament back at F.U. Your final, losing question still galls you: "What is the U.S. state with the largest Indian population?" It had to be Oklahoma—*heck, you still think that it's Oklahoma.* Who would have wagered on New Mexico?

"When Lori and I play, we use a slightly different set of rules," Mike slyly informs you. "We play Trivial Pursuit: The Drinking Game!" he announces, producing a giant bottle of cheap whiskey.

You are relieved. You were worried that they intended to play Naked Trivial Pursuit—or something to that ridiculous effect. You wouldn't put it past them.

"That booze looks toxic," says Timothy McVeigh with a nauseated expression on his face.

"You miss a question, you do a shot," instructs Mike. "And the first person to pass out wins!"

Mike fills four shot glasses from the jug of whiskey.

"Who's the biggest mass murderer in U.S. history?" he asks, reading from a game card.

Lori shrugs her shoulders, giggles, and empties her shot glass.

You don't have the first clue. You take a sip of the whiskey. Good God, that burns, you think to yourself. You push the shot glass away.

"Is it Manson?" replies Timothy McVeigh hopefully.

Mike shakes his head. "Drink up, Sarge!" he commands as your partner gulps down the whiskey.

"The answer is Ronald Gene Simmons, Sr.," Mike announces.

"The bass player from KISS?" Timothy McVeigh asks incredulously.

"No, Timmy, not the guy from KISS," replies an exasperated Mike as Timothy McVeigh begins sticking out his tongue in an obscene imitation of the KISS bassist's stage act. Your partner can be really gross sometimes, you think to yourself.

"Heck, I would have thought it was somebody like Manson—or Ted Bundy," says Timothy McVeigh.

"My turn," says Lori, still giggling. "Who said, 'I never met a man I didn't like'?"

"That's easy," answers Timothy McVeigh. "It was you, Lori!"

Your hostess giggles to herself as Mike shoots an irritated look at Timothy McVeigh.

"No, seriously," says your partner. "It was the great Will Rogers. Oklahoma-born in the Cherokee Nation."

Very impressive, you think. You didn't have the first clue.

"Now everybody takes a drink but Tim," instructs Mike.

The whiskey burns as you down another swig.

"It's JD's turn," says Lori, still giggling.

You glance at the question on your card: "What does a spermologer collect?" Of all the questions in all the world, why did you have to get this one?

"Is it cum?" asks Lori seriously. "Does he collect cum?"

Oh my God, you think to yourself. Why in the name of all that is holy are you getting this question?

You shake your head back and forth, vigorously. Nope. *Not cum.*

Lori begins giggling anew as she gulps down her third whiskey shot.

"I don't have the foggiest notion," says Mike as he slams back the contents of his shot glass.

Timothy McVeigh leans forward and takes a crack at the answer. "We need to think scientifically about this. There's not gonna be some porno question in Trivial Pursuit, for God's sakes," he says, shooting a derisive glance in Lori's direction. "A spermologer must be a person who practices the science—or the art, possibly—of spermology, right?"

That sounds logical, you think to yourself.

"Yeah, like spelunking," says Mike.

"No—it's not like spelunking at all. *It's not about collecting caves,*" says Timothy McVeigh sarcastically. "Sperm is the modus of transportation for semen," he continues. The modus of transportation? *Who is this guy?*

"And semen is the male seed," he continues. "Ergo, a spermologer collects seeds." Ergo? When did your partner adopt the language and demeanor of a Socratic philosopher?

Have you already become so drunk—after two lousy sips of whiskey, mind you—that the world has been turned upside down? That Timothy McVeigh has emerged as the Canyon West Mobile and RV Trailer Park's resident intellectual? *What gives?*

Without warning, Lori suddenly collapses, headfirst, onto the coffee table.

"We have a winner!" Mike proclaims.

So much for Timothy McVeigh's intellectual prowess.

"*A what?*" says Lori, slowly lifting herself up and shaking the cobwebs out of her head.

You observe Mike as he removes a bulging baggie of marijuana from behind the couch. Clearly, a new game is afoot.

"Ah, the potman cometh," says Timothy McVeigh.

"*The what?*" says Lori, giggling to herself.

"I see you're still killing brain cells out here in Arizona," your partner adds. "How many fences do you have to paint to keep yourself in weed?"

"I'm working at the True Value Hardware now," Mike answers, crumbling the marijuana leaves into an old tinfoil pipe. "I've got a regular paycheck and everything. No more welfare or nothing."

"You've certainly come a long way from blowing inspection and doing push-ups back at Fort Benning, then sneaking off with the officers after mess to light up a doobie," says Timothy McVeigh. "Well, perhaps not that far after all," he adds contemptuously.

"This guy was the slickest soldier in our unit," says Mike, gesturing toward your partner. "He did everything better than the other recruits. Better at weapons. Better at tactics. Better aim. Shit, he was even better at calisthenics!"

"Do you remember those five-mile runs back at Fort Ben? Some mornings, I thought we were all gonna die," says Timothy McVeigh, taking a hit from the pipe.

"You were as thin as a rail, man. That's why they called you 'Noodle,' right?"

"'Cause he was thin as a noodle before he was all growed up," chimes in Lori, giggling to herself as she puffs on the pipe. Perhaps she's not as sophisticated as you had previously thought. You make a mental note.

"Yeah, and I'll never forget our drill sergeant screaming at us every inch of the way," Timothy McVeigh recalls. "You pussy motherfuckers!"

That doesn't sound very motivating, you think to yourself.

"Seems like all we did was march and chant, march and chant. All day long," adds Mike, taking a drag on the pipe.

"Blood makes the grass grow!" they yell in unison. "Kill! Kill! Kill!"

Does blood really make the grass grow? you wonder. Is it the nutrients? The water?

Mike offers you the tinfoil pipe. You decline, shaking your head in self-disgust. You've defiled yourself enough for one evening already.

"Noodle!" says Lori. Still giggling.

"Goddamn, we were a bunch of sickos," Timothy McVeigh observes, laughing to himself.

"You ever wonder where those guys are now?" asks Mike.

"Well, Terry's up in the Thumb, of course," answers Timothy McVeigh. "We just saw him."

"Woody Allen in an army uniform!" says Mike. "Only much quieter. And not as Jewish!"

"I wonder what happened to our drill sergeant?" says Timothy McVeigh. "He was a helluva guy."

"Personally, I couldn't stand the bastard," remarks Mike. "He probably joined the mob after leaving the service. Shit, he's probably one of those pussies who ended up in the Witness Protection Program after turning state's evidence on some mook!"

"Sometimes, I truly miss the army," your partner says. "Seriously."

"What do you miss?" Mike asks. "The starchy food? The lousy pay?"

"Kill! Kill! Kill!" says Lori, laughing to herself.

"I miss the feeling of doing something important. Something meaningful," says Timothy McVeigh. "I was scared shitless before

Desert Storm, but once we got there, I felt completely different. The butterflies melted away, I climbed into that Bradley Fighting Vehicle, and all was right with the world. I felt like I was doing something noble and selfless, something patriotic. Probably for the first and last time in my life," he adds reflectively.

The old friends lapse into silence, passing the smoldering joint back and forth, one to the other. Lori begins to snore quietly before dozing off completely on the couch.

You cannot resist asking. You simply have to know.

So what happened, then? you implore your partner, your boon companion, *your friend.* Why did you leave the army?

"I arrived back from Desert Storm," Timothy McVeigh recalls, "to the opportunity of my life. I couldn't believe my luck. The chance to fulfill my greatest dream and join the Green Berets."

"The freakin' Special Forces," adds Mike, reverence in his voice.

"And I dropped out after the second day," your partner laments. "After a lousy five-mile march. Can you believe it? *A five-mile march.* I could have done that in my sleep back at Fort Ben."

"You were still the best I ever seen," says Mike encouragingly.

"Worse yet, I dropped out on account of blisters," Timothy McVeigh continues. "I was such a pussy. I dropped out after getting blisters from wearing brand-new boots. I may as well have been hiking in a pair of fancy wing-tippers."

"You did the best you could, Sarge," Mike intones. "Almost everyone who enters the sequence ends up dropping out or taking a medical. Shit, most of the guys who finish the course aren't even selected. Those are frightful odds in anybody's book."

"I still can't believe it," Timothy McVeigh continues. "How it all frittered away so quickly. But there was nothing left to achieve. Nowhere else to go—*but out.*"

You are staggered by his sorrow. And by the silence—the trailer having grown quiet, save for the occasional snore from the direction of the couch.

"And I still haven't found my way back," Timothy McVeigh says to himself, lost in his own oblivion.

TIMOTHY McVEIGH IS PLAYING HACKY SACK with the neighborhood kids from around the trailer park. You are eating the stale remnants of Lori's Fruity Pebbles in the Fortiers' claustrophobic kitchen, observing from one of the trailer's windows as your partner shifts and dodges with the best of them, doing everything he possibly can to keep the footbag from alighting on the earth.

Timothy McVeigh enters the kitchen excitedly. "I've got a line on selling our entire inventory of flare launchers!" he announces. "We're heading to Nevada. To a little town called Alamo, where our buyer runs a profitable arms business." He seems quite pleased with himself, you think.

"Alamo, Nevada, huh?" says Mike. "It's pretty spooky around those parts."

"That's balderdash," answers Timothy McVeigh. "There's nothing to it. Just a bunch of flyboys getting their rocks off, trekking around in experimental aircraft at supersonic speeds."

Balderdash?

"I've seen the pictures, man," Mike retorts, "and they're pretty convincing."

"Those are pictures taken by drunken rednecks tooling around the desert at night in their dune buggies," Timothy McVeigh responds. "And just because the pictures are printed in the pages of the *Weekly World News* doesn't make it so."

Doesn't make *what* so? you ask.

"Area 51," your partner answers. "Mike is getting his panties in a twist over Area-freakin' 51."

With a grin broadening across his face, Timothy McVeigh hands you the Carolina Panthers cap.

"Let's roll!"

AS TIMOTHY McVEIGH WHEELS the Road Warrior off of the bone-dry streets of Alamo and into the northbound lanes of U.S.-93, the vehicle's trunk is decidedly lighter from the sale of the flare-launcher kits.

"We're going on hiatus," announces your partner with a combination of giddiness and relief in his voice. "Our gun-show days are over for a while."

Up ahead looms the exit for Highway 375. The locals call it the Extraterrestrial Highway. As a white commuter bus with dark, tinted windows passes by in the opposite lane, you see a windblown billboard advertising a novelty shop. "Aliens—and More!"

In the distance, where the sky turns to dusk, you glimpse the Groom Mountain Range—Bald Mountain, Mount Wandell, and, beyond that, diminutive Papoose Mountain—spiraling into the sands of the Nevada desert.

Timothy McVeigh switches on the Road Warrior's driving lights. "We're looking for the famous Black Mailbox," he says.

The what?

"The Black Mailbox. It marks the entrance to Groom Lake Road."

Oh good God, you think to yourself. We're making a detour.

Timothy McVeigh takes a hard left turn onto a long, dirt road. And there it is. An old mailbox jutting out of the dry earth. Just up ahead, you see a cluster of cars, trucks, and motorcycles. A swarm of people circles a campfire along the roadside. You can hear the deafening thump of the music as you get closer. Lawn chairs and ice chests litter a dusty parking lot. It's like a rock concert in the middle of the desert.

As he pulls into the lot, your partner begins laughing to himself. "Great," says Timothy McVeigh, "a whole mess of Fortiers dancing in the desert. Legions of hippies tripping on mescaline and gazing up at the sky for flying saucers." You climb out of the Road Warrior and follow Timothy McVeigh as he makes his way to the campfire.

A long-haired man in denim overalls is filling a mug from a keg in the back of a pickup truck. A wide-eyed, skeletal blonde wearing pink hot pants and drinking from a red sippy cup stands nearby, training a pair of binoculars off into the distance.

"So what keeps you guys from driving across the desert and right on into the heart of Area 51?" Timothy McVeigh asks.

"The G," says Longhair jovially.

"It's your solemn, inalienable right to know what your federal government is up to," your partner remarks. "Anything else is just tyranny."

"The Camo Dudes would be on you in a New York minute," interjects the Skeletal Blonde. The light of the campfire illuminates the deeply etched wrinkles that line her face.

"The *what?*" asks Timothy McVeigh.

"The Camo Dudes," she answers. "They handle security along the perimeter."

"Well, fuck it," says Timothy McVeigh with a touch of arrogance. "We're going in!"

"You're crazy, dude," Longhair cautions. He's right, you think to yourself. *You're crazy, dude.*

"Nobody tells me where I can and cannot go in this country," Timothy McVeigh retorts defiantly. "Especially not a *Camo Dude,*" he adds.

"You fellas are begging for body bags," says Skeletal Blonde disparagingly as you make your way back to the Road Warrior.

As Timothy McVeigh revs up the engine, you hop into the passenger's seat. You pull the Carolina Panthers cap onto your head. It will serve as your battle gear as you blast into the unknown with your partner.

Timothy McVeigh negotiates the Road Warrior along the dirt road. "The Groom Lake secret military test facility," he mutters to himself disdainfully. "What a joke."

"Restricted Area," a bright white sign in red lettering warns. "No Trespassing Beyond This Point. No Photography."

"If we're really lucky," your partner intones, "we can take in an alien autopsy. Or, better yet, we can watch the extraterrestrials carry out one of their notorious cattle mutilations."

That sounds positively grotesque, you think to yourself.

"If we hurry up, we can make the evening tour of Hangar 18," he adds sarcastically. "I'd love to set my eyes on the *Black Manta*—or, better yet, the *Mother Ship.* Maybe they'll let us take a spin on the Anti-Gravity Fighter Disc."

This guy clearly needs to stop watching *The X-Files,* you think. Before it goes to his head.

"The Paradise Ranch, my ass," says Timothy McVeigh. "We might as well turn around. There's nothing to see here."

As if on cue, the radar detector on the dash suddenly explodes into being, emitting a series of high-pitched chirps, its red and green lights popping off like firecrackers on the Fourth of July.

Timothy McVeigh's eyes grow wider as you observe a pair of white Jeep Cherokees coasting in the distance, their spotlights trained on the Road Warrior as it shoots through the desert.

"Swell," says Timothy McVeigh. "Rent-a-cops." The Camo Dudes, you presume.

Up ahead lies a one-story guard shack with a black-and-white security barrier and a barbed-wire fence around its perimeter.

As you brace yourself for the collision, Timothy McVeigh accelerates the Road Warrior, crashing through the wooden security barrier with the Camo Dudes hot on your tail.

"We've got their attention now!" says your partner through gritted teeth as the Road Warrior shoots through the desert night.

The Jeep Cherokees pull alongside the Chevy, their camo-wearing occupants gesturing for your driver to halt.

"Not in this lifetime," says Timothy McVeigh as he slams on the brakes and the Camo Dudes careen on ahead, with the Road Warrior suddenly behind them in their dusty wake.

"We'll have to pass on the alien autopsy," your partner announces. "Sorry about that, pal," he adds as he reverses the Road Warrior.

As he wheels the car around, a mysterious shadow crosses over the Road Warrior and onto the roadway ahead.

What now? you think to yourself as the Road Warrior begins screaming back down the road.

You suddenly hear the low throb of a Black Hawk helicopter's rotors—*foof, foof, foof,* they sing in their slow, eerie cadence—as Timothy McVeigh extinguishes the Road Warrior's headlights in a vain attempt to thwart the Camo Dudes once and for all.

You've clearly seen everything now. Everything there is to see.

Foof, foof, foof go the rotors as Timothy McVeigh races back through the broken security barrier and across the perimeter.

Foof, foof, foof.

The Road Warrior speeds by the warning signs, past the parking lot—now empty—and begins hurtling toward the Black Mailbox, off in the distance.

Foof, foof, foof.

Then nothing.

And just like that—it's over. The Black Hawk has disappeared, with nary a Camo Dude in sight.

Timothy McVeigh pilots the Road Warrior back along Groom Lake Road toward the Extraterrestrial Highway, where he rockets into the night. A ridiculous smile on his face. And on your own.

You have never seen Timothy McVeigh happier. He is ecstatic beyond words. He has beaten the government at their own game and lived to tell about it. For the moment, at least, *he has won.*

You realize—*shockingly, amazingly*—that you feel a kinship with your partner. That you feel something beyond revulsion for your friend.

That you actually *like* Timothy McVeigh.

12 The Hypnotized Never Lie

You are no longer speaking to Timothy McVeigh.

You are sitting on a swivel stool in a Baskin-Robbins ice-cream parlor in Kingman, Arizona, trapped in a one-sided conversation with Evangelina Labio, whose shift ended nearly two hours ago. Her friends call her Angel for short. She lets you call her Angel, too, although you're pretty certain that it's out of a teenager's overdeveloped sense of pity rather than a sincere gesture of friendship. She is a short, frumpy, buxom girl who wears braces and sports a tattoo of a windswept Confederate flag on her upper arm. She loves working at Baskin-Robbins, but, ironically, she cannot stand the feeling of ice cream in her mouth. On account of the braces, that is.

As Junior Assistant Manager of Baskin-Robbins, Angel is your boss.

Angel is thinking seriously of quitting high school next fall, when she turns seventeen. She's sick to death, she tells you, of being known around the campus as "Labia" Labio, and, besides, she doesn't plan to go to college anyway. Kids can really be cruel, you think to yourself.

You spend most evenings listening to Angel deride her parents' insensitivity to her needs. She would like to add a few modest body piercings—lip and nose rings, to be exact—to supplement her tattoo, but her mom and dad won't budge. "Which is hypocritical," she maintains, "'cause everyone knows they're, like, the world's biggest swingers."

She is especially put out with her boyfriend, Cam—which must be short for Cameron, you think. Or Camaro. Or Camshaft—although that doesn't sound right.

"Cam only wants to get in my pants," Angel tells you as you cringe in embarrassment. You are suddenly struck by an image of hairy, disheveled Cam taking a crowbar to Angel's blue jeans in order to pry open the goods. To get at the treasure.

In truth, you're fairly put out with Cam yourself. He recently dropped out of Mohave Community College and landed a job—*surprise, surprise, surprise*—as the night janitor at Baskin-Robbins. Apparently, Angel and Cam are not the college-bound types.

Being a recent college dropout yourself, you're in no position to judge Cam's educational choices. Or Angel's, for that matter. What really bothers you about Cam—what really puts *you* out—is that he's never actually performed his duties as the night janitor.

Never. Not once. *Nada.*

And the reason he never performs his duties as the night janitor is because he spends every evening, without fail, having relations with Angel in the storeroom. Which is ironic, you suppose, because she's always complaining that Cam only wants to get into her pants. Which he does, quite successfully. And with enviable frequency at that.

You think that Angel's logic is rather circular. That it makes no sense. But you keep it to yourself, not wanting to hurt your boss's feelings. At the moment, she's your only friend. And besides, it's none of your business that Angel and Cam are having unprotected sex on the sly at Baskin-Robbins. Apparently, they're too embarrassed to buy condoms, although Angel isn't worried because she's pretty certain that Cam is *the one.* You know—*Mr. Right.* Mr. Hairy Disheveled Right.

And while Cam is getting into Angel's pants in the storeroom, you go about the business of being the surrogate night janitor and sanitizing the ice-cream parlor.

Of cleaning up the god-awful, indescribable things that happen in the Baskin-Robbins public toilet on a daily basis. Of mopping the dirt, grime, and chewing gum off of the parlor's vintage black-and-white tiled floor. Of thawing and throwing out the freezer-burned ice cream. Usually Rum Raisin, which nobody really likes.

And you do these things—night after night, like clockwork, like the fallen Quaker zombie that you have become—because you are no longer speaking to Timothy McVeigh.

STRANGELY ENOUGH, it all started at the lumberyard.

"You guys should stick around for a while," suggests Mike. "What better place to hide out than Kingman—a desert land populated by transients, drug addicts, and derelicts? You can lay low here," Mike continues. "You can blend in with the cactus. You can go unnoticed."

You are not that fond of cactus, although you certainly agree with the idea of blending in. Of going unnoticed for a change.

In short order, Timothy McVeigh lands a job at True Value Hardware—although pointedly not in the storefront, where Mike works.

"About the last thing I wanna do," pronounces Timothy McVeigh, "is spend all day catering to old ladies. 'You can find the rectal thermometers in aisle three, ma'am,'" he jokes. "A real man works in the back," he says mockingly, glancing at Mike. "A real man punches a time card in the lumberyard. Now, that's honest work. That's making a living."

"Don't knock the rectal thermometers," answers Mike. "Ministering to the old ladies of Kingman is God's work!"

"Which makes you—what?—some kind of prophet?" asks Timothy McVeigh sarcastically.

AND THEN, AS LUCK WOULD HAVE IT, you find Timothy McVeigh's dream house in the arid wilderness of suburban Kingman. In Golden Valley. On none other than Hunt Road.

"Hunt Road—I like that!" says Timothy McVeigh. "That's perfect for a shooter and a gunrunner!" He glances at you for a look of approval that will never materialize.

As houses go, the property that you and your partner rent in Golden Valley is about as nondescript as they come. Made entirely out of cinder blocks, the building effects the look of a Southwestern bunker. But without Hitler and Eva Braun in evidence. Only cactus—and plenty of it.

With sagebrush and tumbleweeds casting about the perimeter of the lot, the house seems, vaguely, like a Native American dwelling. Almost adobe-like, with a reddish tan exterior and a salmon-colored tile roof. But inside, it's all concrete—floor to ceiling, unfinished throughout the house.

You are decidedly unimpressed. It will be like living inside a series of interlocking concrete blocks, you think. Like defending Stalingrad against Hitler's relentless *Wehrmacht* morning, noon, and night. You are already developing a siege mentality—but with no foe in sight. Only Timothy McVeigh, with a smile beaming across his face.

To your mind, it looks like a living hell. Like living inside a concrete hell.

"It's perfect!" announces Timothy McVeigh. "It'll be like living inside a bomb shelter. You know—like the 1950s, *Sputnik*, the whole shebang!"

IN SHORT ORDER, your partner goes about the business of transforming the two-bedroom house's drab interior into the contemporary, survivalist *feng shui* of the American patriot. Of the militiaman.

For Timothy McVeigh, the house's most important feature is its wood-burning stove, which he feeds with scrap wood from the lumberyard.

"We'll never be prisoners of the electric company—or the

gasman, for that matter," he informs you. "When the grid inevitably fails, we'll still be sitting pretty while all of those other schmucks are crying for the government to bail them out."

At least the schmucks won't be living inside a cinder-block prison, you think to yourself.

"We're gonna build ourselves a bullet berm for the backyard," your partner adds.

A what?

"A bullet berm," says Timothy McVeigh. "It'll be like the berm up in Michigan where you shot at the soup cans—but with one major difference: our bullet berm will be a defensive countermeasure in case we're ever raided."

Raided? *By whom?*

"We've gotta stop kidding ourselves, JD. The government has declared war on the American public," your partner says, "and they are actively taking our rights away. Do you realize that our homes are going to be our last refuge? Our last sites of defense in order to protect our natural rights?"

That may be true, you think, but you're not sure how you're going to thwart the federal government with water-purifier tablets and a bullet berm. And by living inside a concrete bunker.

In his final stroke of genius, Timothy McVeigh outfits the basement with a 12-volt powered sump pump to prevent flooding. "It cost five bills," he says, "but it's totally worth it. You never know how long you might be trapped down here during a standoff, and we've gotta protect our food and survival gear."

A standoff?

"And check this out," he says, pointing to the far wall of the basement. "I've already bought, like, two hundred cans of food. Soup, mostly. And MREs."

MREs?

"Military term: meals ready to eat," Timothy McVeigh replies, gesturing toward a box labeled "Full Meals, Precooked." "The spaghetti and meatballs is my favorite. It's divine. We could live on MREs for days and never leave the basement."

Sounds swell, you think to yourself, gazing at the cinder blocks that encase you like a concrete coffin.

"We're gonna stockpile as many canned goods and drinks as possible," he adds. "Our goal is to amass a year's worth of food and potable water."

With his secret supply of foodstuffs nestled in the basement, Timothy McVeigh takes you on a tour of the house's hidden armory.

"People have to protect themselves," your partner announces to no one in particular. "We can't just depend on the government to protect us. I've placed shotties behind the bedroom doors," he tells you, "and you'll find your AirLite underneath one of the couch cushions. For good measure, I've placed knives and pistols above the ceiling tiles."

As Timothy McVeigh pulls back one of the ceiling tiles in his bedroom to show off his arsenal, you notice that he has Garfield the cat sheets. How precious, you think to yourself.

"I've also duct-taped a rifle underneath the sink in the bathroom," he adds. There's a sense of satisfaction in his voice as he gazes around the house. "Guns are the most important investment we'll ever make. When currency is gone, guns will be like legal tender. It'll be the most lucrative market around."

You make a note on your "Jot It Down" pad.

"And don't kid yourself. Every single one of these guns is locked and loaded," he says. "Why prepare your munitions if you're not ready and willing to act—to use them at a moment's notice? When trouble comes, you don't need to be toying with the safety. You don't want to be fumbling around for shotgun shells when they're taking a battering ram to the front door. *Capiche?*"

Capiche.

YOU WALK INTO THE KITCHEN wearing your sparkling white uniform from the ice-cream parlor. The name Daryl is stitched across the left breast pocket in light blue cursive letters.

"Oh my God," remarks Timothy McVeigh. "You're the Good Humor man."

That's actually kind of funny, you think to yourself. Humorous, even.

For the first time in your insular, sheltered life, you have a job. Your job at Baskin-Robbins may not be a real job in the conventional, pension-plan, contributing-to-the-good-of-society sense, but it's a job nonetheless. Besides, it's a job that you can do. Heck, it may be the *only* job that you can do.

As Timothy McVeigh shakes his head in mock disgust, the telephone begins to ring. "Don't answer that," he says curtly. "Let the machine pick it up. We don't want anyone to know we're here," he continues. "We don't want to give up our edge."

Our edge over what? you wonder. *Over whom?*

As the telephone stops ringing, the answering machine crackles into life with the voice of Timothy McVeigh. "I have but one lamp by which my feet are guided, and that is the lamp of history," he says. "Leave a message."

Patrick Henry, you think to yourself. Nice touch.

The caller hangs up without leaving a message.

"And that, gunrunner, is why we don't answer the phone," says Timothy McVeigh, a hint of paranoia growing in his voice.

YOU ARE WANDERING THE AISLES of True Value Hardware. Past the giant bins of nuts and bolts, past the electric drills and drill bits. You are searching for the entrance to the lumberyard. As you stroll through the back exit of the store—past the lawn mowers, hedge clippers, and other assorted yard-care equipment—you smell the warm, sweet odor of sawdust. You must be getting closer, you think to yourself.

Timothy McVeigh is standing next to a stack of plywood. He is sweating profusely from his brow. His T-shirt—which depicts a drawing of a six-gun above the words "We Bring Good Things to Life"—is soaking wet.

"You wanna see what laziness looks like?" your partner asks. "Look over there—across the parking lot. Next to the Dumpster."

In the distance, you see Mike Fortier talking to a bearded, oafish-looking man wearing a garish Hawaiian shirt and tan shorts. He cuts an awkward figure, standing in the Arizona sun behind True Value Hardware. They are smoking pot with a trio of True Value Hardware stock boys.

Yes indeed, you think to yourself. That looks like laziness all right. You make a mental note.

"I want you to meet the loser talking to Mike," he says.

That's not really necessary, you think. You don't need to meet the loser.

"That loser's been supplying us with scrap firewood for our stove," Timothy McVeigh continues. "And that loser's coming over tonight with Mike and Lori. They're coming over to the house in Golden Valley for an impromptu party."

But how can it be impromptu, you wonder, if we're already in the planning stages? If we've already scheduled the party?

You follow your partner toward the vicinity of the Dumpster. Balding heavily, with gigantic plastic glasses, the loser looks even worse up close than he did from a distance.

When you and your partner arrive, the stock boys scatter to the wind. Perhaps it's the awesome power of your Good Humor outfit coupled with the dangerous vibes emanating from your Carolina Panthers cap? Or maybe they're just frightened by Timothy McVeigh's perspiration. Perhaps they're afraid of work?

"My name is Stagger Lee," he mumbles, shaking your hand. His fingers are oily to the touch. Sweaty, even.

Stagger Lee? Wasn't that the name of a song?

Stagger Lee went home. And he got his .44, you think to yourself automatically.

"My daddy named me after a trick play," says Stagger Lee, apologizing for his bizarre handle. As if he has had to go through this very same exercise with every stranger he meets. Strangers like you and Timothy McVeigh. Strangers like anybody.

"My daddy loved football," Stagger continues, laughing to himself. "He thought it was a clever name, although it could've been worse," he adds. "My momma wanted to name me Enos."

Enos Lee, you think to yourself. That's definitely worse.

"I've seen a lot of football in my time," says Timothy McVeigh incredulously. "What the hell kind of play is a Stagger Lee?"

"Oh, it's a football play all right," chimes in Mike. "Quarterback laterals to the running back for a big-yardage pass. Unless the play fails, that is. In which case, it's a fumble. Loss of possession. Usually deep in your own territory."

"So are you a big-yardage pass or a fumble?" asks Timothy McVeigh.

"At the moment, the book is still out," answers Stagger Lee. "But to be honest," he says, crinkling his nose slightly, "it feels mostly like a fumble so far."

Enos Lee or *Stagger Lee*—it doesn't make any difference.

You are suspicious beyond words—even more suspicious, if that's possible, than you are about Roger Moore. Or Dakota Fish, for that matter.

You are decidedly unimpressed.

13 A Tooth for a Tooth

"This has become quite a little fortress!" announces Mike after touring the house in Golden Valley with Timothy McVeigh. He is standing in the living room with your partner, nursing a can of Pabst Blue Ribbon. Lori is sitting on the couch, leafing through a copy of *Soldier of Fortune*. Oblivious to the conversation.

Timothy McVeigh is clearly nonplussed by Mike's reaction. By his verdict about the state of preparedness on Hunt Road.

"Listen up, Mike," says your partner. "This place has a fully-functioning bullet berm in case of an attack to the rear of the property. I've got weapons strategically located throughout the house in order to carry out a protracted room-to-room struggle."

Is that likely? you think to yourself. A protracted room-to-room struggle?

You can tell that Timothy McVeigh is getting angrier by the minute. He's nearly frothing at the mouth. "And I can hold out in that basement—excuse me, *we can hold out in that basement*—for six months without so much as breaking a sweat," he continues. "By the time we come up for air, the A.T.F. and the satellite trucks will have left, having been defeated by boredom."

"Like I said," Mike remarks. "This is some fortress you've got here!"

"What's the A.T.F.?" Lori asks, giggling.

"The Bureau of Alcohol, Tobacco, and Firearms," answers Timothy McVeigh tersely. He's really smoldering now.

You are interrupted by a knock at the door. It's Stagger Lee, still wearing the Hawaiian shirt from this afternoon at the lumberyard. He's carrying a crumpled paper bag. Mike hands him a wad of cash, and he's gone almost as quickly as he arrived.

Isn't Stagger Lee sticking around for the party? you wonder to yourself.

"So this is crystal," says Timothy McVeigh, staring into the paper bag. "What is meth, anyway?" he asks.

"It's an ampha—," says Lori, attempting to pronounce the multi-syllabic word.

"An amphabetalmine," she tries again, giggling to herself.

Dear Jesus, make it stop, you think to yourself.

"An amphetamine," says Mike, bringing Lori's misery to an end. "It's an amphetamine. An upper."

"Could I lose my mind?" asks Timothy McVeigh. "Could I die?"

"Absolutely!" sings out Mike.

How can that be a good thing? you think.

"You go first," your partner tells Mike hesitantly. "I'm not sure we can trust a guy named after a trick football play."

"Anchors aweigh!" says Mike, placing the crystal gingerly into his tinfoil pipe and running his Bic lighter back and forth over the bowl. The crystal bubbles and foams inside the receptacle. Satisfied, he holds the tinfoil pipe to his lips and takes a healthy drag.

"Why is JD so pious?" Mike asks Timothy McVeigh. "And why is he so god-awfully quiet all the time?" He leans back on the couch, handing the tinfoil pipe and the lighter to your partner.

Doesn't he realize how awkward this is? you think to yourself. How rude it is to speak this way about someone in their presence?

"Well, let me tell you," Timothy McVeigh answers, winking in your direction. "JD here is a member of the Religious Society of Friends."

"The *what?*" says Lori, giggling.

"He's a goddamned Quaker!" says Timothy McVeigh as he runs the Bic lighter underneath the pipe.

"And what's *your* religion?" Mike asks.

"Science," your partner answers. "Science is my religion. The gospel of logic and reason." He takes an extended puff from the tinfoil pipe and hands it to Lori.

"I would have thought your bible was *The Turner Diaries,*" says Mike, laughing uproariously at his own joke.

"That's a good one," says Timothy McVeigh. "And there was a time when that would have been true—would have been right on the money. But I see things in a simpler light these days," he continues. "You reap what you sow. There's nothing mystical about that. Pure science and logic."

"But isn't that a religious argument in itself?" asks Mike. "Like 'an eye for an eye'?"

And a tooth for a tooth, you think to yourself automatically. Lori hands you the pipe and the lighter. You have nothing left to lose, you think. You are invisible here. You begin clumsily lighting up the crystal.

"Does that make you a scientist or a zealot?" asks Mike.

"The way I see it," answers Timothy McVeigh, "is that it makes me a little bit of both. As a scientist, I know that for every action there is an equal and opposite reaction. That things don't happen in a vacuum in this world. That there are forces to be reckoned with."

You take a slow, lengthy drag on the tinfoil pipe. You are already feeling a slight euphoria. A buzz of your very own.

"But as a zealot," Timothy McVeigh continues, "I know that there are untapped passions out there waiting to explode. That there is a Day of the Rope out there for all of us. The day the hangings begin. The day on which we're called to task for the things that we've done. The ways that we've been living. And you can read about that," he says, staring Mike down, "in *The Turner Diaries.*"

Your partner's demeanor suddenly begins to change. "I feel like my heart is about to burst out of my body," he announces. "Is that normal?" he asks Mike breathlessly.

"Just let it happen, Sarge," says Mike. "Let your mind soar. You're just sketching out, that's all."

"This is incredible," your partner exclaims. "My mind is racing. I'm remembering every obscure little thing that's ever happened to me. Christmas at my grandfather's house, hiking the cliffs above the Lower Niagara River, random math formulas from high school."

Without warning, your partner rattles off the quadratic formula:

$$x = \frac{-b \pm \sqrt{b^2 - 4ac}}{2a}$$

You don't need crystal meth to transport you back to math class, you think to yourself. You can do that completely sober.

As the euphoria takes over your body, all you can remember is Gina—*Gina, Gina, my pretty ballerina!* Lying on the chaise lounge with a midriff that goes on forever. Her downy hair setting your heart aflame. And the sight of poor Dakota Fish fighting for his life beneath his French textbooks. Bullet holes in dorm rooms followed by endless nights on the road with Timothy McVeigh.

It seems like a million years ago. Although sometimes it feels like yesterday. And at this moment—as the meth courses through your veins—it feels like right now. *This very instant,* as you relive it all over again.

You drift off into oblivion. Into a crystal haze.

MIKE IS LYING ON THE COUCH, his body contorted in his sleep. His mouth agape.

And Timothy McVeigh is nowhere in sight.

You shake yourself out of your delirium, dragging your body into the bathroom that separates your bedroom from Timothy McVeigh's. You gaze into the mirror, your vision seemingly altered by the crystal, your facial features distorted by the aftereffects of your euphoria. And then your reverie is interrupted by a sudden, libidinous moan.

You can see them through the open doorway of your partner's bedroom. Two bodies draped in a gloomy, nocturnal haze.

Timothy McVeigh is crouching behind Lori. His fingernails gripping into her shoulder blades. Piercing them. Clearly, this is your partner's position-of-choice—his fetish. He's doing Lori, forcefully, in the rumpled Garfield the cat sheets.

"I love to fuck!" she screams. "You are my fuck machine, Noodle!" She giggles.

Watching your partner having relations is getting increasingly stale, you think to yourself as you hide in the adjoining bathroom. And it's getting worse by the minute. Wasn't there a time in this story, you recall, when you were the one having all the sex?

Oh, Garfield, you lament. Oh, Lori.

You continue manning your post at the bathroom door. Still lost in your euphoria. *In their euphoria.* In spite of yourself.

AND THE NEXT EVENING—*the very next evening*—things fall apart completely.

You return to the house in Golden Valley after a long, interminable day at Baskin-Robbins, where you are being harassed by—of all things—a bully. At your age.

Your bully's name is Petey Van Horn. Admittedly an unlikely name for a bully, but you don't get to choose your bullies—or their names. You merely get to suffer them.

Petey calls you Daryl the Retard. Which doesn't bother you all that much. It also doesn't bother you that he's all of twelve years old. Or that he purposely spills his ice-cream sundae on the parlor's exquisite black-and-white tiles. Or that he urinates all over the bathroom floor on purpose. Just for you—the surrogate night janitor.

What bothers you is that his harassment of Angel—your boss, the only friend you have who doesn't have weapons stashed behind the toilet—is markedly worse. It's not just that she has braces. Or that she is dating a hairy mess of a person named Cam. Or that she's verging on becoming a high-school dropout and an unwed, single mother.

It's that she desperately needs her job at Baskin-Robbins—with its horrible hours, its mind-numbing sameness, and its thirty-one flavors. "This job is all that I have," she confides in you, "and Petey Van Horn isn't helping matters by calling me *brace-face* and pissing on the side of my momma's Chevette." She sobs quietly to herself. "What am I going to do, Daryl? What am I going to do when the baby comes?"

At times you imagine yourself exacting a little revenge. You fantasize about bringing the AirLite to work and dealing Petey Van Horn a lethal jolt of justice during your lunch hour.

But you don't, of course. You may be a fallen Quaker, but your heart still beats with the blood of a pacifist.

WHEN YOU RETURN HOME that evening—well after midnight, well after *Letterman* has already ended—Timothy McVeigh is waiting for you on the living room sofa.

"Kill the lights!" he commands.

You kill the lights.

"There's a car across the street," he whispers. "I think someone's staking us out." He has the Glock in his right hand. Cocked and ready to go.

You glance through the blinds, hoping to glimpse your pursuer. Your shadow.

Before you can say *Dragnet,* Timothy McVeigh is out the front door, the screen door slamming abruptly in his wake. He is off and running—like a proverbial shot. You had no idea he was this fast.

He is chasing a car down Hunt Road. You can see the red taillights in the distance—along with your partner, hot on the vehicle's trail. Running like a madman with a handgun through the streets of Golden Valley. Desperate to avenge.

You remove the AirLite from its hiding place underneath the couch cushion. And wait for your partner to return. You wait, as always, for further instructions.

When Timothy McVeigh finally comes back—breathless and dejected, covered in sweat—he is strikingly different. His face has changed. His features have shifted somehow. He is no longer your partner. He is someone else.

"What are you hiding from me, JD?" he asks menacingly.

You stare at him blankly, the AirLite resting loosely in your hand.

"Are you with me or against me?" he says, placing the barrel of the Glock against your chest and removing the AirLite from your grip in one easy motion.

You can feel your heart beating uncontrollably as Timothy McVeigh tosses your revolver aside and presses the barrel of the Glock even harder against your upper body.

"Who the fuck are you, Quaker?" he asks in a careful, deliberate tone—the careful, deliberate tone of a man who is becoming increasingly unhinged.

You cannot tell him, of course. You don't have the first clue.

AND THAT WAS 21 DAYS, 17 hours, and 31 minutes ago. You are purposely keeping your distance from Timothy McVeigh. You are no longer speaking to him. You are still cohabiting with him—*what choice do you really have?*—but you choose to come and go as you please, working later and later hours at the ice-cream parlor in order to carve out a space of your own. For yourself.

A few mornings later, after Timothy McVeigh has left for the lumberyard in the Road Warrior, you slip into his room.

The rumpled Garfield the cat sheets are still there, as is a well-thumbed copy of *The Anarchist Cookbook,* lying open on the nightstand.

I am an Antichrist, you think to yourself automatically. *I am an anarchist.*

There is blush and eyeliner on the dresser—Lori's makeup, you presume. So that's still going on.

And lying on the dresser are mounds of receipts. From filling stations, mostly, across the Heartland. There's a receipt for $2,775 worth of nitromethane gas—*whatever that is*—from an Ennis, Texas, racetrack. And another for ammonium nitrate from a farm co-op in McPherson, Kansas.

And then you see it: a handful of crystals lying in a baggie in the top dresser drawer. A stray meth pipe and brown paper bags. *Numerous brown paper bags.* Ghastly evidence of Stagger Lee's nightly visits to Golden Valley.

Timothy McVeigh is gone, you think. *Too far gone.*

THE NADIR OF TIMOTHY McVEIGH'S weirdness—of his vast and consuming psychological breakdown—occurs in the blistering heat of July, when you arrive home, courtesy of Angel and her borrowed, much-maligned Chevette, to the peculiar sight of your demonic, paranoid partner crouching on the roof, rifle in hand, staring blankly into the nighttime sky. You half expect him to say, "Who goes there?" like some deranged Beefeater keeping watch outside the royal estate. But he says nothing, of course. He's become too incoherent for anything like that. For anything lucid.

From the porch, you can see that the house is dark, save for the deep-red flames licking through the slats of the wood-burning stove's wrought-iron doors.

Timothy McVeigh climbs down from the roof and joins you in the front yard, rifle still in hand, his vigil unabated.

"Get in the car, JD," he orders. Insensate, without emotion, you do what you're told. Like you always do.

You climb into the Road Warrior. Into your familiar spot in the passenger's seat. You've actually sort of missed it, you think to yourself. You would never have thought that was possible. But there it is.

"I see that you're wearing your Good Humor getup," he says with a flicker of normalcy in his voice.

You remain silent.

Timothy McVeigh drives the Road Warrior through the quiet, dimly lit streets of Golden Valley. The morning sun is just beginning to present itself on the horizon.

He pulls the vehicle into the driveway of a stately house on a quiet, tree-lined street. A brick-and-mortar mailbox identifies the residents: "Van Horn."

How did you know? you ask.

"I know everything," he says, without a hint of cockiness. Without a hint of *anything*. "I know what happened before, since, and what will happen in the future," he continues. "I am a scientist and a zealot."

And you were a shooter, you think to yourself automatically. And now you are a crazy person. *A paranoid lunatic.*

Timothy McVeigh exits the vehicle and knocks, loudly, on the front door. He motions for you to join him.

A middle-aged woman answers, her hair in curlers, a cigarette flapping loosely in her hand.

"What?" she says gruffly. Without a care in the world. As though you've interrupted reruns of *Dynasty.* Or that you were there to sell her a vacuum cleaner.

But then she sees the rifle in Timothy McVeigh's hand. He suddenly holds her complete and unwavering attention.

"Listen very carefully, ma'am," he says with a terrifying tone in his voice—a remarkably controlled yet terrifying tone that you've never heard him emit before. "If your son doesn't stop the shit that he's doing around town—and he knows what I'm talking about—then keep this in mind: I know exactly where you live. And I'm going to burn your fucking house down."

His business concluded, your partner abruptly turns on his heel and heads back to the Road Warrior, leaving Petey's mom thunderstruck in your wake.

You ride home, wordlessly, as Timothy McVeigh wheels the vehicle back to Hunt Road. To the relative safety of his cinder-block fortress. For your part, you cannot imagine a more dangerous place on earth.

You mumble your thanks to him as he returns to the porch.

"Don't mention it," he says. "And by the way," he announces as the screen door slams behind him, "I'm getting a lock for my bedroom door."

THE MISERABLE FARCE of your life in Golden Valley—of your existence on Hunt Road—comes to an end during, of all things, a wedding.

The wedding of Mike and Lori Fortier. With infant Kayla as their unwilling flower girl and Timothy McVeigh—of all people—as Mike's best man.

If he's the best man, you think to yourself, then what does that make you? The second-best man? The best man's former partner? *The Invisible Man?*

Timothy McVeigh acquits himself admirably—summoning up a halfhearted toast about friendship and loyalty, about good tidings and good fortune, for the bride and groom. Most of the renegade staff of True Value Hardware is in evidence, including Mike's trio of pot-smoking, stock-boy sycophants. And Stagger Lee is there, too. How could you have your wedding without inviting your favorite drug dealer?

During the reception, Timothy McVeigh holds court among the other right-wingers—guys from the hardware store, mostly, along with Mike and Lori's flag-waving parents. He trolls over the usual subject matter—about the New World Order and the loss of American values. The assault-weapons ban and the tragedy of Ruby Ridge. And as they all get drunk, they become increasingly troubled about the nasty state of the world, about the loss of everything that was once pure and good about the republic.

And for all his vitriol, Timothy McVeigh is in fine form. Perhaps it's the brief respite from the crystal trafficking its way through his veins. Who the devil knows.

"America is in serious decline," he pontificates to the other guests, their attention shifting between his words of patriotic zealotry and Lori's triple-layer bridal ice-cream cake. "We have no proverbial tea left to dump in this country. Should we instead sink a ship full of Japanese imports? Is a civil war imminent?" he continues. "Do we have to shed blood to reform the current system? I hope it doesn't come to that, but it might."

Bravo, you think to yourself. Kudos for your pithy diagnosis of the contemporary American malaise.

With nothing left to do—and nowhere left to go, *no place to be somebody*—you stand off to the side, bystander that you inevitably are, and find yourself becoming increasingly distant. And eventually—*mercifully*—you slip away from the wedding altogether. You call Angel, who picks you up in her mother's world-weary Chevette.

You go straight home and pack your stuff—what little stuff you own, that is. *You do not pass Go. You do not collect $200,* you think to yourself automatically.

You resolve to strike out on your own path. You are growing increasingly fatigued by Timothy McVeigh's afflictions. Of making his paranoia and psychoses your own.

You slip into the darkness.

14 The Candy Store

Terry Nichols is standing in front of the entrance to Baskin-Robbins. He is wearing a black turtleneck sweater, black trousers, and black shoes. And—lest you forget, *how could you forget?*—a ridiculous dreadlock wig. He couldn't look any more preposterous if he tried. You wonder if anyone has called the police yet.

"Sarge is in trouble!" he declares with about as much emotion as he can possibly muster. "He desperately needs our help." What appears to be a black bowling bag sits at his feet.

He is staring at the breast pocket of your Good Humor getup. "Who the eff is *Daryl?*" he asks, a look of deep confusion on his face.

I am Daryl, you think to yourself. *Daryl Bridges.* And you, Terry, are wearing the most unconvincing, fake-looking dreadlocks that the world has ever seen.

"You need to come with me," he continues.

No way, José, you think. Not in this lifetime.

"I need you to get into my Honda," he implores. "Now. *Please.*" He gestures toward the beat-up, pale blue Honda Civic idling in front of the ice-cream parlor. It barely looks roadworthy.

Terry is putting on an absolutely terrible display, you think to yourself. A truly god-awful performance.

"Nobody's ridden with Timmy as long or as far as you," he adds. "If you don't help me, nobody will."

What about James? you think. Or Mike? Or Andy the German? You are not your brother's keeper, you tell him. You are no longer ministering to Timothy McVeigh.

"I'm afraid I'm going to have to insist," he tells you as he reaches down to unzip the bowling bag. In short order, Terry is training an Uzi on your white Baskin-Robbins smock.

An Uzi? In front of Baskin-Robbins? In Kingman, Arizona?

"Now," he adds sternly. "Get into the Honda. *Please.*"

You have no choice, really, but to cooperate.

You get into the Honda.

Terry nonchalantly sets the Uzi on the armrest between you and begins checking the mirrors—first the rearview, then the side-view—before easing into traffic.

"Are you buckled up?" he asks quietly.

Where are we going? you implore your kidnapper.

Terry begins to fidget uncomfortably.

To the house out in Golden Valley? To True Value Hardware?

"Not hardly," he answers.

To another state?

"Affirmative," he says, nodding his head.

To Kansas? Missouri? To the Thumb?

"Try Arkansas," he replies brusquely.

YOU HAVE BEEN SPENDING one sleepless night after another on the soiled, grimy couch in Cam's apartment. You have clearly reached your lowest low. You have bottomed out. And now you are sitting in the passenger's seat of Terry's beat-up Honda Civic. Driving across the country to Arkansas. More than a thousand miles in the company of the one person who talks even more rarely than you do.

How is this possible? you wonder. How do these things keep happening to you?

You turn on the radio in disgust. "All for Love," the syrupy collaboration by Bryan Adams, Rod Stewart, and Sting, is playing. Terry glances at himself in the rearview mirror, absentmindedly fingering his mustache.

I will defend, you sing along automatically. *I will fight.*

But defend against *whom?* And fight *what?*

AS TERRY PILOTS THE HONDA through Henryetta, Oklahoma, pop. 5,872, you interrupt the deafening silence.

What are we going to do in Arkansas? you ask.

"We're going to the Candy Store," Terry mutters without shifting his attention from the interstate.

The what?

"The Candy Store. It's our code word for Bob Miller's stockpile of guns and gold."

You pause for the rest. You can only imagine what's next.

"And we're going to empty it clean out," he continues.

And why, pray tell, is that?

"'Cause Timmy says that Bob—*Roger Moore*—is an effer," he answers without hesitation. Without betraying any emotion whatsoever.

A heifer?

"No!" says Terry harshly. "An effer. You know what I mean—*a fucker.*" The irritation is palpable in his voice.

A fucker. Indeed. And how, you ask Terry, does that necessitate a robbery?

"Because Timmy says that he's an effer," your kidnapper continues, "and he's got what's coming to him."

You remain silent. What more, really, can you say?

"And what he's got coming to him," Terry remarks, "is *us.*"

And with that, he leans across your lap and opens up the glove compartment, revealing your AirLite hidden snugly amidst a slew of poorly folded maps, a Twinkie, and an old tire-pressure gauge.

So this is going to be an armed robbery, you think to yourself.

AS YOU PULL INTO ROYAL, ARKANSAS, pop. *unknown*, you spy a group of boys playing baseball on a dirt diamond with a crude, chain-link backstop, their rattails and Mohawks on full display. They're using an old tennis ball and a broom handle. There are no baseball gloves in evidence.

Terry parks the Honda on a side street.

"We're getting out here," he announces.

Where's Roger Moore's ranch? you ask. All you can see is a dirt road leading back to the baseball diamond and a pasture that stretches, off in the distance, toward a forest preserve.

"We're going on foot," he replies. "We're heading thataways," he says, gesturing toward the grassland. And, beyond that, the woods.

As you wait in the car, Terry puts on what appears to be clown makeup, a black ski mask, and his black dreadlock wig.

Isn't that overkill? you ask him. Any one of them—the makeup, the ski mask, the wig—would constitute a disguise, but all three? That's just plain ridiculous, you tell him.

He hands you a ski mask and a wig. You climb out of the Honda and tuck the AirLite into your waistband. A bumper sticker affixed to the vehicle's heavily dented posterior suddenly catches your eye. "Is your church A.T.F. approved?" it reads.

You put the ski mask on underneath your Carolina Panthers cap, but there's no way—*not in this lifetime*—that you're going to wear the dreadlocks for Terry Nichols. And you're not even going to talk about the clown makeup.

"Suit yourself," your kidnapper says as he fiddles with the Uzi, nonchalantly removing and replacing the cartridge.

"We're ready to roll," Terry announces, gesturing silently toward the pasture. Like the S.W.A.T. guys do on television. Wordlessly. And with a sense of deadly purpose.

You are wading through the pasture with Terry Nichols. An active, well-used pasture after what appears to have been a very heavy rain. You cannot imagine how ridiculous the two of you must look. Wearing ski masks in the clear light of morning. Terry in his dreadlocks, you with your Carolina Panthers hat. Not to mention the Uzi and the AirLite.

As you go deeper into the pasture, the grass gives way to mud. And the mud gives way to hogs. Everywhere. Giant razorbacks. Docile, for the most part, but emanating the most repugnant odor you've ever encountered.

Terry attempts to shoo the razorbacks away, using his Uzi like a miniature driving tool. You look on in amazement at the bizarre figure standing before you.

How did you find your way from the relative tranquility of Friends University to this pasture, you wonder to yourself, with this man— *this man!*—wearing dreadlocks and corralling a posse of hogs with a submachine gun? It absolutely boggles the mind.

As you enter the forest, Terry removes his ski mask. Gasping for air beneath the clown makeup and the dreadlocks, he leans forward on the Uzi.

"When we get to the house," he tells you, "I'll go inside and roust Bob." Terry is visibly straining to catch his breath. He squats on his haunches, wheezing uncontrollably, gulping for oxygen.

"I'll blindfold him and then come get you," he continues, still panting. "Whatever you do, don't foul this up. If Bob recognizes us, it's curtains." Terry snickers to himself for a moment. "Although killing him would certainly be a bonus," he adds, grinning through the absurdity of his clown makeup.

You follow Terry through the forest until you see a large ranch house and a smattering of outbuildings. A blue-paneled van and a shiny Ford LTD are parked beneath a nearby carport.

As Terry prepares to make his way toward the ranch house, you see a gray-haired man wearing a white vest and matching trousers walking from the carport toward the barn. It has to be Roger Moore. Who else could it possibly be?

Without hesitation, Terry makes a beeline for the man in white. Covering some thirty yards in a matter of seconds, he aims the barrel of his Uzi at Moore's face.

"Lay on the ground," he barks.

"My dear boy," says Moore, "I had no idea the circus was in town. How good of you to come all the way down from Little Rock just to entertain an old man."

"Lay on the ground!" says Terry. With Moore lying on his stomach, his turkey wattle jogging at full tilt, Terry places the Uzi on the back of his captive's neck.

"Is there anybody else in the house?" Terry asks. As Moore shakes his head, Terry forces him to crawl on all fours into the ranch house, where he covers his victim's eyes with a strip of duct tape.

With yet another S.W.A.T.-like hand gesture, Terry motions for you to follow them inside. As an extra precaution, Terry throws a jacket over Moore's head before binding his hands and ankles with plastic, police-style handcuffs.

You stand over Roger Moore as Terry restrains him, brandishing your AirLite as fiercely as you can possibly muster. You are the Quaker Patty Hearst, you think to yourself. Perhaps that will be your defense at the eventual trial? *Terry made you do it. You were brainwashed—you had no choice but to go along. To save your own life.*

"Are you expecting any company?" Terry asks his captive.

"Yes, some folks are coming from Hot Springs for an early lunch," Moore remarks with a voice as sweet as pie. Without betraying a hint of fear.

As Terry begins rifling through his victim's home, Moore complains about the stench. "My dear boy, you smell absolutely like a pig yard."

"Shut the eff up, old man," says Terry. "Where's the money?"

"It's right inside the bedroom—on the computer desk," says Moore. This guy is as cool as a cucumber, you think to yourself.

"And where are the keys to the van?" Terry asks.

"They're right next to the money," answers Moore, his voice muffled by the jacket over his head. "But please, I beg you, don't take my van," the old man continues, his turkey wattle starting and stopping. "I just had it customized. Why not take the LTD instead? It's a lovely automobile."

"You can shove your LTD," Terry barks. "We're taking the van."

Following Terry's lead, you begin carting Roger Moore's possessions, one after the other, to the van outside. You empty out the man in white's treasure trove of rare gold and silver coins, his bounty of diamonds and emeralds, and a veritable mother lode of pistols, shotguns, and rifles—nearly ninety weapons in all.

"These plastic handcuffs are absolutely paralyzing me," Moore interrupts. "Would you be so kind as to remove them? Surely, the duct tape would suffice for an old man like myself."

"Where's the Winchester?" Terry demands.

"Are you a fed?" Moore counters.

Terry chuckles through his ski mask. "The Winchester repeating rifle," he says with growing exasperation in his voice, "where is it?"

"It's in my study," says Moore. "Inside the walk-in safe."

"You'd better not be lying to me, old man," says Terry.

"Why would I lie?" he asks. "If you tell the truth, you don't have to remember anything," Moore replies somberly.

"What's the effin' combination?" Terry asks.

"Four—nineteen—seventy-five," answers Moore calmly.

Terry pauses for a second.

"April nineteenth, seventeen seventy-five," says Terry thoughtfully. "The shot heard 'round the world. The day that the American Revolution broke out in Lexington, Massachusetts."

"So you're a history buff?" Moore inquires.

"Well, that don't make you a patriot," replies Terry derisively.

Don't it? you think sarcastically.

"I suppose that it doesn't," says Moore.

"You're an effin' profiteer, not a patriot," says Terry. "And ain't nothing else gonna make a lick of difference." What's with the folksy demeanor? you think to yourself. The man spends one minute talking about the American Revolution, and then he transforms into Timothy McVeigh and every other backwoods militiaman out there. *What gives?*

Moments later, Terry returns from the walk-in safe with the Winchester.

He glances around the room for a moment, then down at Roger Moore, still handcuffed on the living room floor. Without warning, Terry carefully aims the Winchester at the back of his captive's veiled head.

What the eff are you doing? you scream at Terry Nichols.

"Shut up, dude! I know what I'm effin' doing," your kidnapper replies.

The eff you do! you retort.

"Eff you!" Terry snorts through his ski mask.

You are suddenly caught up in the great battle of the teetotalers. Where words act as thermonuclear devices.

"It'll be a mercy killing," Terry exclaims as he steadies the Winchester. Roger Moore's turkey wattle comes to a sudden halt.

The heck it will, you think to yourself.

With your hand shaking, you place the barrel of the AirLite against the nape of Terry's neck.

Terry stares back at you menacingly. You can feel the heat of his gaze through the dark fabric of the ski mask, through the garish veneer of the clown makeup.

He finally lowers the Winchester. "This ain't over," he informs you, gritting his teeth in disgust. "Not by a long shot."

Terry returns his attention to Roger Moore. "I might have killed you just now," he tells his captive.

"The fear of death follows from the fear of life," Moore replies. "A man who lives fully is prepared to die at any time. And I have certainly lived fully," he adds.

"Now listen up, old man," says Terry. "There's another guy out there with a shotgun. We're coming back for the rest later."

Roger Moore grunts beneath the jacket, twisting his hands together in a desperate attempt to break free of the handcuffs.

"And you don't have to worry about your guns," Terry adds, grinning to himself. "They're going to the gangs."

"Apparently, there is nothing that cannot happen today," Moore sighs to himself. "Nothing, nothing, and yet more nothing."

"Let's get the eff out of here," Terry snarls in your direction.

Yes sirree, you think to yourself.

With Roger Moore's worldly goods stowed safely away in his newly customized, freshly stolen van, you get the eff out of there.

15 Back to the Future

As you look on in amazement, Terry Nichols begins transferring your booty from Bob's robust paneled van to the beat-up, road-worn Honda.

You glance over at the posse of boys who are still playing baseball on the dirt diamond. Oblivious to your crimes. Oblivious to the two men in ski masks shuffling back and forth between the vehicles.

The weight of Bob's precious metals and weaponry is exerting an observable effect on the Honda, which is now sagging dangerously close to the ground, particularly around the trunk and the rear bumper.

You have no idea how Terry's dilapidated Honda is going to be able to make its way out of Royal, much less out of the state of Arkansas while bearing such a heavy load.

Why don't you just keep the van? you ask Terry.

"Because that would be grand-theft auto," he replies.

But you don't acknowledge American statutes, you counter, so how could it be a crime?

"Yeah, but stealing a man's vehicle is wrong," answers Terry.

You just cleaned the guy out of some ninety weapons, you reply, not to mention the gold and silver. Was that a wrong thing to do?

"But that was the mission," your kidnapper retorts. "That was our intended goal." A look of confusion crosses his face.

That's fine and dandy, you point out, but if you believe that it's wrong to steal Bob's van, then how—*in the name of all that is holy*—do you justify the fact that you almost blew the man's head off?

"Like I already told you," Terry responds, with deep exasperation growing in his voice, "Timmy said that Bob is an effer—you know, *a fucker.*"

And?

"And that effin' effer is expendable," says Terry. "He's the scourge of the gun movement. Bob is a shameless profiteer, and I don't care how many facts the guy memorizes about the American Revolution. *He does not get it, he is not a patriot, and he is expendable.*" Terry is frothing at the mouth. He is pointedly staring away from you, looking off into the distance as if he were simply too upset to maintain eye contact with you. With his new-found enemy.

It doesn't hurt, you counter, that Bob is also a potential witness against you—*against us*—does it? Does that make him even more expendable? you ask.

Terry stares at you with pure disgust in his eyes.

"I have absolutely nothing else to say about the matter," he replies.

AND TERRY NICHOLS doesn't say another word—not another syllable, not even so much as a grunt—until he wheels the Honda into Herington, Kansas, pop. 2,685, some nine hours later. It's a remarkable feat, really. Sustaining all of that silence for so long—and without so much as a wayward glance in your direction.

Even the simple act of being back in Kansas—of being within a few hours of Wichita—riddles you with anxiety. You are only a matter of miles—eighty-five of them, to be precise—from the site of your greatest despair.

You are overwhelmed with the fear of being discovered, of being captured and forced to atone. And yet, *at the very same time,* you are desperate to effect your homecoming. To be punished for wading into the river of no return.

You want nothing more than to be redeemed. *To rediscover the light.*

TERRY EASES THE HONDA into a storage facility located on a remote hilltop overlooking Herington. "If anybody asks," Terry confides, "my name is Shawn Rivers."

And I am Daryl Bridges, you think to yourself automatically.

Spotting a newsstand in front of a business office, you glance at the headlines out of force of habit. Your crimes down in Wichita have surely grown stale by now—sodden and dusty with age—and your mischief in Arkansas is simply way too fresh for news coverage, especially in these Kansas backwaters. "President Dedicates Pan Am Flight 103 Memorial," trumpets one of the headlines in the *Wichita Eagle.* "Israeli Prime Minister Yitzhak Rabin Assassinated at Tel Aviv Peace Rally," announces another.

Oh, irony of ironies, you think. Murdered at a peace rally. In the broad light of day.

Terry steers the Honda to a halt in front of storage unit number two. "It's go time," he exclaims as he climbs out of the abused, beleaguered Honda.

When did you rent this thing? you ask Terry.

"Oh, me and Timmy have them all over the place. We've had them for months—some of them for years."

Glancing furtively from left to right, Terry unlocks the storage unit. Some of the clown makeup still clings to his sideburns and the outskirts of his face. With the first hint of dusk settling in for the evening, it makes for a ghastly sight.

With an awkward lurch, Terry lifts the garage door open and turns on the unit's overhead light. What looks to be around 40 bags of ammonium nitrate fertilizer are stacked neatly in the corner.

McPherson, Kansas, you think to yourself. *The farm co-op.*

Following Terry's lead, you begin unloading the spoils of your robbery into the storage unit. Your muscles are aching from hauling the guns—back and forth, from one vehicle to another—all day long. Shifting Bob's gold from the Honda into the storage unit doesn't make things any easier.

It's been a long day's journey into night, you think to yourself.

Your work completed, Terry extinguishes the overhead lamp and shuts the garage door. He is still panting from the effort exerted in unloading the Honda.

That robbery made for a nice bit of payback, you remark to Terry as you settle into the car.

"Payback?" asks Terry. "Payback for what?"

Payback, you tell him, for the way Roger Moore banned your erstwhile partner from the gun show back in Missouri. For threatening Timothy McVeigh's livelihood. His God-given, American right to earn a living as he sees fit.

"I may not have been entirely truthful about that," Terry admits. "That most certainly wasn't payback, and that wasn't just a robbery either," he adds.

Then what, pray tell, did you do back in Arkansas? you inquire.

"That was a fund-raiser."

A what?

"For the operation," he continues. "It was a fund-raiser. We're going to need a budget. You can't do these things on the cheap."

What things?

Terry looks absolutely flummoxed. The color has drained entirely from his face. He begins nervously fingering his mustache.

"That's really all I can say," Terry answers, almost whispering. "I've said too much already."

He sits quietly for a moment.

"Please don't tell Sarge I said anything," Terry pleads. He is on the point of begging. "I really had no right to say anything to you. I just needed your help so badly for this mission—and Timmy hasn't been available."

The crystal, you think to yourself. He's too far gone on the crystal.

And the hate. And the paranoia. And God knows what else.

"BACK TO KINGMAN," your kidnapper announces as he shifts the Honda into gear.

You are struck by a whim. You ask your driver to drop you off in Wichita—to his surprise as much as your own. Sometimes you astound yourself. You really do.

"Sarge's instructions were pretty clear," Terry answers with a hint of concern in his voice. "He wants you back, safe and sound, in Arizona."

Anywhere in Wichita would be just fine, you implore Terry. Or anyplace along the way.

Any way the wind blows, you think to yourself automatically. *Doesn't really matter.*

Terry is fidgeting demonstrably with the steering wheel.

"I don't know, dude," he answers. "Timmy was real adamant about you coming back to Kingman."

You remove the AirLite from your waistband and place it, gently, against your driver's torso.

He certainly hears you now.

Why does it always come to this? you think. To threats of violence and duress. Whatever happened to fulfilling a simple human request? Where is the harm in that?

TERRY BRINGS THE HONDA to a stop near the golf course that marks the outer fringes of your misplaced studenthood. Of Friends University.

You reach across the armrest and grasp his right shoulder, lightly, with your hand. As kidnappers go, Terry Nichols hasn't been all bad. He never tortured you, for one thing. And when push came to shove, he didn't pull the trigger—he didn't blow Bob's head off. Of course, you were training your AirLite on him at the time, but that's a minor detail.

In the grand scheme of things, Bob is still alive—only decidedly lighter in the gun and gold departments—and Terry hasn't become a murderer. You may have just saved his mortal soul from eternal damnation. Not bad for a few days' work, you think to yourself. JD—1, Soul-Destroying Afterlife—0.

Still staring straight ahead, Terry nods his head twice as you touch his shoulder. As if to tell you that he understands.

As if to say good-bye.

YOU ARE STANDING AT the main entrance to F.U. It is dark and quiet, with nary another person in sight, save for the occasional student trudging like a snail, backpack dangling across one shoulder, to the library.

If anyone paused to look at you, you would make for an incredible sight.

You are still wearing your Carolina Panthers cap—your battle gear. The AirLite is nestled in the waistband of your Good Humor outfit, with its matching white smock and trousers. Your nom de plume stitched in friendly blue letters for all to see.

You stroll across the campus—through the vacant parking lots, past the classroom and administration buildings, and beyond the library to the dormitories.

And there it is. The Academic Village.

You cross the street, briskly, and take the steps, two at a time, to the security door. You remove the lonely dorm key from your pocket. Nine months in mothballs, waiting to be used.

As your apprehension begins to get the best of you, you turn the key in the lock. And then—nothing.

Nothing happens in the slightest. No sirens. No plainclothes security guards bursting from the woodwork. Just you—*fugitive you*—gaining entrance to the site of your most notorious crime against society. At least so far.

You walk across the silent lobby—vacant, save for a pair of coeds studying together—and climb the back staircase to the second story. To the dorm room you once shared with one Dakota Fish, an American citizen of near-charter lineage. And your sworn enemy.

You try the key in the lock, your anxiety quickening as you wait for the siren call of the campus police. But again, nothing happens. Nothing whatsoever.

And nothing awaits you on the other side of the door either. No yellow crime-scene tape. No chalk outline on the dorm-room floor. Not even a commemorative plaque.

And certainly no Dakota Fish. Oh, there are occupants all right—a pair of college students snoozing away, oblivious to your trespass—your trespass against them. Dakota Fish's grammar books are gone—vanquished, it seems, by the voluminous textbooks of a biology major. The poster of a busty blonde in a shiny red swimsuit adorns the far wall—Pamela Anderson perhaps? Although you can't be sure through the haze.

With the exception of the occupants of your dormitory room, the Academic Village seems remarkably unchanged. You are troubled by this sameness, as if your footprints in Wichita have already vanished. That you have been disappeared. *That you have been made invisible.*

YOU ARE WALKING ALONG the deserted streets of Wichita, making your way toward Gina's boardinghouse. You will locate Gina, you think to yourself, and you will strive for atonement. You will seek out the light—even if it is only the disquieting light of a fallen Quaker in her eyes. *Two fallen Quakers.*

You are still wary about your presence in Wichita, as if the authorities have already been alerted to your arrival in their jurisdiction. But it is a quiet evening in the city, and you hear nothing—save for the occasional blaring television set or a dog's authoritative nighttime bark.

Like the Academic Village, Gina's boardinghouse seems utterly timeless in your world. Her chaise lounge still rests quietly in the backyard. Your heart is racing, palpably, as you climb the steps to Gina's front door. You are addled in your anxiety. What will she say? How will she react to your sudden return? To the ghosts of your traumatic past?

You knock on the door—your anxiety having been displaced by a sense of excitement, an urgency, an enthusiasm, strange as it may seem, for what might happen next. If only—

But then you see it: the unmistakable sign of Gina's exit from Wichita's environs. "For Rent" reads the notice in the window. Simple, direct, and to the point.

She is gone.

16 Feed Your Head!

For the first time in months, you wake up in the cool morning air of Wichita. And you are sore—terribly, painfully sore. Staring into the sun—into the bright light of a new day—you are reclining in Gina's backyard. On the chaise lounge to which, once upon a time, she had brought so much glory. The chaise lounge where you slept last night, restless and beset. And, as usual, dreamless.

You lift your body out of the chaise lounge's wooden clutches. You can hear the sound of Gina's neighbors stirring, and you realize that you had better leave—*pronto!*—before you attract any undue attention. Before you sound any unnecessary alarms.

You are wandering the streets of Wichita. You will become a wanderer, you think to yourself whimsically. A wandering Quaker. Spreading the good word—and trying your darnedest, *as always*, to stamp out the bad ones.

A few blocks away, a mailbox catches your eye. "Wilson" it reads. "*Bonjour!*" proclaims the welcome mat lying in wait before the front door.

Madame Wilson! Who else, really, could it be?

You ring the buzzer, giddy with anticipation. Desperate to see a friendly face. To see some evidence of your erstwhile Wichita existence made real.

The door opens to a tallish brunette, graying slightly around the temples. A pair of stylish green bifocals perched lazily upon her nose. A friendly face, if ever there was one. *Finally.*

"Well, if it isn't JD!" she exclaims with a hint of good cheer rising in her voice. So far, so good.

"You're not here to shoot up the place, are you?" she adds, adopting a mischievous tone.

YOU ARE DRINKING a *caffè latte* with Madame Wilson on her back porch. It occurs to you that it may be the first nourishment, of any kind, that you've had in days. You are famished, yet you are also experiencing a sense of contentment that has become foreign to you. That doesn't seem quite real.

"So, who is Daryl," she asks, "and what is with the costume?"

Je m'appelle Daryl, et je sers la glace à Baskin-Robbins, où je suis aussi le concierge de nuit.

"Ah, *très bien!*" she says. "Your French is still in fine form." She pauses for a moment. "You have developed a nasty habit, you know, of running off my best students." Peering over the edge of her eyeglasses, Madame Wilson fixes her stare on you.

You finally blurt it out. You cannot help yourself. *You simply must know.*

What happened to Dakota Fish? you ask. You can hardly breathe as you wait for her answer—her verdict, even—on the results of your crime spree. Your great loss of self-control. Your great loss of faith.

"He has transferred to another school," she replies. "In Oklahoma— near his reservation."

So he's not dead?

"Of course not," she answers. "Why would he be dead? He's so young—like you. He was just homesick—and uncertain, to be sure, about his religion. Who can blame him, no?"

Were your bullets—straying and splaying across the dorm

room—the catalysts for Dakota Fish's escape? you ponder to your-self. For his journey of self-renewal?

And what about Gina? you ask Madame Wilson, your voice shud-dering and quaking as you struggle to say the words.

"She's gone to live with her mother—in Hannibal, Missouri," says Madame Wilson. "You shouldn't be surprised," she adds.

You are confused. What, pray tell, could that possibly mean?

"A lot of young women leave the life," Madame Wilson continues. "They want to get on with things, have boyfriends, fall in love. They become disenchanted, so they—*how do you say it?*—they delve into promiscuity. They drop out of school. This is nothing new under the sun. There are scholarly studies on the subject—written by men, mostly, which is rather perverted, if you think about it."

You should read more, you think to yourself. You suddenly feel so uninformed.

"That is what happened with you two, no?" she adds. "She dangled it in front of you, and you took it. Or it was forced upon you—it doesn't matter which. The result remains the same."

But how can you be so understanding? you ask Madame Wilson. What allows you to see things so clearly, so objectively?

"You forget, *mon chéri*," Madame Wilson replies, "that I am not a Quaker."

YOU ARE WALKING THE STREETS of Wichita with a skip in your step and a song in your heart. It may seem corny, you think to yourself, but it is true.

You may be a lot of things, but you are not a murderer. A crimi-nal—*most certainly*. But you are not a destroyer of life. And now you know that explicitly. And you know it within the deepest soundings of your heart.

As you stroll back toward the campus, you are struck by the cruelest of mirages. No more than fifty yards away, idling in front of a filling station, is a silver-colored Chevy Geo Spectrum.

The Road Warrior. *It just has to be.*

"I DROVE ALL NIGHT," Timothy McVeigh informs you. "As soon as I got the word from Terry, I hit the trail. I've been looking all over town for you. I tried your old dorm room first," he continues. "By the way, I really scared the shit out of a couple of guys when I came in unannounced. I had to hightail it outta there. Almost had to break out the Glock. But no biggie."

No biggie?

Timothy McVeigh is piloting the Road Warrior out of Wichita. Away from the site of your greatest desolation. You've certainly been here before, you think to yourself. And at least this time you didn't have to traipse through a godforsaken Dumpster.

You cannot believe how glad you are to see him. To see Timothy McVeigh—replete with his paranoia and his obsessions.

You really are the Quaker Patty Hearst, you think to yourself. You cannot stop yourself from clinging to your veritable Symbionese Liberation Army—*your Timothy McVeigh*—like the victim of some mind-numbing Stockholm syndrome. His welfare has become your own. How the devil does that happen? you wonder.

You really have no idea. You don't have the first clue.

What you do know, though, is that you will accept this earthly reprieve. That you will be grateful for Dakota Fish's survival. That you are thankful that you cannot hit the broad side of a barn.

You will honor Dakota Fish's existence by living the life of reverence for which you were destined.

You will redouble your energies on Timothy McVeigh's behalf. You will never allow yourself to stray from his orbit again. There's simply no other way.

"'**FEED YOUR HEAD!**'" Timothy McVeigh sings as he speeds along I-40, thirty-eight miles outside of Amarillo in Vega, Texas, pop. 840, on a direct, westerly route toward Kingman, Arizona.

Your partner wheels the Road Warrior off of the interstate to use a pay phone in the back of an old Dairy Queen.

"I'd like to make a person-to-person call in the name of Robert Kling," he tells the operator.

"Hey, dude," he says into the receiver. "This call is code red. Terry and JD did Bob. We're ready to roll. You need to scramble into action. We'll be there in about nine hours. It's code red, *hombre*. Don't even think of letting me down on this, you hear?

"Fortier's on the bubble," he tells you as he hangs up the telephone. "He's with us—then he's not with us. It's back and forth with him anymore."

What gives?

"What gives," Timothy McVeigh replies, "is that he got married. That he's pussy-whipped. He used to be a crack infantryman—when he wasn't stoned, that is—but now he's a shadow of his military self. He's become a woman."

A woman?

"And there's no room for a woman in this man's army," your partner exclaims, winking in your direction.

YOU ARE BLAZING with Timothy McVeigh across New Mexico in the Road Warrior. The winter winds are whipping across the plains, battering the tiny Chevy like a Matchbox car.

But Timothy McVeigh has other things on his mind.

"Don't even think about fretting over Bob," your partner says. "He got what's coming to him."

You can say that again, you think. *We've all got what's coming to us.*

"Bob would surrender his guns meekly to any federal agents who came along," he says, "and you and I both know it. Those guns were doing no good in his possession."

Amen, Brother McVeigh, you think to yourself.

"You guys deserve to be congratulated," he continues. "The Candy Store robbery went off without a hitch—well, save for one thing."

Is it because we didn't steal Roger Moore's nifty customized van and ditch that worn-out old Honda? you wonder to yourself.

"It's a shame that Terry neglected to kill Bob," says Timothy McVeigh. "That would have been the icing on the cake."

You have no idea how close that came to being true, you think. How close Terry came to offing Roger Moore. *How close he came to eternal damnation.*

"Everybody has their own Day of the Rope," Timothy McVeigh continues. "And Bob's number came up with you guys. Sure, nobody strung him up," he adds, "but it's the same principle."

You glance outside the passenger's seat window as the New Mexico landscape goes tumbling by. A gas station here. A rest stop there. Mile after mile of repetition and sameness.

"It's a day of atonement, to be sure, but it's much more than that. It's about dealing a blow to the system," Timothy McVeigh continues. "Not a deathblow perhaps, but a crippling blow that forces us to reconsider our political positions, which seem like they're rooted in concrete, when in reality they're rooted in quicksand. And if we're not careful, we're going to keep sinking into that quicksand until it suffocates us. Until we drown."

That's a lot of quicksand, you think to yourself. *That's a lot of suffocation.*

"And this here U.S. of A. of ours is chin-deep in the stuff," he adds. "We're in the quicksand up to our snouts."

Up to our chinny-chin-chins, you think to yourself automatically.

"In *The Turner Diaries,*" says Timothy McVeigh, "Dr. William Pierce gets to the heart of the matter."

Your partner has adopted the formal tones of a college professor, you think. Of a mindless pedagogue like Dr. Swearingdon. You can't help but wince.

"'What is really precious to the average American,' Pierce writes, 'is not his freedom or his honor or the future of his race, but his pay-check.' Just think about that for a moment," says your partner. "The almighty dollar has become the be-all and end-all of our existence. As if nobody or nothing else matters."

How will we know when the Day of the Rope has arrived? you ask Timothy McVeigh. You're being serious for a change. Sincere, even.

"According to Pierce, the Day of the Rope is 'a grim and bloody day, but an unavoidable one.' A day of hangings from every lamp-post, of paying the ultimate price for your sins against humanity. But it's more than that," says your partner. "It's a metaphor for getting your comeuppance. Your well-deserved retribution for living the way that you do."

So what's your Day of the Rope? you ask. Have you experienced it yet?

"Damn straight," says Timothy McVeigh. "I most certainly have."

You are a little surprised by his admission. *By the simple fact that he's admitting to anything.*

"And it was not long after you moved out of the house on Hunt Road," your partner continues. "I was driving home from True Value, from the lumberyard, when I suddenly didn't know where I was. Stagger Lee had loaded me up at work. With the crystal. And I was wasted. I was out of my mind."

He pauses for a moment. New Mexico keeps hurtling by your window. The Land of Enchantment. Some enchanted evening, you think to yourself, in the land of hope and plenty.

"I was nervous as hell," says Timothy McVeigh. "I was sweating so hard, I could barely grip the wheel of the Road Warrior. And, JD—*God help me*—I went home in that condition. But the problem was, you see, that I went home to the *wrong goddamned house.* And there were people there, of course. Entirely innocent people that I'm suddenly mistaking for interlopers. And I've got my Glock out by now, and I'm hollering at them to hit the ground. A mother. Father. Couple of kids. Six, seven years old. Maybe younger."

He is sighing to himself. Catching his breath. Stirring up the courage to go on.

"And I'm screaming 'Sit the fuck down!' to the kids—a girl and a boy, I think. And the parents are trying to get to them—trying to save their children, and all hell is breaking loose. And suddenly, I'm trying to restrain the father. I've got him down on his stomach, lying flat, and I place the heel of my shoe on his neck. And I'm pressing down with everything I've got, and he's gurgling. Loudly. And I place the barrel of the Glock against his cheek—'cause I've got to, like, shut him up. 'Cause I've got to stop the gurgling, see?"

You can hardly believe your ears. Can scarcely believe what he's telling you.

"And then I hear this little voice—this little voice saying, 'Daddy. Don't kill my daddy.' And it's like a light went off," your partner continues, his voice cracking perceptibly. "Like the shutter of a camera—opening and closing from one microsecond to the next. And I realize that I'm in somebody else's house. That I'm not at our place on Hunt Road. And that I'm about to blow this guy's head off that I've never even met before in my life."

And then what? you ask. *What happened next?*

"That's when I quit smoking crystal meth," says Timothy McVeigh. "I was donesville—right then and there." He is shaking, visibly, as he steers the Road Warrior through the dusty plains of New Mexico.

You are impressed by this change of heart in your partner. Amazed by his resolve.

You will fight for Timothy McVeigh, you think to yourself. You will minister to his very soul—*even if it kills him.*

Even if it destroys the both of you in the process.

17 Ascending Mount Carmel

You are riding with Timothy McVeigh across the barren Texas plains, gradually making your way into the comparatively fertile environs of the hill country. Mike Fortier reclines in the backseat of the Road Warrior, his feet dangling outside of the vehicle's passenger's side window. Lost in a deep sleep since Albuquerque, he has proven to be an unobtrusive third wheel—quiet, unassuming, and compliant. The sun sets at your back as you travel eastward, through Amarillo and Wichita Falls. Toward the outer reaches of Waco.

Timothy McVeigh pilots the Road Warrior across the Brazos River, its waters silty and unmoving. On the far side of town—only a few scant miles from the Tradinghouse Creek Reservoir that feeds Waco—your driver leaves the main highway for the decidedly more rural Farm Road 2491. And beyond that, the infamous Double-E Ranch Road.

"I wore a special T-shirt for this occasion," your partner announces as he turns the Road Warrior onto a gravel road. "F.B.I.—Federal Bureau of Incineration" is emblazoned across Timothy McVeigh's chest.

"We're here, boys," he exclaims as he parks the car on the side of Double-E Ranch Road. Mike climbs lazily out of the backseat, rubbing the sleep from his eyes. As you walk away from the vehicle, Timothy McVeigh hands you the AirLite. "It's zero hour," he warns, "and this is posted government land." You observe the Glock resting casually in the holster draped across your partner's shoulder. You can only assume that Mike will have to make do with hand-to-hand combat, should it come to that. From the looks of him—with his eyes droopy and glazed over—you'd be surprised if he even knows he's in Texas.

You are astounded by the lack of security. There is no one else around—not so much as a tractor or a combine in the vicinity. Just a simple perimeter fence, with a crude rectangular sign as its only deterrent: "No Trespassing. Contaminated Zone."

Following Timothy McVeigh's lead, you leap over the flimsy wooden barrier, with Mike loping off to the rear. Still lost in his post-somnambulant haze.

"The compound was off on the hilltop to the right," your partner announces, gesturing in the direction of a gentle grade sloping off to the east through the brushland. A dirt road snakes its way from Double-E Ranch Road to the rear, toward the hillock in the distance. Toward your destination. Toward Mount Carmel.

Hiking along the dirt road, Timothy McVeigh breaks into an impromptu narration. "This is a crime scene, fellas. A cover-up," he says. "I'm surprised there isn't yellow tape around the premises."

The sun is setting in the west as you stroll toward the hilltop. "Welcome to the hallowed ground where the federal government of these United States of America declared war on the American people," says Timothy McVeigh.

You turn around slowly, gazing at the panorama that unfolds before you. The primitive swimming pool is still there, brimming over with brown, dirty water. Oozing in its staleness. Off to the right lies the rusting hulk of a school bus, oxidizing in the unforgiving Texas sun.

Before you sits a motorcycle, still standing erect on its kickstand, the weeds growing through its spokes and threading their way, slowly but surely, among the putrefied innards of its engine. In the extreme background, you can make out the exposed remnants of a series of underground tunnels snaking their way through the decaying foundation.

Yet another school bus, semiburied in its earthly tomb, rises off to the left. Its absent roof, having been sheared from its frame, leaves the vehicle's interior—*strangely, inexplicably*—exposed to the elements. Like its counterpart, it has been rudely discarded to suffer the Texas weather in all its brutal whimsy.

In the foreground lies a corroded bathtub perched awkwardly on its side. Random and out of place, it seems somehow emblematic of the vanquished compound in miniature: lost and off-kilter—the virtual shadow of its former, living self.

Aside from the prairie brush and the rampaging weeds, there is really nothing to see. Only history's unspoken, silent misery.

Timothy McVeigh trolls about the site as if he were exploring the vagaries of some ancient Mediterranean ruins. Giving them their reverential due as if he were staring at the lifeless, stonelike bodies of Pompeii. Their final moments frozen for all time.

But there are no bodies, of course, at the former home of the Mount Carmel Center. Only the weeds—scads of them. Growing as high as an elephant's eye.

"It started over there," says Timothy McVeigh, pointing to an area just beyond the dirt road. "A slew of cattle trucks roared in from the highway. For the Branch Davidians, they may as well have been arriving from outer space. They were loaded to the gills with A.T.F. agents. Here to arrest David Koresh, the Davidians' spiritual leader, on illegal weapons charges and allegations of child abuse."

You follow your partner as he strolls about the compound's decrepit, crumbling foundation. Mike lingers just behind.

"Never mind the fact that they could have arrested Koresh at virtually any time. He went into Waco nearly every week. They had a warrant—they could have busted him at will. But instead, they came out here—to his homestead. To the homestead of nearly one hundred people pursuing their inalienable right to enjoy life, liberty, and happiness. *Like everybody else."*

Timothy McVeigh pauses for effect. "And they came out here like hit men. Not like federal agents dispassionately doing their jobs. There were seventy-five A.T.F. agents in full combat gear rushing onto the scene like an invasion force. At the same time, a convoy of some eighty vehicles rumbled into the area, including an unholy trinity of helicopter gunships circling overhead like vultures. *Helicopter gunships to corral a splinter sect of Seventh-day Adventists!* You can throw in another dozen or so Texas Rangers, along with snipers training their sights on the compound from various locations around the prairie. And what you have is a turkey shoot. *All in an effort to bring down a single, solitary guy."*

Timothy McVeigh stakes out a position where the compound's front stoop once existed. "Imagine what it was like to stand right here on February twenty-eighth, nineteen ninety-three, watching your government shower hell down on you from out of nowhere. Do you know what the Davidians were doing when the attacks started?" he asks. "They weren't breaking out their arsenal. They weren't rushing for the priest holes. *They were praying.*

"And the first thing that the A.T.F. agents did was shoot the compound's pets—Alaskan malamutes, mostly," says your partner. "They executed a dynamic entry, hurling flash-bang grenades into the compound—into the vicinity of dozens of families. Within spitting distance of a houseful of innocent men, women, and children. *More than forty children.* You have the A.T.F. agents itching to serve a warrant, and, meanwhile, the Branch Davidians think that the End Times are upon them. It was the perfect prescription for wholesale death and destruction.

"And that's before the psychological warfare even started," Timothy McVeigh continues. "Before the A.T.F. teamed up with the F.B.I. and built a gigantic PA system around the perimeter." He gestures off into the distance to where the agents erected the scaffolding. "With amplification appropriate for a Led Zeppelin concert, they projected the mind-bending sounds of seagulls and sirens, of bagpipes and crying babies, of dental drills and rabbits being slaughtered. All to the titillating soundtrack of Nancy Sinatra singing 'These Boots Are Made for Walkin'.' Throw in the *über*-bright stadium lights that they set up around the compound, and we're talking about brute human torture. Cruel and unusual punishment doled out, over and over again, throughout the fifty-one-day siege.

"And when it all finally ended, on April nineteenth," your partner adds, "there was no mercy. There was no reprieve for the troubled souls still trapped inside. There was the deployment of one hundred canisters of highly concentrated CS gas—tear gas that is especially toxic and highly flammable in close quarters like, say, the wooden Branch Davidian compound. On that final day, the government brought in Bradley Fighting Vehicles and a pair of M1 Abrams Battle Tanks, specially fitted with battering rams, in order to punch holes in the building and shoo the Branch Davidians out of their home. And by noon, the fate of some seventy-six people was sealed as smoke billowed out from the compound. And there they died, trapped like rats. Surrounded and trapped like worthless, disenfranchised rats.

"And I'm here to tell you that nobody deserves to be burned, gassed, and killed for their religious beliefs—no matter how whacked-out they are," he continues. "This wasn't routine police work. It was out-and-out warfare. Where is it written in the Constitution that the government has the right to wage war against its own citizenry?"

As Timothy McVeigh speaks, you can almost glimpse the flames licking at the wooden compound. You can feel the heat rising up from the final conflagration. "How was this any different from the liquidation of the Warsaw Ghetto?" he asks. "At the end of the goddamned day, do you know why they did it?" asks Timothy McVeigh. "Why they burned this whole place to tarnation?"

You have no idea, really. You stare at him blankly.

"'Cause the Branch Davidians were just a little too weird. Just too different for decent folks like you and me. This wasn't a cult. It was just a bunch of people living together, raising a whole mess of children, and sharing their fascination with the Good Book.

"So tell me, JD, *where is God in here?* And how can our government—*how can this government*—be the defender of virtue and all that is good in the world if it can do something like this?" he asks, gesturing toward the silent wreckage, the smattering of brush, and the empty Texas plains.

This must be a rhetorical question, you think. How could it possibly be otherwise?

As dusk settles over the ruins, you find it hard to imagine that the annihilation of Mount Carmel went down only twenty months ago. Right here on this very spot. This quiet and lonely spot in the hills just outside of Waco. An eerie silence, accented by the whirring buzz of cicadas, begins to set in. And with Mike straggling behind, you and your partner hike the short distance back to the junction at Double-E Ranch Road.

YOU OBSERVE—in a kind of awe—as Timothy McVeigh hastily sets up camp in a clearing just beyond the roadside. Gathering up a parcel of stones to create a fire ring, your partner fills the interior with stray brush and twigs for kindling. A pile of yellow wooden boards—slats from the perimeter fence perhaps?—serves as his tinder.

Fetching a trio of bedrolls from the trunk of the Road Warrior, he unfurls them and arranges the bedding in a semicircle around the fire pit. Meanwhile, Mike tends to the growing fire with the skill and dexterity of a confirmed pyromaniac.

"This is a military mission now," says Timothy McVeigh, producing a fistful of MREs. "We've got to start acting the part." He proceeds to tear open a package of instant spaghetti and meatballs with his teeth.

A military mission? How does he figure that? you wonder. As if to validate your confusion, you glance over at Mike, who turns away from your stare, gazing blankly off into the distance. As if he were scanning the horizon in search of relief.

Timothy McVeigh hands you a packet of instant chicken tetrazzini, tossing Mike a container of chicken and dumplings in the bargain.

Bon appétit, you think to yourself.

AFTER SUPPER, you sit around the campfire, the flames licking up—higher and higher—into the darkling night.

"I can't stop thinking about the CS gas," says Timothy McVeigh. "It's not just tear gas, you know. It's a low-grade chemical weapon designed for the sole purpose of plunging its victims into spasms of coughing and nausea."

As your partner speaks, Mike absentmindedly drags a stick across the fire-red coals, stirring up the burning embers, the kindling back-talking to him in hisses and crackles.

"When we were at Fort Ben," Timothy McVeigh continues, "they locked ten recruits at a time into a tiny, enclosed room, where we were outfitted with gas masks. And then they pumped in the fumes. As part of the training exercise, you were ordered to remove your mask and scream out your name and Social Security number. Most of us tried to hold our breath as long as we could. I closed in on two minutes before I couldn't take it anymore. Mike here nearly made it to three," he adds, gesturing at the Third Wheel.

"But ultimately, you couldn't stop the dry, peppery gas from invading your lungs. You start to cough uncontrollably at first. Then the vomiting begins. Your nose runs, your eyes glue themselves shut, and your skin feels like it's about to burn clean off your body."

Listening to his old friend recount the horrors of chemical-warfare training, Mike nods knowingly. "Sooner or later, you figure out the trick, which is quite simple, really," says Mike. "You have to stave off panic. Keep your wits about you. Don't lose control. It's easier said than done, of course, but it works. Eventually."

"But what if you were a child," intones Timothy McVeigh, "a child, say, at Mount Carmel, with the government blaring the sounds of hell at you all day and all night. And suddenly, this terrible, noxious gas is billowing into your living room. And you can't do anything about it. You didn't train with the other recruits back at Fort Ben," he continues. "You're just some kid in the Texas hill country, and the government you were taught to pledge allegiance to—*one nation, under God*, the whole bleeding thing—is trying to gas you out of existence.

"Could there be anything more horrible that you could experience?" wonders Timothy McVeigh. "That you could do to a child?"

As you gaze across the campfire at your partner, you glimpse the flames shooting up from the embers, as if they were licking and clawing at his face, which is transforming, slowly, into an orange, deadly visage.

"There's only one play, really, when faced with such tyranny," says Timothy McVeigh. "*It's payback time. Dirty for dirty. You reap what you sow.*" He pauses for a moment. "And why not? Your aggressor doesn't speak any other language. So you need to communicate in the most blunt, unambiguous idiom possible—the language of violence and demolition. A wake-up call for the masses."

Point taken, you think to yourself as Mike sighs across the campfire. Timothy McVeigh glares back at him with the eyes of living, unadulterated hatred.

You make a note on your "Jot It Down" pad.

THE NEXT MORNING, you climb into the Road Warrior for the long journey back to Arizona. As you prepare to depart Waco, Timothy

McVeigh stops the vehicle at a filling station on Farm Road 2491, not too far from the gravelly entrance to Double-E Ranch Road.

"Do you get much traffic around here?" he asks the round-faced, bespectacled attendant. "Any Lookey-Loos coming out to take a gander at Mount Carmel? To see what happened way the heck out here?"

The attendant laughs quietly to himself as he fills up the Road Warrior's tank. "Not that many people, really. You'd think there'd be a helluva lot more. If out of a sick sense of curiosity as much as anything else."

The name tag on the attendant's blue jumpsuit identifies him as Billy.

"What bothers me is that this was a lot of fuss over nothing," he says. "Those people had been here for a long time and never bothered nobody.

"And now," Billy continues, "it's like they were never here at all. Like they been done swept off the face of the planet. How's a thing like that happen?" he asks, a look of confusion washing over his hearty, uncertain face. "I still don't get it," he adds, shaking his head. "It doesn't compute."

"WE'RE NOT GOING BACK to Kingman just yet," Timothy McVeigh exclaims. "We're heading north instead. There's something you've gotta see," he says as he settles into the driver's seat.

With the Third Wheel holding up the rear, you climb into the Road Warrior. And with cold, steely vengeance in his heart—not to mention the fearsome Glock cradled inside his shoulder holster—Timothy McVeigh eases his trusty Chevy onto I-35.

Toward Oklahoma City.

18 Anarchy in the O.K.

Timothy McVeigh is guiding the Road Warrior down the Centennial Expressway off-ramp. The Oklahoma City skyline looms just ahead in the distance. A low-lying fog drifts among the office buildings, evoking the impression that the cityscape is floating in a sea of clouds.

Timothy McVeigh steers the vehicle along Harrison Avenue before turning onto Northeast Sixth Street, past the old rail yards, across a parcel of vacant lots and nondescript concrete parking structures. Road-weary after years of toil on the nation's highways, the Road Warrior's frame creaks audibly as your partner negotiates the sharp left turn onto North Robinson Avenue. With relative finesse, he brings the car to a halt at the edge of a large, well-appointed courtyard that fronts Northwest Fourth Street.

It's lunchtime in workaday America, the men and women in their business attire mixing freely with the denim-clad day laborers. Eclipsing class barriers for a relaxing repast on the park benches, they nestle among the courtyard's stately oak trees and expertly manicured shrubbery, which the city has decked out with Christmas decorations—plastic candy canes, mostly, with a smattering of snowmen—for the rapidly encroaching holiday season.

And just to the north, a rectangular, nine-story office complex rises out of the plaza. At the building's center, a massive, protruding elevator shaft shoots skyward, poised like a multistage rocket waiting on its launching pad for further instructions from Mission Control.

"That shaft is gonna be a problem," says Timothy McVeigh to nobody in particular. "It's like a bulwark. Or an anchor." He shakes his head with concern.

Shifting the Road Warrior back into gear, your partner wheels the vehicle around the North Harvey Avenue side of the plaza, making a hard right turn onto Northwest Fifth Street, where he idles along the front curb.

From this vantage point, you can no longer see the elevator shaft imposing itself upon the building. Instead, you are treated to a spectacular view of the reinforced concrete structure—seven stories of dark tinted glass rising straight up out of a dramatic two-story recess in front of the entryway.

"Alfred P. Murrah Federal Building" read the words on the plaque affixed to the concrete edifice. The midday sun collides with the windows, creating a black, impenetrable glare. Across the street, lunchtime patrons stroll into the four-story redbrick building that houses the Athenian Restaurant.

Who was Murrah? you ask Timothy McVeigh.

"A federal judge," he answers.

"Appointed by whom?" Mike inquires. Has the Third Wheel suddenly become a junior political scientist? you wonder to yourself.

"F.D.R.," says Timothy McVeigh.

How do you know this? you ask.

"Leafing through the *Encyclopædia Britannica* at the Mohave Branch of the Kingman Public Library," answers your partner. "*Any more questions?*" he asks, the bile clearly rising in his voice.

"Why are we casing this building?" Mike inquires, squirming in the backseat.

"Because it's a federal office complex," Timothy McVeigh responds. "But more importantly, because there are field offices for the A.T.F. and the F.B.I. on the premises. Rumor has it that the orders for Waco were delivered—if not hammered out and designed—on this very spot."

All right then, you think. The paranoia has returned. *And with a vengeance.*

Your driver gestures toward the commercial drop-off zone in front of the Murrah Building. "I wonder if you could fit a truck in there," he says cryptically.

"You could probably fit three trucks in that space," says Mike, who continues fidgeting rather conspicuously in the backseat. All this talk about Waco and casing federal office buildings clearly has him flummoxed.

"This is officially a black-bag operation," says Timothy McVeigh. "You're either with us or against us."

A black-bag operation? How are you possibly involved in black ops? You don't have a decoder ring, a poison pen, or elaborate sleeping powders at your disposal. *Heck, you don't even own a cellular phone.*

"And with any luck," Timothy McVeigh adds, "it will set off a general uprising in the United States—the opportunity to knock some people off of the fence and urge them to take some action of their own against the federal government."

You can hear Mike sighing loudly from the rear. As your partner accelerates the Road Warrior away from the curb of Northwest Fifth Street, you glimpse a most unexpected figure. A deathly mirage.

The long dark hair. A stylish headband. Strolling toward the revolving entrance of the Murrah Building with all the confidence in the world—*and strutting his stuff for all the world to see.* A cool customer, if ever there was one.

It's Dakota Fish. And very much alive—in all of his arrogant, narcissistic glory. *Who else, really, could it be?*

Oklahoma City is nowhere near the reservation, you think to yourself. Has the great-great-grandson of the Shawnee nation found employment with the federal government? Perhaps he translates top-secret documents for the D.E.A.?

In a moment of pure fantasia, you imagine Dakota Fish deciphering government wiretaps of Mike's telephone conversations with his drug dealer. As if your former roommate were trying to make sense out of the cockeyed grammar exemplars in one of his beloved French-language textbooks.

Mike Fortier: *"Je voudrais acheter des méthamphétamines."*

Stagger Lee: *"Voulez-vous de la marijuana aussi?"*

Mike Fortier: *"Oui, oui. C'est une bonne idée!"*

"It's probably not even him," says Timothy McVeigh, staring at you intently across the front seat of the Road Warrior. *As if he were reading your mind.*

"Let's face it," your partner continues, "Injun Joe would have to be off the reservation—quite literally—to be here in Oklahoma City."

That's true, you think. No self-respecting Shawnee would work for the selfsame government that revoked his tribal lands. That effected the Holocaust of a proud and ancient people.

Would he?

TIMOTHY McVEIGH PULLS the Road Warrior away from the curb, crossing in front of the Murrah Building and stopping, briefly, for the red light at North Robinson. When the traffic clears, your partner accelerates through the intersection.

A giant inflatable Santa Claus marks the entrance to an alleyway that bisects the buildings fronting North Robinson—the location of the city's old, multistory Y.M.C.A. facility—and North Broadway. The twelve-foot, Plasticine Kris Kringle is waving at passersby with an absurd smile frozen upon his face. With his swollen bag full of goodies dangling over his shoulder.

He was chubby and plump, you think to yourself automatically. *A right jolly old elf.*

Without warning, Timothy McVeigh suddenly hits the gas, shooting the Road Warrior down the alley at an unholy pace. Only slightly wider than the Chevy itself, the narrow alleyway echoes with the roar of the vehicle's turbocharged engine. At one point, your driver clips a pair of vinyl trash receptacles, sending their contents—pizza boxes, beer cans, and discarded fast-food cartons of all shapes and sizes—bounding in your wake. Meanwhile, the Third Wheel is screaming bloody murder in the backseat, while you brace yourself against the dashboard, clinging for dear life.

Timothy McVeigh halts the Road Warrior, briefly, at the edge of Northwest Sixth Street. As soon as the traffic clears, your partner tears down the alley once again—and the insanity begins anew. With the Third Wheel bouncing around the backseat spewing derision, not to mention a slew of clever expletives, in your driver's direction. With pedestrians narrowly avoiding certain death as they duck in and out of the alleyway, Timothy McVeigh's silver shuttle rockets by their feet.

Up ahead, where the alley intersects Northwest Seventh Street, a rusty green pickup truck rolls into your path. But suddenly, without warning, your partner peels off to the right, through a vacant lot and across a driveway onto North Broadway. After hightailing it for a few more blocks to the north—with yet more pedestrians shuck-ing and jiving to stave off their slaughter—Timothy McVeigh brings the Road Warrior in for a landing next to an unkempt city parking lot, overgrown with weeds, that signals the end of your breakneck journey from the Murrah Building.

"What—the—fuck—was—that?" snarls Mike.

"That was my escape route," answers Timothy McVeigh calmly. "Every caper has an escape route. And that was mine."

We're calling this a *caper* now? you think to yourself.

"How do you think you're going to stash a getaway car down here if you're busy ferrying a bomb around the streets of Oklahoma City?" Mike asks curtly.

A bomb? What bomb?

"That's simple," your partner replies.

"How's that now, Slick?" answers Mike, still seething from Mr. McVeigh's Wild Ride.

"The way I see it," your driver explains, "is that there are two possibilities. On the one hand, Terry and JD could follow me down here in the Honda a couple of days earlier, and I could park the Road Warrior right here." He gestures toward a remote corner of the parking lot. "When zero hour arrives, I can hop right into the car and disappear into the thin air of the American interstate-highway system.

"On the other hand," he continues, "Terry and JD could follow me in the Road Warrior, and we could make this parking lot our rendezvous point. Either way," he adds, "we get the hell outta Dodge before the cavalry comes."

The Third Wheel nods slowly to himself. "You've obviously got it all figured out," says Mike. "I gotta admit I'm impressed."

"The key to the getaway plan is having something sturdy between me and the blast," your partner observes. "And the Y.M.C.A. building near the entrance to the alley looks like just the cushion I'll need. Of course, Santy Claus won't be much help," he continues. "He'll be long gone by then."

The blast? you ask Timothy McVeigh. *What blast?*

"It won't be a hindrance," your partner responds. "I'll be wearing earplugs to block out the sound of the blast—the roar of the explosion. I've got to keep my wits about me every step of the way."

Mike has started banging his forehead in obvious frustration against the back of the passenger's seat headrest. *If he doesn't stop doing that,* you think to yourself, *he's going to develop a brain cloud.*

"You have got to be kidding me!" says Mike before continuing to pummel his brow on the back of your headrest.

With his forehead aflame from his bout of self-flagellation, the Third Wheel begins glaring at Timothy McVeigh from the backseat. "Jesus Fucking Christ, Sarge, when were you gonna tell him?"

They must be talking about the wake-up call, you think. *For the masses.*

Mike is absolutely beside himself with anger. Overwhelmed by his irritation with your partner, he stares at him with a look of all-consuming disgust.

"You can shut the fuck up, Mike," says Timothy McVeigh. "JD here comes and goes as he pleases. He's a free agent, dude."

That's right, *dude*, you think to yourself.

"Have you bothered to tell Terry what you have in mind?" the Third Wheel asks incredulously.

"You're starting to get on my nerves," your partner answers. "Terry's been privy to every detail. He was there for the racing fuel, for the ammonium nitrate. Shit, he was there when we busted into the rock quarry and heisted the blasting caps."

The rock quarry? The blasting caps? *What gives?*

"You need to step back and give me a fucking break, Mike. I'm running this operation by the seat of my pants," says Timothy McVeigh. "You've been off getting married. Getting laid. Getting stoned. You name it."

The Third Wheel has grown quiet after your partner's tongue-lashing. But as for you—your mind has suddenly broken wide open. You have been awakened to the reality of your life with Timothy McVeigh. Of your life beyond society's grid.

And you'll be darned if Timothy McVeigh is going to succeed in pulling this caper off with you in the picture. In blowing some-thing—*or somebody*—sky-high.

He can give it the old college try, that's for certain—but there is a world of difference between planning and doing.

Not on my watch, you think.

No way, no how.

AS TIMOTHY McVEIGH STEERS the Road Warrior back toward the Centennial Expressway, something suddenly catches his attention.

"That's it!" he cries out. "That's the truck I wanna use!"

The truck? What truck?

Timothy McVeigh is staring, his mouth agape, at a yellow Ryder rental truck in the oncoming lane.

"That looks like a sixteen-footer," the Third Wheel announces, adopting a deferential tone. As if he were estimating the length of the bass you just reeled in on your line. As if he were impressed by the size of your catch.

"Only one size bigger," says Timothy McVeigh. "I wanna get the twenty-footer—the one where the back portion of the truck sits directly on top of the wheel well. The one where the cab and the cargo bay are welded into a single unit. It's stronger that way, more durable. It can manage a heavier load."

You observe the Ryder truck as it quietly motors beyond your field of vision. As it lumbers its way into the city.

Meanwhile, Timothy McVeigh wheels the Road Warrior toward the interstate. Away from downtown. Away from the Murrah Federal Building.

All told, you have been in Oklahoma City fewer than twenty minutes.

19 The Battle of Fort Er

Timothy McVeigh is leaning his body into the stovetop in Mike and Lori's eat-in kitchen, scrubbing and scouring as hard as he possibly can.

"This is—*bar none*—the nastiest shit I have ever seen," he exclaims.

It always amazes you, you think to yourself, when your partner morphs into Felix Unger. When he transforms into an unmitigated neat freak.

You are sitting in the living room of the Fortiers' trailer, playing Nintendo with Mike. You are lost in the high-octane world of commercial plumbing. In the land of turtles and mushrooms with which the Mario Brothers must contend. The Third Wheel is playing the heroic Mario while you are scrapping your way through as Luigi, his craven younger brother. With the game's ecstatic, funky soundtrack whirring away in the background, each successive level is a master class in survival as you—in a desperate effort to avoid your own extinction—attempt to exterminate the pests and the other creepy-crawlies that seep from the pipes. So that you can survive—*your brother and you*—in order to plumb another day.

You couldn't be happier, really. *You are in gaming heaven.*

A back issue of *Shotgun News* sits on a nearby coffee table, not far from the discarded tinfoil pipe—disquieting evidence of Stagger

Lee's malingering presence at Fort Er. There is also a well-thumbed copy of *The Spotlight* newsletter, chock-full of advertisements for contraband assault weapons, gun-modification kits, and various militia groups. You've never heard of *The Spotlight*, which is peculiar, given your elite gunrunner status.

Lori is snoring loudly on the couch—her mouth hanging open in bizarre repose, as if she were in the act of being surprised. Or frightened.

Baby Kayla is curled up against Lori's thigh, dozing away in tandem with her cataleptic mother. Their melody of raspy exhalation rises and falls in unison, as if they were a well-rehearsed choir.

Somewhere, off in the distance, a neighborhood dog issues an unruly bark. His animal sound echoing across the lonely desert evening.

Looking around the trailer, you can't help wondering if this isn't the picture of a typical American household—*of a prototypical night in the life of suburban America.*

TIMOTHY McVEIGH IS SQUATTING in the shade behind the Fortiers' trailer. As you look on with deep concern—if not outright fear and agitation—your partner begins building a crude bomb.

"We're gonna test this bitch out in the desert tonight," he announces with a sense of enthusiasm verging on pure glee.

Timothy McVeigh carefully balances an empty Gatorade jug on his knee. He slowly fills the container with pellets the size of BBs. With his free hand, he starts gently pouring a sweet-smelling liquid into the jug.

Ennis, Texas, you think to yourself. *The racetrack.*

Your partner cautiously inserts a blasting cap into the container, along with a lengthy segment of green-colored fuse.

How does it work? you ask, innocently enough.

"It's fairly simple, actually. You combine the prills with a hydrocarbon accelerant," he instructs, like a seasoned chemist. "But of course, that only gets you halfway there," Timothy McVeigh continues. "You still need a gigantic shock to the system to make the whole thing go boom. Which is why we have the blasting cap to create the primary ignition."

That's a wicked-looking contraption, you think to yourself.

"It's a wicked-looking *bomb*," corrects Timothy McVeigh. "And there's no reason why it shouldn't explode to kingdom come. If it works in the micro," he adds, "why wouldn't it work in the macro? The physical laws stay the same."

You shrug your shoulders. In truth, you don't have the vaguest idea what he's talking about.

"It's all a matter of scale," your partner remarks. "If I can successfully ignite the Gatorade jug here, then there's no reason why I can't blow up a truck full of explosives, right?"

TIMOTHY McVEIGH IS PILOTING the Road Warrior into the desert night. You are reclining in your usual station in the passenger's seat, with Mike and Lori sitting in the back, giggling uncontrollably to themselves. They have brought along an ice chest filled with Pabst Blue Ribbon in order to mark the occasion. And from the looks of things, they are already well on their way to achieving wholesale inebriation.

Your partner steers the vehicle along Highway 68, beyond your old haunts in Golden Valley and just a few miles shy of Bullhead City. He exits the highway near Union Pass, coasting into the foothills of the Black Mountains, which have been gutted over the centuries by a series of old, abandoned gold mines. After parking the Road Warrior behind a convenient hillock, Timothy McVeigh begins transporting his homemade bomb—with as much care as he can possibly muster—into the rough and arid terrain that skirts the mountainside. Off in the distance, you can just make out the nighttime lights of Kingman, gleaming in the darkness like a miniature train set.

Mike and Lori linger in the rear, carrying the ice chest between them and guzzling cans of Pabst Blue Ribbon. Their frivolity is clearly getting on your partner's nerves.

"This is what happens when you bring a pair of stoners to do a man's job," says Timothy McVeigh derisively. "If we had a collective brain between the two of us, we'd strap the Gatorade bottle to their goddamned ice chest and light up the Arizona sky the old-fashioned way."

Your partner eventually selects a test site some two miles away from the highway. With Mike and Lori looking on in astonishment, he deftly positions the jug underneath a medium-sized boulder.

"That looks like a whole lotta trouble," says the Third Wheel anxiously. "Lori and I are gonna take in the show from the mezzanine," he announces as the couple edges their way into the background.

Timothy McVeigh gingerly inspects the components of his deadly contraption. You can hear Mike and Lori giggling off in the distance as your partner sets up the explosives.

"This is a one-minute fuse," he explains. "That'll give us plenty of time to scoot out of harm's way. Hopefully, those two jackasses won't wander back into the kill zone while we're looking out for life and limb over yonder."

Removing a Bic lighter from his pocket, Timothy McVeigh lights the green-colored fuse. The acrid smell of gunpowder quickly fills the cool mountain air.

With your partner leading the way, you walk briskly several hundred feet away from the bomb site.

A burst of light illuminates the nighttime sky. You hear the roar of the detonation, followed closely by the sound of sand and rocks falling earthward in the explosion's wake. The ambient noise created by the bomb is quickly displaced by the sound of Mike and Lori, hooting and hollering as if they were spectators at a tractor pull.

"Nice shot, Deadeye Dick!" screams the Third Wheel, intoxicated beyond all sensibility.

"Obviously, we've succeeded in impressing the peanut gallery," says Timothy McVeigh as the two of you make your way back to the test site.

To your great amazement, the topography at ground zero has been changed—*changed utterly*—by the force of the detonation. A fine mist of newly atomized sand blankets the surrounding area. But nothing compares to the state of the boulder itself, which has been sheared clean in half by the power of Timothy McVeigh's explosives.

"Mission accomplished," he whispers, clearly taken aback by the awesome power of his experiment in the desert.

THE NEXT MORNING, you are awoken by the awful noise of human moaning. Of what you perceive to be the sounds of terror and abject pain.

Tiptoeing your way outside of the Fortiers' claustrophobic guest bedroom, you trace the agonized sounds to the double-wide's tiny bathroom. What you are hearing, of course, is the unmistakable vim and vigor of sexual congress.

The mathematics are remarkably simple. With the Third Wheel safely ensconced at the hardware store, his wife and Timothy McVeigh must be having relations in the shower. Which is a terrible idea, you think to yourself, given the room's unbearably tight dimensions. You could put an eye out—*or something much worse, something much more debilitating.*

To be exceedingly frank, you are astounded by the depths of your partner's unchecked libido. He espouses ethics in almost every aspect of his life—*until it comes, that is, to the delicate issue of getting it on.*

"Fuck me, Timmy!" your hostess bellows from the bathroom.

As you kneel in the trailer's slender hallway, you can't stop wondering about the ceaseless limits of human desire.

Why are people always on the make? you think to yourself. *Why can't we ever take a break from checking each other out? From sniffing each other's bottoms?*

MUCH LATER, after the Third Wheel returns home from a lazy day's work at True Value Hardware, Timothy McVeigh holds court in the living room at Fort Er. It will be his grandiloquent statement, his Gettysburg Address, his Sermon on the Mount. But in terms of Mike and Lori—two of his oldest and most devoted Apostles—it will be nothing short of Little Big Horn. His own miniature Waterloo at the Canyon West Mobile and RV Trailer Park.

Timothy McVeigh's treatise starts out with a bang as he outlines his case against the federal government in excruciating detail. Fortunately, you spend much of your partner's oral presentation playing *Mario Bros.* with Mike. Trying your darnedest to outsmart the vermin that are bound and determined to destroy you. Not to mention the Third Wheel.

As your partner prepares to deliver his oration, Lori puffs blithely on the tinfoil pipe, allowing the crystal to winnow its way, unimpeded, through her veins.

"Let's get down to business," Timothy McVeigh intones. All seriousness. No fooling.

"This will be an act of tactical aggression," he announces. "We're timing the blast for 11:00 a.m. in order to synchronize the event with the lunchtime crowd. So as to maximize our body count."

"At first, it will seem like Pearl Harbor," your partner continues, "with Americans realizing—once again—how defenseless our nation really is. But then, as things begin to sink in, it will seem more like the bombing of Hiroshima, an action in which many civilians died—but in the service of a larger good. This kind of extremism will save lives in the long run by raising awareness about the tyranny of the federal government. About the war that it is already commandeering against its own people."

At this juncture, Lori is staring off into a narcotized space of her own making, while the Third Wheel is mesmerized in his bid to defeat Luigi—*a.k.a. Daryl, a.k.a. JD.*

"The federal building in Oklahoma City is an easy target," Timothy McVeigh proceeds, oblivious to his audience's indifference, "and my sources tell me that it houses some of the people, the agencies, that were involved in the Waco raid."

What sources? you wonder to yourself. *James Nichols?*

"It has to be a shaped charge," he explains as he gathers together a dozen cans of Campbell's soup, with their familiar red-and-white labels, from the pantry. He arranges them in a triangle formation on the living room floor, as if they were positioned inside the cargo bay of a twenty-foot rental truck.

"Each one of these cans represents a fifty-five-gallon drum," your partner continues. "I have the bomb ingredients secreted away all over the Heartland in storage facilities, and I'm gonna need help putting them all together. We're talking about seven, maybe eight thousand pounds of explosives here."

Herington, Kansas, you think to yourself. *Storage unit number two.*

"It'll be like the Nuremberg War Trials for the A.T.F.," he adds. "It's about time somebody exacted some justice for their crimes against the nation."

An eerie quiet pervades the living room, save for the clicking of the game controllers and the occasional sigh from Lori on the couch.

"Forget it," Mike suddenly interrupts. "No sale." He carefully puts down his controller, leaving Mario's fate in the hands of chance.

"And you claim to be a patriot," mocks Timothy McVeigh, still stunned by Mike's rebuff. "What happened to you, dude? What happened to your integrity?"

"I would never dream of doing anything like that," replies the Third Wheel, "unless there was a U.N. tank in my front yard."

"And what about the people?" asks Lori. "The people working in the building, getting ready for lunch?"

"Those people are like the Imperial storm troopers in *Star Wars*," Timothy McVeigh explains. "They may be individually innocent, but because they are part of a larger, evil empire, then they are guilty by association. Sure, they're collateral damage—but they're collateral damage for a greater purpose."

"You're talking about committing suicide," says the Third Wheel. "This is stupid. What you need to do is keep standing on street corners and telling people about Waco—about Ruby Ridge. Over the next ten years, you'd be much more effective than doing something like this."

"I'm no longer in the propaganda stage," your partner protests. "I'm freakin' done with passing out papers. I'm in the action stage."

Mike and Lori are shaking their heads in disgust. For all of the vacuity and incompetence that they exhibit in their day-to-day lives, their resolve is surprisingly unyielding. Perhaps he should have bribed them with a lifetime's supply of meth? you think to yourself.

"I am the master of my fate; I am the captain of my soul," Timothy McVeigh announces to Mike and Lori, echoing his disappointment over their inability to strike up the courage to join his plan. "What the fuck are you guys?" he asks. "Are you committed to anything outside of getting drunk and getting stoned?"

Your host and hostess stare at your partner in a dissembling silence. They are clearly at a loss for words. Lori has even stopped giggling—at least for the moment.

"Take a long look around, JD," says Timothy McVeigh, beet-red and seething with anger. "These two misfits aren't gonna have us to kick around anymore—that's for damned sure."

Turning slowly on his heel, your partner retires to the trailer's guest room with the angry slam of a door acting as his final word on the matter. At least as far as the Fortiers are concerned.

As Timothy McVeigh instructed, you take a long look around the room, glancing panoramically from the eat-in kitchen to the living room, where Mike and Lori are still staring straight ahead, beguiled in their speechlessness, to the trailer's minuscule, death trap of a bathroom. With its lingering aura of sex and duplicity.

YOU JOIN TIMOTHY McVEIGH in the guest room. Your partner is wrapped up in his fury and anger.

"Did you see how they looked at me back there?" he asks, his voice crackling with a venom he can barely contain. "They looked at me like I am some kind of trash—some kind of gun-nut trash."

"Let me tell you something," Timothy McVeigh announces, his voice hovering just below a controlled shout. "I am not *gun crazy*. I am not *a right-wing nut.*"

He stares at you with the intensity of near-hatred.

"I told you before. I am a shooter. A *shooter*. And there's a world of difference between a shooter and freaks like Terry and James."

A lump is building in your throat. You make a mental note that Timothy McVeigh is making you feel uncomfortable—very uncomfortable. *Not as uncomfortable, say, as outside the bathroom this morning, but uncomfortable nonetheless.*

"A shooter," he continues, "isn't some haphazard, misbegotten thing. A shooter is exact, precise, a freak of nature."

You're never quite sure what to make of Timothy McVeigh when he goes on one of his harangues. His anger seems to be overwhelming him. If he's not careful, you think to yourself, he might develop a brain cloud.

"When the gun nuts and the militia guys get busted, the government cleans out their gun safes, all the cabinets and the nooks and crannies in their basements, and they're out of business. They go to prison, and there's a halfway house out there somewhere—*already out there somewhere*—with their name on the mailbox. Or worse— there's a standoff, and innocent women and children die. That's what happens. That's what *always* happens. Mark my words."

You dutifully make a note on your "Jot It Down" pad.

"But when the shooter goes off, he doesn't get caught unawares. He is machinelike, accurate, prepared for the larger battle after the battle has already begun."

Timothy McVeigh pauses, attempting to catch his breath, to sort out his argument. To focus his mind-set.

"When the shooter goes off, he already knows what the target is—
and what it takes to bring his man down, once and for all. That's what
the shooter does. And that's why the shooter isn't just some gun-toting
ideologue." He pauses again. "That's right—I know some big words,
too, JD."

Ideologue. Very impressive.

"The shooter is for keeps—not just for show. *Not just for gun
shows.* When the shooter breaks into action, it's for all the chips on
the table."

Timothy McVeigh is working himself into a lather. Somebody
needs to put a muzzle on this guy, you think. *Before it's too late.*

"Don't underestimate me, JD—like everybody else does. Don't get
confused by the flotsam and jetsam of these here adventures we share.
There's a larger thrust to our story, right? Don't tell me you haven't felt
it. That you haven't felt the pull of history, of *forever* in our story."

A FEW HOURS LATER, Timothy McVeigh awakens you out of a deep,
dreamless sleep. You are rubbing your eyes in confusion, trying to
make sense, bleary-eyed, out of your surroundings. Out of the nighttime world in which you suddenly find yourself.

"You better never back out on me. *Never,*" Timothy McVeigh
warns. He is clearly intoxicated. Drunk as a skunk from Pabst Blue
Ribbon, presumably. "Those stoners are one thing," he adds, "but
you're another. Let's not forget who rescued you the night you tried
to off Injun Joe."

You'll never forget, you think to yourself. *How could you possibly
forget your darkest moment on this earth?*

"*Capiche?*" asks Timothy McVeigh, purposely directing his voice
in a level, impenetrable monotone. He is staring at you expectantly
with his cold, blue, unwavering eyes.

Capiche.

20 Tattoo You

You push your way, forcefully, through the double doors of the biker bar, with Timothy McVeigh following closely on your heels.

"It's time," he announces confidently.

You look at him incredulously. *Does he ever stop?* you wonder to yourself.

"It's time all right—time for a little R&R. And why not?" he adds. "We're young. We're vigorous. We're reasonably good-looking."

He glances up and down the room, at the sea of bikers clad in leather vests and caps, blue jeans and shiny black pants—not to mention the tattoos. *Legions of them.*

"Shit, we're at least as good-looking as this crew," your partner remarks.

He looks in your direction. "Take you, for instance. You're intelligent, educated. You're quiet—you're reserved. Let's call it 'mysterious.' Chicks dig that."

You cannot believe that you're hearing this, you think, as you rub your throbbing left arm with your free hand.

"Now let's take me. I'm tall, handsome. Ruggedly handsome at that. And I'm a skilled tactician. A soldier."

A shooter, you remind him.

"That, too," he responds. "Either way, it's gotta rate us some pussy."

BACK IN KINGMAN, the Fortiers had very little to say in the wake of your partner's tirade. But Timothy McVeigh—as usual—had one more trick up his sleeve.

The next morning, with the Campbell's soup cans still arranged in their menacing triangular design on the living room floor, he played his final trump card at Fort Er.

"If you won't help me build the thing," he informs Mike, "then the least you can do is help me empty out the storage locker I rented over in Golden Valley."

"Fair enough," exclaims the Third Wheel. As if he were in a hurry to get you and your partner out of his hair. It occurs to you, for the first time, that Mike and Lori are afraid of Timothy McVeigh. That he's like a rabid dog that keeps wandering back onto their property.

What, then, does that make you?

A FEW HOURS LATER, your partner and the Third Wheel return from the storage shed, the trunk of the Road Warrior filled to the brim with blasting caps and long, cylindrical devices labeled Tovex.

"They look like big pieces of sausage!" says Lori, giggling, as she stares into the trunk.

"Oh, that's not sausage," Timothy McVeigh cautions his hostess. "Not by a damned sight."

"Sausage—but not sausage!" Lori laughs to herself.

"That's Tovex," your partner replies. "It's a water-resistant, gel-based explosive. Along with these blasting caps here, it could blow the King right out of Kingman."

Now why would you want to go and do something like that? you wonder to yourself.

"Sausage—but not sausage!" repeats Lori, still giggling to herself.

Adopting the soft touch and delicate demeanor of a couple of heart surgeons, Timothy McVeigh and the Third Wheel gently transport the Tovex and the blasting caps into the trailer. With the explosives arrayed on the kitchen table, your partner produces a roll of Scotch tape, a pair of scissors, a trio of packing boxes, and a roll of Christmas wrapping paper.

Without waiting for instructions, Lori begins filling the boxes with the explosives, then wrapping them with the blue-and-white paper adorned with silver-colored doves of peace.

"Sausage—but not sausage!" she laughs to herself.

Is she drunk? you think. Stoned possibly?

"We need to disguise them as Christmas presents," Timothy McVeigh announces, "until we have a chance to deposit the contents in the Herington storage unit. That way, we can maintain the illusion if Johnny Law comes a-callin'."

The illusion of what? you think to yourself. *Of Christmas? Of having a happy holiday season?*

With the faux Christmas gifts stowed safely away in the trunk of the Road Warrior, your driver wheels the vehicle away from the Canyon West Mobile and RV Trailer Park for the last time. Glancing over your shoulder, you notice that Mike and Lori have already drifted back inside the trailer. No lingering good-byes for the Fortiers, you think. No sentimental *bon voyage.*

"I HAVE A DREAM," Timothy McVeigh proclaims as he pilots the Road Warrior eastbound along the interstate. "A dream about wide-open spaces. About free living. *About wild biker babes.*"

Kingman had wide-open spaces, you think to yourself. The living was fairly cheap, for that matter, and your partner seemed to be getting along scandalously well with your hostess. Although you have to admit, come to think of it, that she falls well short in the biker-babe category.

"I am dreaming," your partner continues, "of Grand Rapids, Michigan."

Of what?

"And the Tenth-Annual Winter Cycle Enthusiasts Rally. Featuring the famous Pancake Breakfast, the Snow Rumble, the Charity Bike-a-Thon, and—*did I neglect to mention?*—the Western Michigan Gun and Knife Show. We can even get commemorative patches and body art!"

So we're back on the gun circuit, you think to yourself. Back in business after lo these many months.

It'll be just like the old days—hitting the trail with your boon companion. Driving across the country. Getting into adventures. *Ready to explode.*

BUT FROM THOSE VERY FIRST HOURS on the road to Michigan, it wasn't like the old days at all. For starters, you don't exactly have any stray guns to hawk. Only a handful of leaflets and bumper stickers, not to mention a trunk full of combustible Christmas presents.

And then there's the matter of your partner's increasingly diminished capacity. In his post-crystal days, he has become healthier and more focused, to be sure. And certainly less paranoid. But something is missing from his former self. His youthful whimsy has been displaced somehow by his uncompromising desire for revenge. *For playing dirty for dirty,* his resounding mantra for the New World Order.

And quite frankly, you're not entirely convinced about the necessity of chasing after biker babes in the frozen wilds of Michigan.

"Try to imagine the possibilities," Timothy McVeigh argues.

You are trying your darnedest to imagine the possibilities. But nothing is coming. Nada. *Nil.*

And besides, you and your partner don't know the first thing about motorcycles. You couldn't tell an old-school Kawasaki hightail chopper from a Harley-Davidson Roadster. If you and your driver owned a motorcycle, you would undoubtedly have a three-wheeled sidecar. Like the ones you see in the old war movies.

You briefly imagine the two of you riding across the Urals, with Timothy McVeigh behind the handlebars and you reclining in the sidecar. Going from one Russian gun show to another, from the Kazakh Steppe to the Arctic coast. Selling Kalashnikovs to the Cossacks.

YOU ARE STANDING OUTSIDE a tattoo parlor in Comstock Park, Michigan, pop. 6,530, working up the nerve to follow your partner inside. You are actually breaking into a cold sweat from the fear and uncertainty of what awaits you. Gazing at the flickering neon sign above the door, you wonder how you keep finding yourself in these predicaments. In these unfathomable situations with Timothy McVeigh. "All-American Tattoos. Ink, Needlework, Body Piercing & Massage" reads the sign.

"Let's call this a loyalty test," Timothy McVeigh pronounces as you slowly, warily, enter the tattoo parlor with its fusty smell of mildew and decay.

Loyalty for whom?

"Loyalty for you and me," your partner answers. "Everybody else may have deserted us—Mike, Lori, Terry, and James, even Roger Moore—but at least we've got each other. It'll be like a blood oath between blood brothers."

We should be getting drunk for this, you caution your partner.

"What's that?" he asks incredulously. "I thought you didn't touch the sauce."

The Third Wheel recommends that you get drunk before going under the needle, you remind him.

"Fortier's a pussy, and you're not," says Timothy McVeigh. "And I am most certainly not a pussy," he adds with a glint of arrogance.

Right—you're a shooter. *How could you possibly be a pussy?*

"That would be like asking for Novocaine—or laughing gas," he continues, "and I don't need anything to mediate my pain for me. I can take it like a man. Bring it on!"

You are impressed with his bluster. His fearlessness in the eye of the inkmaster's needle.

The far wall of All-American Tattoos is covered, floor to ceiling, in tattoo designs of all shapes and sizes. Your blood brother takes all of five measly seconds to choose his body art. "The Playboy Bunny," he announces merrily. "On my right arm!"

Not surprisingly, it takes you considerably longer to make your selection. You scan over each and every one of the samples. There are thousands of flowers to choose from—roses, mostly, but stunning just the same. There are Celtic designs and butterflies, vintage automobiles of every make and model, tribal totems, and angels—whole rafts of them. There are kanji symbols and the obligatory anchors, hearts and skulls, and hundreds, nay thousands, of crucifixes.

Praise be, you think to yourself.

There is barbed wire of nearly every gauge, panthers and bears, and ankh symbols beyond all comprehension. And the King of Rock and Roll—more Elvis than you can shake a stick at—is clearly in residence at All-American Tattoos. But what really catches your eye is a Komodo dragon tattoo with its forked tongue and the flames licking at its wicked tail. It's a thing of beauty—and scary, too.

But then you see it. A fiery, blazing phoenix rising from the ashes of death. Verging, mystically—almost magically—upon its rebirth in a brave new world of its own creation. Now, that's the tattoo for you—for JD. For Daryl. *For whomever you happen to be at the moment.*

Timothy McVeigh settles into the adjustable tattoo chair as Summer, the busty tattoo artist, prepares to do her client's bidding. She is wearing a tight yellow T-shirt that reads "Cock-a-doodle-do-me." An easel with the Playboy Bunny design sits nearby.

And then the unthinkable happens.

As Summer steadies the needle above your partner's exposed, sanitized arm, Timothy McVeigh faints. And he doesn't just lapse out for a moment. He blacks out, fully unconscious to the noise and the mayhem of the tattoo parlor.

After Summer revives him with smelling salts, your partner lies down on an empty massage table nearby. Blinking and unblinking his eyes as he attempts to regain his senses.

Taking your turn in the adjustable tattoo chair, you marvel at Summer's array of gadgetry. There are the usual certificates hanging, haphazardly, on the wall. And then there is a device that looks vaguely like a pressure cooker. "That's an autoclave," Summer explains, "for sterilizing my instruments." A complicated lighting assembly hangs overhead. And then there is the tattoo machine itself, a rotary model with a series of electromagnetic coils attached to the needle.

As Summer dons a pair of rubber surgical gloves, you find yourself oddly aroused by the image of her leaning over you, ministering to your every bodily art need. You remove your white Baskin-Robbins smock for the procedure as Summer applies a stencil to your upper left arm in order to trace the image of the phoenix upon your naked bicep.

And then it starts. The full-on pain as Summer activates the needle—the *iron,* as she calls it—and begins applying the pigment to your skin. You experience an entire spectrum of pain, ranging from an initial stinging sensation followed by a deep, penetrating burn. Eventually, the fire in your upper arm gives way to a scratchy feeling, and, as Summer puts the finishing touches on her masterpiece, you feel an unremitting itch growing up and down your left arm. You really should have been drunk for this, you think to yourself.

But in truth, you hardly even care. You adore your body art and the renegade feeling of *being bad.* Of feeling unconventional and—*let's face it*—a tad bit notorious.

As Timothy McVeigh wheels the Road Warrior away from All-American Tattoos, you can't help staring at your arm. You are enamored with your bravery—with your chutzpah at being able to stomach the pain. You carefully remove the bandage that Summer affixed to your arm and gaze at your prize, at the emblem of your courage. *At the symbol of your depravity.*

DESPITE HIS RECENT BOUT of unconsciousness, your partner recovers well enough to attend the gun and knife show at the massive DeltaPlex Arena. Timothy McVeigh doesn't take any chances at the registration booth, introducing himself to the attendant as Mike Havens.

"And this here is Joe Kyle," he continues, gesturing in your direction. "We'd like a pair of day passes to the gun show."

Joe Kyle, you think to yourself. *I am Joe Kyle.* You hastily cover up the insignia on your Baskin-Robbins smock with your right hand. As if you were listening to "The Star-Spangled Banner." Or pledging allegiance.

As Timothy McVeigh traipses off ahead of you into the throng, you begin trailing your partner around the showroom. By now, the gun-show racket has become old hat for you. All of the usual players are in attendance. Off in the distance, you see Tosh Berman hawking his wares. And then there's Andy the German—no doubt engaged in some heartfelt conversation about thwarting the New World Order and dismantling the influence of the Third Reich on foreign shores.

The usual spate of gun collectors is here, not to mention one booth after another devoted to survival gear. Your partner was clearly ahead of his time when he predicted the rise of postapocalyptic paraphernalia in the gun-show hierarchy. You are a little surprised by the number of skinheads on the premises. With their jackboots and their dour expressions, they lend an unwelcome air of ennui and despair to the proceedings. At least as far as you're concerned.

You follow Timothy McVeigh to the far corner of the showroom, where a giant banner adorns the wall above the vendors. "Protect the Gun-Show Loophole," it proclaims. "Or Die Trying!"

And there he is. *The purpose of your visit, you can only presume.* Grandpa Walton.

It's Snow, you think to yourself, of Snow City Pawns. He's wearing a bolo tie with a rhinestone clasp. And he's handing Timothy McVeigh—your partner and recently initiated blood brother—a Converse shoebox.

"It's been a pleasure doing business with ya!" says Grandpa Walton, shaking hands with Timothy McVeigh. "See you at the rendezvous."

What rendezvous? What can he possibly mean?

"Good to see you, Daryl," says Grandpa Walton, with a friendly glance in your direction.

What was that all about? you ask your partner as you make your way out of the showroom.

"Oh that?" says Timothy McVeigh. "That was our fence." He pauses for a moment, smiling to himself. "And I am delighted to report that the matter involving the Candy Store is officially closed."

"WE JUST GOT OUR MONEY back for the Winchester and then some," your partner announces, sitting on a stool at the biker bar in Grand Rapids. "And we've still got the Winchester to boot!"

And what about Bob's gold? What about the precious metals?

"Snow bought every last morsel," says Timothy McVeigh. "Shit, he would have bought Bob's van, too, if Terry hadn't scuttled it. We'll chalk that up to experience!" he adds, laughing to himself.

A dark-eyed brunette is sitting on the barstool next to you. She is wearing shiny red leather pants and a T-shirt proclaiming that "Jesus Saves."

Jesus saves? *In a biker bar?*

Here you are once again, you think to yourself. Hanging with the freaks and the ghouls.

A youngish blonde sits on the stool next to your partner. She is wearing a black leather bra underneath a matching leather jacket, stylishly zipped open to her midriff.

You are clearly in the presence of wild biker babes, if ever there were any.

As you engage in small talk with Red Leather Pants, Timothy McVeigh rolls the dice, going for broke in the tradition of gamblers everywhere. As he stares, unblinkingly, into the eyes of Black Leather Bra, he makes his sad, pathetic wager.

"OK, we've just met," he says. "We could sit here for three hours, wasting money on drinks, or we could just go now and get laid." The silence coming from the direction of Black Leather Bra is deafening. In short order, she gathers up her matching leather purse and walks away. Biker Babes—1, Timothy McVeigh—0.

You hate it when he does that.

I hate it when you do that, you say to Timothy McVeigh. Out loud, no less.

"I'm gonna go shoot some pool," he says with a familiar terseness in his voice.

As your partner strolls away, Red Leather Pants begins fondling your thigh underneath the bar. It turns out that she's partial to fallen, unemployed Quakers on the lam.

"Is that a tattoo?" she asks, slowly fingering the cuff of your Baskin-Robbins smock where it folds above the fiery figure of the phoenix.

You are blushing in embarrassment as she caresses your arm. And you are even more embarrassed when she invites you back to her room.

As you leave the biker bar with Red Leather Pants, you catch Timothy McVeigh's eye. Pausing in midair with his pool cue, he smiles and begins shaking his head, slowly, back and forth.

As if to say, *What gives?*

21 The Road Warrior's Last Stand

Timothy McVeigh is flying across the frigid Michigan terrain in the Road Warrior. Rushing headlong toward the Prairie State. Toward the rendezvous point with Snow in Cairo, Illinois.

Of all the places, you think to yourself, why Cairo, Illinois?

As Timothy McVeigh drives across southern Michigan, you pass through one small town after another, their once-thriving city centers boarded up and overcome by rust and neglect. Your partner begins chuckling to himself as he glances at a heavily bundled black family sitting on the front stoop of their decaying row house.

What's so funny? you ask.

"I used to know a guy who called them porch monkeys," he replies, "back when we drove our route as security guards with the Burke Armored Car service in Buffalo. Not far from where I grew up."

Timothy McVeigh is from New York? *You had no idea.*

"Every time that we'd see them on our route, he'd say, 'God-damned porch monkeys. They sit out there all day long, waiting for those welfare checks to come pouring in while we do the real work out here in the real world. The real America.'"

What work is that? you wonder. Real work like we do—like getting tattoos and hooking up with random, skanky women in biker bars? *Who is he kidding?*

"But you know what?" says Timothy McVeigh. "I see things differently now. I don't think that they're lazy or failures or losers or whatever my buddy was whining about. Shit, I think they're smart for not wanting to get off of the porch in the first place. For staying home and not dipping their toes into the putrid, soul-destroying pool that we call modern life. More power to 'em—that's what I say."

Your driver pauses for a moment, collecting his thoughts. "And God help 'em the day the Bradleys start pulling up their street. When the helicopter gunships come a-callin'. Don't tell me it couldn't happen," he adds, "especially when it comes to citizens sitting around their own homes, minding their own business."

You make a note on your "Jot It Down" pad.

"But you know what's even more fucked-up than my buddy's knee-jerk racism?" he exclaims. "I would have killed anybody in defense of that armored car. Anyone who crossed our path with so much as an awkward glance. And for what reason? To protect and preserve a bunch of money. *A bunch of paper.* Stacks of funny paper that our society has given imaginary value to. It might as well be Popsicles—or balsa wood. *Or whatever.*"

Popsicles. You love them—*why lie about it?* If only you could say the same about balsa wood. *But alas—*

"The point is that I would have done anything to fight for that money," he continues. "Kill, maim—you name it. And the truth is that it's nothing but a pile of paper. We only say that it has value because we have an agreement—*within our society*—to say that it has value. *When it doesn't. When we don't even have a gold standard to back it up anymore.* It boggles the mind when you think about the things that men will do—the inhuman lengths that we will go to— for a bunch of fancy-colored paper. *And to have more of that paper than the next guy does.*"

The lights on the Road Warrior's dashboard radar detector suddenly erupt into being. The machine starts beeping like crazy—*blinking like Christmas tree lights on Christmas morning*—and, before you know it, a police car eases up behind you with its flashing lights in full bloom.

Sausage—but not sausage! you think to yourself as the police car closes in behind the Road Warrior. What will happen when they rifle through the trunk? you wonder to yourself.

"No worries," says Timothy McVeigh. "They don't have probable cause, so there won't be any Christmas presents for Johnny Law." Your partner gazes at the police cruiser in the rearview mirror. Fingering the strap of his shoulder holster, staring them down—*daring them to pull you over.*

But just as quickly as the police car appears, it accelerates into the passing lane, shooting ahead of the Road Warrior, its lights flashing, then disappearing into the rapidly encroaching dusk.

"He must have had another call," says Timothy McVeigh, an audible hint of disappointment in his voice. As if he were yearning for some sort of epic, final confrontation with the authorities.

As the cruiser shoots off ahead into the night, you let out the longest exhalation of breath in your entire life. A powerful sense of relief bordering upon euphoria.

Only to be undone, in the very next instant, by the searing noise of metal crunching against metal. The backbreaking sound of the Road Warrior being struck, violently from behind, wrenching forward at an unnatural angle as Timothy McVeigh desperately attempts to right the vehicle. To keep it from going off of the highway and into the drainage ditch that runs parallel with the interstate.

Sausage—but not sausage! you think to yourself automatically.

In an act of nearly superhuman will, Timothy McVeigh brings the wounded vehicle to a halt near the precipice of the drainage ditch. The screeching sound of tires. The odor of carbon monoxide. Then silence.

Your driver gazes at you across the front seat of the Road Warrior, the blood drained entirely from his face.

"We should be dead, my friend," your partner reports. "Dead as Dillinger."

You wait for the sound of the explosives. For the last sound you'll ever hear.

In your heart of hearts, you are almost hoping for it. *Hoping for detonation.*

But there is no sound of detonation, of course. Only the noise of metal collapsing against the pavement. And the bewildered tones of an unfamiliar male voice—a trucker, it turns out, who fell asleep at the wheel.

And then the sound of your partner as he climbs out of the Road Warrior to inspect the damage.

"Well, dog my cats," says Timothy McVeigh over the apologies—steadfast and true—of the trucker. "This thing is totaled."

Joining your partner on the side of the highway, you observe the mangled carcass of the vehicle. The back end of the car—of Timothy McVeigh's beloved Road Warrior—twisted into an unrecognizable heap, the crunch zones in the backseat crumpled into oblivion.

You pass the rest of the evening in a haze, nestled in the cab of the tow truck with your partner as you make your way up to the Thumb. To the Nicholses' farm, where the driver dumps the Road Warrior's disfigured corpse in a clearing next to the silo.

For all of the damage, the Christmas presents in the trunk are surprisingly intact, save for a crease in one of the package's corners. A single, solitary crease.

"We should be dead," Timothy McVeigh repeats. "Dead as Dillinger."

As you gaze at the dismembered Road Warrior in the clearing, James Nichols drives up in a gray, heavily battered 1983 Pontiac station wagon. Will you ever be able to see James Nichols, you wonder to yourself, without involuntarily conjuring up the image of Lady Godiva slithering upon her silver stripper's pole?

With his crazy eyes aglow, James Nichols signs over the pink slip to the sputtering, road-weary vehicle for the unholy price of four bills, which Timothy McVeigh dutifully extracts from the Converse shoebox. Terry Nichols stands sheepishly nearby throughout the transaction. Sending an occasional wayward glance in your direction, as if he's afraid of being noticed. Of being involved, even.

"This'll get you to Cairo!" says James Nichols with a broad smile across his face.

We'll be lucky if the Pontiac gets out of the Thumb, you think to yourself disdainfully.

The only thing worse than the station wagon's corroded body is the vehicle's interior, which smells precisely like the Nicholses' barn, where it has been in deep storage for God knows how long. You find yourself literally gasping for air as you settle into the passenger's seat while your partner stows the Christmas presents away in the Pontiac's cargo bed.

Ho ho ho, you think to yourself automatically.

BY THE NEXT AFTERNOON, you're back on the road to Illinois, speeding across lower Michigan and skirting the rim of northern Indiana. For all of its foibles and eccentricities, the station wagon turns out to be an able-bodied successor to the Road Warrior. It certainly isn't as fast—and it smells like the dickens, to be sure—but there's no denying the vehicle's resilience. Timothy McVeigh is hell on wheels, and he puts the car—any car—through its paces. Wild hairpin turns, hard lefts, sharp rights, full-blooded stops. And the wagon takes everything your partner dishes out, and then some.

As midnight beckons, Timothy McVeigh is steering the station wagon into sleepy Cairo, Illinois, pop. 4,846. Right on time, and no worse for wear—unless you count the untimely loss of the Road Warrior, which is immeasurable, of course.

Your blood brother exits the interstate and drives into the sleepy town. Cairo's murky street lamps cut through the darkness, illuminating the city's ornate collection of postbellum redbrick homes. Taking the wheel with his left hand, Timothy McVeigh extracts a piece of soiled paper from his pocket.

"We're looking for Levee Road," he says. As he pilots the station wagon through the city streets, the mighty Mississippi rolls into view just beyond the passenger's seat window.

M-i-s-s-i-s-s-i-p-p-i, you think to yourself automatically.

A tugboat pushing a barge, loaded to the gills with tractor-trailers, chugs upriver as your partner turns onto Levee Road and brings the station wagon to a stop near a clump of trees. The river, brown and silty, ambles slowly by. Rolling down the window, the only sound you hear is the nighttime noise of the cicadas.

And then, suddenly, you catch a glimpse of a cigarette lighter being activated, then extinguished, three times in quick succession.

"That's our signal," Timothy McVeigh announces. "That's Snow." Your partner climbs out of the vehicle, strolling confidently in Grandpa Walton's direction, which, by your admittedly amateurish calculations, is no more than a few hundred feet away.

You step out of the station wagon to await your partner's return. To enjoy the cool evening air and the river's natural rhythms. Its ebbs and flows.

And then he's back. And after only a matter of moments—if that.

"Snow is a fed," says Timothy McVeigh, walking back toward the car. He is shaking his head, staring up into the sky. Chuckling to himself ever so slightly, a sly grin unfolding across his face.

Grandpa Walton? you think to yourself. Not a chance!

"I shit you not," says Timothy McVeigh, still smiling. "Take a look at the bushes over yonder—around twelve o'clock, near the tree line. Look for the glint in the moonlight. That's his backup. They're probably training their Colt M16 assault rifles on us right now. And I guarantee you that Snow is wearing a wire, hoping for me to admit something on tape. Something about the action."

That isn't going to happen, you reply.

"You're sure-shittin' it ain't," says Timothy McVeigh.

He sighs audibly. His disappointment is overwhelming him even as he stands before you on the dark pavement of Levee Road.

"Here's how it's going to go down," he says, glancing back at Snow with a friendly wave in the older man's direction. "I'm gonna stroll over and give an Academy Award–winning performance for our friend Grandpa Walton, and then I am going to walk, slowly, back to the car and drive on outta here. Under the speed limit the whole way. Real nice-and-easy-like."

WITHIN MINUTES, the Pontiac is coasting up Levee Road, with Timothy McVeigh shifting back and forth uncomfortably in the driver's seat.

"Snow must've been playing me for years," your partner laments. "Every last transaction, every goddamned gun deal—all of it was in the service of getting into my kitchen. In gaining my confidence." He pauses, shaking his head in disgust. "When this is over, I'm gonna personally shoot that motherfucker right between the eyes. I'll be the last thing Grandpa Walton ever sees."

Why were we meeting Snow, anyway? you ask. What was so important that he was able to lure us out here—to Cairo, Illinois, in the middle of nowhere—and be caught so unawares?

"He told me that he had some top-secret information about the New World Order," Timothy McVeigh admits, exasperation in his voice. "He said he had intelligence about a clandestine U.N. military incursion in Gulfport, Mississippi."

And you believed it? you think to yourself. *You actually believed that the United Nations was going to launch an unprovoked attack on U.S. domestic soil?* Your partner's thirst for conspiracy and paranoia simply knows no bounds.

How could you tell that Snow was a fed? you implore Timothy McVeigh. Maybe your driver misread the situation—perhaps

Grandpa Walton is Grandpa Walton after all?

"Because the first thing that the stupid son of a bitch asked me about was the action. He didn't beat around the bush or nothing," says your partner. "The least he could have done was make small talk about Gulfport. Which is what got our asses out here to the sticks in the first doggone place."

Timothy McVeigh is really fuming, you think to yourself.

"Snow has a lotta fuckin' nerve—I'll give him that," your partner continues. "Why not just go ahead and say, 'Would you be sure to speak directly into the microphone for me, Timmy? Yeah, just like that. That's a good boy, Timmy. That'll really help when we turn this over to the grand jury, you patriot piece of trash.'"

But how do you know for certain that Grandpa Walton was referring to the action? you plead with Timothy McVeigh. Did Snow make any references to Oklahoma City? About rousting Bob back in Arkansas? *Can you really be sure?*

"Because the fucker asked me about the liquid nitromethane," he responds with desperation in his voice. "And who the fuck else would know about that?" he asks.

Ennis, Texas, you think to yourself. *The racetrack.*

Sitting there in the nighttime silence, as Timothy McVeigh steers the station wagon back toward the relative safety of the interstate, you register a conspicuous change in your partner's demeanor.

The usual bravado is gone, only to be replaced by a gnawing sense of dread and uncertainty. Your partner has been visibly shaken by the events back in Cairo. And as he wheels the Pontiac through the dead of night, you can tell that Snow's betrayal is beginning to eat him up inside.

"This story is starting to get really sad," your partner whispers forlornly across the front seat. "Do you think there's any chance that things'll get better—that we'll ever find our way out of these troubles?"

You hope so, you tell him. *You surely hope so.*

22 The Girl Can't Help It

As Timothy McVeigh drives along the interstate—leaving the quiet streets of Cairo and its stealthy posse of federal agents in your wake—your blood brother becomes increasingly wary about heading in the direction of the Sooner State. At least just yet.

"It's code red, dude," says Timothy McVeigh as he steers the Pontiac along the Great River Road, with the murky Mississippi streaming by in the moonlight. "We need to find a place to hunker down for a few days and sort this shit out."

You know just the place, you tell your partner. The very place where no one would think to ferret you out.

AS DAWN BREAKS OVER THE MISSISSIPPI, Timothy McVeigh motors into Hannibal, Missouri, pop. 18,004.

And while your blood brother is locked in a desperate search for a hideout, you have other things on your mind entirely. You are hoping to be reunited with your lost ballerina love. You are in search of Gina—and the chance, slim as it may be—to recast your fate. The destiny that you divined, that you thwarted, some thirteen months ago in a fit of passion and misplaced jealousy. The very same mangled destiny that sent you spiraling into a life of crime. That sent you into the arms of Timothy McVeigh.

Driving across the pristine, oak-lined streets of Hannibal, your partner stops at a convenience store so that you can locate the Watsons' address in the local white pages. While Timothy McVeigh soothes his aching nerves with a cherry Slurpee, you glance absentmindedly at the newsstand. "Mississippi Ratifies Thirteenth Amendment," reads the headline. What is this—*1865?* Have we gone back in time? you wonder to yourself.

The old Watson place is nestled on stately Hill Street. Not too far—as the crow flies—from the "Unsinkable" Molly Brown Museum and a converted house called the Gilded Age Inn. Whatever that means. As you pull into the Watsons' circular driveway, a wintry wind is whipping up the front yard, the weeping willows swaying to and fro.

You knock on the house's massive, oaken door as Timothy McVeigh paces near the station wagon, glancing this way and that for the *Federales.* They never materialize, of course, but that doesn't stop your partner from being on high alert. From drifting toward the nightmare scenario of DEFCON 1.

A gray-haired, pencil-thin woman pulls opens the heavy wooden door. She is wearing a formless, light blue dress with a belt loosely cinched about the waist. She has a pale and bloodless complexion— perhaps the palest and most bloodless complexion you've ever seen.

It's none other than Regina Watson—*the original Gina,* you think to yourself, *the pre-Gina Gina*—who lost her husband, a riverboat captain, when your pretty ballerina was only twelve years old. Which makes her the Widow Watson, for all intents and purposes, of Hannibal, Missouri. Captain Watson's untimely demise left young Regina to raise her daughter on her own. And raise her she did—with the finest of Quaker upbringings and living the good life in the historic district.

And there you are: wearing your Good Humor outfit, complete with your Carolina Panthers cap. And in the background, marching at an anxious, uneasy gait, is Timothy McVeigh, sporting a hunter green T-shirt proclaiming "Peace Through Superior Firepower." A beige Windbreaker barely conceals his shoulder holster and his trusty Glock.

To be perfectly honest, it's a wonder that the Widow Watson lets you into her home in the first place. At best, you look like a pair of ruffians. And at worst—well, at your worst, you look like a pair of criminals on the run. Criminals who have scarcely slept for days. Or bathed or eaten, for that matter. You must make for a sorry sight indeed.

Standing in the foyer of the house, you stretch out your hand to introduce yourself.

"I know who you are," the Widow Watson interrupts. "You are JD, and this must be your anti-government friend." Timothy McVeigh smiles sheepishly at this last remark. "Gina has told me all about you," the Widow continues. "You are welcome in our home."

You follow your hostess into the living room, where a young girl, her strawberry-blonde hair yoked back smartly in a bun, is reading a book while sitting on a plush Victorian sofa. She is the spitting image of Gina. You are thunderstruck simply to be in her presence.

"Who's Daryl?" she asks, staring at your Baskin-Robbins smock.

I am Daryl, you think to yourself. *Daryl Bridges.*

The Widow Watson and her young companion stare at you in utter disbelief.

"It's too complicated to explain," interrupts your partner. "Do you mind if I pull my car around back?" he asks the Widow.

Two minutes inside the house on Hill Street, you think, and Timothy McVeigh's paranoia is already in full throttle.

"I'm Rachael," the sofa girl announces, closing her book. She's reading *A Girl of the Limberlost,* according to the spine. Rachael is staring at you expectantly. "Are you in love with my sister?" she asks. Without emotion, without pity—*only wonder.*

Gina, Gina, my pretty ballerina! you think to yourself automatically.

You don't know what to say, of course—you so rarely do.

After several uncomfortable moments of silence, you are saved—
deus ex machina-like—by the sudden reemergence of Timothy
McVeigh, who is cradling the Christmas presents in his arms. Looking for a place for safekeeping. *For avoiding premature detonation.*

"You can store those in the mudroom behind the kitchen," the
Widow Watson instructs your partner. "And then the two of you can
go upstairs and get cleaned up properly," she announces, emotion-
lessly, as she stares in your direction. Still sizing you up.

AFTER WASHING UP in the Watsons' elegant guest bedroom suite,
you stroll about the property, nervously awaiting Gina's appear-
ance. A late winter snow is fluttering down upon the quiet streets of
Hannibal, blanketing the town in its pure, white, unsullied powder.
Timothy McVeigh is making snow angels in the front yard with
Rachael, a precocious nine-year-old with the unquenchable spirit
of God in her heart and an inalienable belief in Jesus Christ, Our
Savior, conducting a symphony in her mind.

They are playing in front of the family's old Italianate house.
Tall and regal in its day, the building has become faded with age. A
shadow of its former self. A beat-up skiff, barely seaworthy, sits in
the backyard, the snow slowly filling up its interior. The name *Delta
Queen* is stenciled upon its emaciated wooden stern. As you amble
behind the house, you spot a white, cedar gazebo off in the distance.
And there, bundled up tightly against the brisk winter wind, is your
erstwhile Wichita lover. The lost ballerina of your dreams.

She is sitting alone in silence, staring at the wooden floorboards
as you approach. She has clearly reverted back to her Quaker self—
prim and proper, appropriately attired.

Gazing at her on the gazebo bench, you haven't a doubt in the
world that you still love her. *That you will love her for all time.*

Gina eventually breaks the silence. "I'm so sorry, JD," she says.
Her voice as sweet and true as ever.

Why is she apologizing? you think to yourself. You're the one, after all, who brandished a weapon. Who sent Dakota Fish packing in a hail of bullets.

"I'm just an effed-up girl," Gina sobs. "That's all I ever was."

She is wearing her staid blue dress of old beneath a black winter cape, and you are shivering in your Good Humor outfit.

"That's a nice tattoo you got there," she says, staring at your left bicep, averting her eyes from your face. You begin absentmindedly tracing the contours of the skin of your upper arm.

"God has entered my life," she announces. Or perhaps *reentered* her life, you think to yourself, given her obvious reconversion to the faith. The Widow Watson has clearly done her work.

"I am holding fast to the light," she continues. "And I won't be letting go again," she says, peeking up at you from under the hood of her cape. Hoping for a gesture of approval. *Or reconciliation?*

The last time you saw her, she was naked and writhing on top of you in her boardinghouse bedroom. A million years ago in Wichita. Now she's dressed like a Pilgrim. The difference is simply staggering.

Where's Dakota Fish? you ask, attempting to drain all of the emotion from your voice. As if you were merely asking about the location of a local rummage sale. Or about the weather.

"I lost track of him several months back," she answers nonchalantly. "Last I heard, he has a day job in Oklahoma City—in one of the big office buildings downtown. He's working for the Social Security Administration, if I remember correctly. Takes a bus into the city from the reservation every day."

She suddenly loses her train of thought and begins taking a long, awkward look at your Baskin-Robbins smock.

"Who's Daryl?" she asks, confusion in her voice.

But before you can reply, you are interrupted by a shriek from the direction of the house. The sound of a young girl in danger. *Rachael—it just has to be.*

YOU ARE STANDING in the mudroom with Gina and the Widow Watson. Rachael is squatting on the floor, frozen in the act of opening one of your partner's clandestine Christmas packages.

Was it merely curiosity? you wonder to yourself. Or was she dreaming of a belated Merry Christmas, courtesy of your blood brother?

Timothy McVeigh is kneeling in the kitchen doorway, his Glock drawn from his shoulder holster and positioned in his hands, combat-style. He is eyeing his prey like a hard target. Like an enemy combatant.

And Rachael is frightened out of her wits, verging upon catatonia. A tiny pool of urine has sullied the floorboards below her petticoats.

What are you going to do—shoot her? you think to yourself. *For opening an unmarked Christmas gift?*

The Widow Watson's voice interrupts the scene like the sound of the Almighty. "Put away the gun, Timothy," she commands. Cool and quiet. All business. "There's no place for it here."

Almost robotically, your partner returns the Glock to his holster, stands up, and walks back toward the kitchen. For her part, Rachael falls backward in relief. And Gina just stares at you. With eyes of love? With derision? You can't even begin to know.

As Gina and the Widow Watson tend to Rachael, you leave the house in search of Timothy McVeigh. As it turns out, your quest for your partner is decidedly short. He is leaning, head in hand, against the Pontiac.

Perhaps he has seen the error of his ways? you think. *Perhaps he's not too far gone this time?*

But your relief, alas, is to be short-lived.

"Did somebody move the car?" Timothy McVeigh asks. "I don't remember parking it here."

You moved it yourself, you remind him. So that it wouldn't be parked on Hill Street. You know—for all the world to see.

"I can't shake the notion that we're being followed," he continues. "That they're out there somewhere. In the bushes. In the streets of Hannibal."

Who would be following us?

"The feds, JD. They're on to us now," he replies. "They were on to us back in Cairo, and now they're here. Probably watching us right now through their telephoto lenses. Taking notes. Hatching stratagems. The works."

Was Grandpa Walton *really* a fed? you suddenly wonder to yourself. You feel guilty for even questioning your partner's veracity—for doubting his mental capacity. But what else do you have to go on, if not Timothy McVeigh's brute impressions of the world?

BY DAYBREAK, you are on the road again. The road that you have seemingly never left since joining Timothy McVeigh's bizarre employ lo those many months ago.

But before you depart, you are joined by the Widow Watson in the circular driveway, while your partner warms up the station wagon nearby.

"Perhaps there is still hope," she says. "There is always hope, JD."

How can you forgive him so easily? you ask. How can you forgive a guy you only just met after he waves a gun at your daughter?

"Forgiveness is easy," says the Widow Watson. "It's living that's difficult—living with regrets, living with the things that we've done when we know that we might've done better."

You make a note on your "Jot It Down" pad.

And then you begin weeping quietly to yourself. You are crying for everyone now—for Rachael, for Gina, for Timothy McVeigh. Heck, even for Terry Nichols. Lonely, forlorn Terry Nichols. And yes, even for yourself—for yourself who has been lost on this interminable highway for so very long. And the end doesn't even seem to be remotely in sight.

"Remember," says the Widow Watson, "what the caterpillar thinks is the end, the butterfly thinks is the beginning."

You will remember, you think to yourself. What else, really, can you do?

AS TIMOTHY McVEIGH steers the Pontiac out of Hannibal, he is already in fine form, maniacally stringing his words together and blathering, nonstop, about your shadowy enemies. "We can't stay here anymore—on account of the feds," he says. "But we can't go back to Kansas or Oklahoma City yet either—'cause we both know that they'll be hot on our trail."

So what happens next? you wonder to yourself. *What now, then?*

"What happens now," replies Timothy McVeigh, "is that we get the hell outta Dodge and seek our refuge in Oklahoma's own little Shangri-La."

Elohim City—now *that's* a solution that you can live with, you think to yourself. Perhaps there really is hope after all? Perhaps you will be like the butterfly and effect a new beginning?

AS TIMOTHY McVEIGH pilots the Pontiac along I-44, just outside of Carthage, Missouri, pop. 10,747, you happen upon a scene of bloody carnage. A distorted, broken carcass lies prone upon the blacktop. Your partner brings the station wagon to a halt just beyond the wounded animal.

It's a white-tailed deer. Still breathing—*barely.* Lying in a pool of its own blood on the side of the highway.

Roadkill, you think to yourself. *Gross.*

Timothy McVeigh approaches the deer cautiously, kneeling down on the road beside the animal. He begins weeping quietly to himself as he cradles the deer in his arms. He is petting the animal about the nose and ears. Comforting it.

"Some fuckin' tractor-trailer driver shoots across the interstate, going God knows how fast, and Bambi here is done for. What the fuck is this country coming to?" he asks. "After the last umpteenth gas crisis, we shoulda gone back to the railroads. Instead we have a million eighteen-wheelers carrying the commerce of the nation on their backs. And for what?" he continues. "So that we can buy a Big

Mac on every street corner? So that we can stuff our faces and fill our pockets with—*with stuff?*"

By this point, the deer is bleeding all over the front of your partner's T-shirt, dribbling in a thin, red, dotted line onto his black jeans.

"And this guy here," he says, gesturing toward the deer dying in his lap, "is left to bleed out in the gutter. On the side of the road, like garbage. When will we ever learn to value what really matters?" he asks disgustedly.

"When I was eight years old," he continues, clearing his throat, "I was playing near a small fishing pond. And this friend of mine comes along—Ethan Shay, an older kid from the neighborhood. And he's carrying a burlap sack, which he proceeds to hurl into the drink. So I asked Ethan what it was, and he tells me that his cat had kittens and they had to get rid of them somehow. And then I had to stand there and watch while that god-awful burlap bag wriggled and wrangled on the surface until it slowly sank into the pond. It was the most horrible thing I've ever seen. Shit, even after Desert Storm, it's still the most horrible sight I've ever witnessed."

Sighing to himself, Timothy McVeigh removes the weapon from his shoulder holster. With a single, deadly blast from his fearsome Glock, he finally puts the animal out of its misery. But your own misery—*your shared misery*—seems to endure beyond all reason.

Dear Jesus, how can you possibly keep your partner on the straight and narrow? How can you save Timothy McVeigh from losing his mind?

23 Escape to Elohim City

"Welcome," says Timothy McVeigh, "to the Month of the Bull." He is steering the Pontiac across the craggy eastern plains of Oklahoma and into the foothills of the Ozark Mountains. And you—*you are holding on for dear life.*

Your partner pilots the station wagon into the parking lot of an old filling station, where he uses a pay phone next to a stack of dusty tires labeled "For Sale—New!"

They don't even look roadworthy, you think to yourself. *How can they be new?*

"I'd like to make a person-to-person call in the name of Robert Kling," he tells the operator.

"Is Andy the German there?" he says into the receiver. What kind of salutation is that?

"It's Tim Tuttle," he continues, "and I need to get a message to Andy the German. Tell him, 'Tim Tuttle says it's code red, and he's comin' in from the cold.'"

The shooter who came in from the cold, you think to yourself automatically.

"Let's roll," says Timothy McVeigh, hanging up the telephone. "Let's make it happen."

We've got to make it happen, you think. You're hanging on by a thread here, and you've just got to find a way—impossible as it may seem—to unravel the Day of the Rope.

AS YOU ENTER ADAIR COUNTY, your blood brother wheels the Pontiac off of the highway, through a nondescript aluminum gate, and onto a large parcel of unincorporated land. The locals call it the City of God. But as far as you and your partner are concerned, it's Elohim City, Oklahoma, pop. *unknown.*

"So much for Andy the German's security," says Timothy McVeigh, chuckling to himself. "The A.T.F. could roll their Bradleys in here without so much as a beaver to break up the proceedings."

After traveling several hundred yards into the compound, your driver brings the station wagon to a halt next to a quintet of Ford pickup trucks. In front of you sits a large, vine-covered building that is enclosed with an absurd polyurethane-foam roof. And just beyond that, a half-dozen silver Airstream trailers form an awkward semicircle, the daylight glinting off of their aluminum skins as if you were looking into the maw of the sun.

You climb out of the Pontiac—and directly into the arms of the Elohim City welcoming party. Guns drawn, anger in their eyes.

The cast of Elohim City makes for a fascinating portrait. From left to right, you have an elderly, gray-bearded gentleman pointing a nasty-looking shotgun in your face; and then you have a humongous, stout fellow, his hair dyed platinum blond, lunging forward with a tommy gun, complete with its signature circular magazine; the picture is rounded out by a petite blonde training a wicked-looking Luger on your partner.

This must be Elohim City's finest, you think to yourself.

"I'm Tim Tuttle," your partner announces cautiously, his hands raised high above his shoulders. "And this—this is Daryl Bridges."

I am Daryl Bridges, you think to yourself. *And it is as hot as blue blazes out here.*

And then you see him. In his immaculate blue suit, Andy the German cuts an awkward figure as he walks across the rugged, dirt road to greet you. He is sweating profusely in the springtime sun, wiping his forehead periodically with a handkerchief.

"Welcome, my friends. Welcome!" says Andy the German. "You see," he adds, waving his hands in the air, gesturing at the unforgiving surroundings, "it really exists. Elohim City isn't a mirage—it's a reality!"

This isn't a mirage, you think to yourself. *It's a bunch of mobile homes.* You half expect Mike and Lori Fortier to peek out from behind one of the Airstreams with a case of Pabst Blue Ribbon and their trusty tinfoil pipe.

"**PLEASE ACCEPT MY APOLOGIES** for our little display back there," says the gray-bearded man. "We're always at the ready in case of a raid. The rumors are flying that we're next on the A.T.F.'s hot list."

"I am the Right Reverend Robert G. Millar," he says, extending his hand in your direction. "But everybody calls me Pappy."

"What does *Elohim* mean, Pappy?" asks Timothy McVeigh.

"It translates, loosely, as Divinity or God," your host replies. "We're filled with the Holy Spirit here," he pronounces. "People often confuse us with bigots or separatists. But in truth, we're purists. And there's not a lot of room left in these United States for pure, freedom-loving people. The only thing that seems to matter is driving a Japanese import and carrying an American Express card."

"What kind of security do you have on the premises?" your partner inquires. "We drove right on in here without encountering so much as a land mine."

With a nod from Pappy, Andy the German erupts into speech. "We're not so naive that we believe we can keep the feds away with a few automatic weapons," he says, removing a camouflage tarp that conceals a vintage World War II howitzer.

"Well, how do you like them beans?" says Timothy McVeigh, staring at the centerpiece of the Elohim City armory.

It's a formidable weapon, to be sure. Gray-colored, with a deadly-looking barrel capable of delivering 105mm shells. It might not stop an M1 Abrams Battle Tank, you think to yourself, but it would make a heckuva lot of noise.

"Don't get me wrong," says Pappy. "I am a man of peace. But a civil war is brewing in which we must contend with the Jews and their Western sympathizers. It will be a time of great reckoning for their pact with the devil."

"How would you describe your beliefs?" asks Timothy McVeigh, clearly trying to make conversation.

"We're a Christian Identity sect," answers Pappy.

What does that mean? you ask your partner discreetly.

"Means they're racists," he whispers. "But you know—the fun-loving, recreational kind."

Your blood brother suddenly turns in Pappy's direction, extending his right hand in a gesture of friendship and benevolent peace.

"We are humbly requesting sanctuary," says Timothy McVeigh. "And we are at your service."

Beaming proudly in the Oklahoma sunlight, Pappy grips your partner's hand. "Son, you and your friend here are welcome to stay in Elohim City as long as you like," says Pappy, winking in your direction. "But remember, we're all in God's hands—and He has a plan for each and every one of us."

Sanctuary is sanctuary, you think to yourself. This may not be Brigadoon, but it'll have to do.

LATER THAT EVENING, you are relaxing in the vine-covered building—or the Worship House, as your fellow Elohimians call it—listening to classical music on an old Sony turntable.

Sounds like Wagner, you think sardonically. *Or Strauss.*

A pair of wooden ceiling fans circle overhead, doing absolutely nothing to cut through the sweltering heat.

You are standing in a corner of the building's social room, drinking Liebfraumilch with Timothy McVeigh.

"Hot damn!" he says, staring across the room at the petite blonde, who has traded in her Luger for a crystal wineglass. "That is some *shiksa!*"

She is wearing a black halter top, and a swastika tattoo is visible on her right shoulder blade.

"My name is Carol," she says, joining you and your partner in your quaint corner of the social room, "and you must be Tim and Daryl, the talk of the compound."

"That's right," says Timothy McVeigh admiringly. *Lustily.* "We're the flavor of the moment. How'd you find yourself in Elohim City?" he asks.

"See that tall drink o' water over there?" she replies. "That's Dennis the Menace," she says, pointing toward the platinum-blond gentleman from your greeting party earlier in the day. "He's the beloved leader of the White Aryan Resistance. He'd just as soon kill you as make you a Denver omelet."

Why would we want to eat a Denver omelet? you wonder to yourself. *They're terribly greasy.*

"Anyways, I came to the compound several months ago with Dennis," she continues, "but that went south, and I'm still here. Rusting away with the holiest of holies in the new Third Reich."

"Why'd you break up?" asks Timothy McVeigh inquisitively. "What went wrong?"

"I thought he was a real man," she answers. "A real man of action. But it turns out that he's all talk with a big gun. A big, dumb gun."

"To sin by silence when they should protest makes cowards out of men," says Timothy McVeigh, clearly trying to impress your new blonde acquaintance.

Abe Lincoln, you think to yourself. *Nice touch.*

"You can say that again," says Carol. "So what brings you guys to these parts?" she asks with the slightest hint of suspicion in her voice.

"Andy the German," your partner responds. "We know him from the gun-show circuit, and we've been dying to check this place out. He says it's the last frontier for a freethinker in this hemisphere."

"*A freethinker?*" says Carol incredulously. "Sorry to burst your bubble, boys, but Andy the German is the biggest Nazi here—and that's saying a lot."

"You must be misinformed," says Timothy McVeigh. "He emigrated to this country to stamp out illegal exports of Nazi propaganda back to Germany."

"Not hardly," answers Carol. "If anything, he's the largest importer of Nazi paraphernalia on the U.S. market. Here's a news flash for you: Andy the German's grandfather was a founding member of the Nazi party, fellas. And don't bullshit yourselves—those roots run deep."

You glance around the social room at the other guests. And as if things couldn't get any more surreal, you catch a glimpse of none other than the man in white. Arkansas's favorite son.

Roger Moore at three o'clock, you whisper to your partner.

"Jesus freakin' Christ," answers Timothy McVeigh with obvious irritation in his voice. He begins walking in Bob's direction as you trail closely behind. *Like you always do.*

Roger Moore is sitting off in the corner, slowly swaying to and fro in Pappy's antique rocking chair. Dressed immaculately in a white seersucker suit, he is leaning forward on an exquisite white cane. He seems like a shadow of his former self. Like a broken man.

He is gazing across the room as you and your blood brother stroll in his direction. He has no idea, you think to yourself—no idea that you helped Terry clean out the Candy Store.

"I was so sorry to hear about the robbery," says Timothy McVeigh. "You must be sick about losing all those guns."

"What happened at my ranch was the lowest form of human indecency," Roger Moore exclaims. "It was enough to make a body ashamed of the human race."

"It was undoubtedly the feds that rousted you," says Timothy McVeigh. "You have our deepest sympathies. We're all in this together, dude."

Having given his former mentor's hand a vigorous shake, Timothy McVeigh excuses himself—anxious to return, no doubt, to Carol's sweet vicinity.

After a few moments, your companion breaks the silence. "Take a look at your partner," says Roger Moore. "Do you see what I see?"

You are confused. You don't have the first clue what Roger Moore sees. The last time you saw him, Roger Moore was staring, up close, at the interior of the jacket that Terry Nichols had swaddled about his face.

"Young Timothy has what we used to call, back in the service, the Thousand-Yard Stare. There's nothing like it," Roger Moore continues. "It is uniquely its own phenomenon. It is the eerie, vacuous look that a soldier gets in his eyes. The unfocused gaze of a battle-weary soul. Of a man who is marching on his last legs. Fighting the last, most important battle of his life. His final, desperate stand."

We're all battle-weary souls, you think to yourself. *When will it ever end?*

EARLY THE NEXT MORNING, as you and Timothy McVeigh relax in your guest quarters in one of the Airstream trailers, your partner can't stop talking about the sexy blonde poster girl for the New Right.

"Riddle me this," says Timothy McVeigh. "What's a babe like that doing in a sausage fest like Elohim City?"

Sausage fest? That's a truly disgusting phrase, you think to yourself.

As Timothy McVeigh waxes and wanes in his infatuation over halter-top Carol, you notice an envelope peeking underneath your bedroom door.

In as much time as it takes for you to cross the six short feet from your Murphy bed to the doorjamb, you grasp the envelope and begin examining its contents. The letter itself is nothing more than a single, narrow strip of paper inscribed with a hasty, penciled scrawl: "Beware. Trouble is brewing. Keep a sharp lookout." The letter is signed "unknown friend."

Unknown friend, you think to yourself. That's a new one—you're not entirely sure that you have any *known* friends, much less any *unknown* ones.

"Well, goddamn!" says Timothy McVeigh. "We've been infiltrated yet again."

Do you think that they're feds? Or agents? Or, worse yet, special agents? you ask your partner.

"They're all *special* agents in the A.T.F.," Timothy McVeigh wryly observes. "But to answer your question, JD, it's bad—*real bad.*"

Your money's on Carol, you tell him.

"Then your money's no good," he replies. "It's freakin' Bob. How much of a coincidence is it that you and I show up here, out of the blue, only to find Roger Moore sipping wine in Elohim City? It's uncanny."

Carol's the oddball in the compound, you tell him. Well, Carol and your own Quaker self—but that's another story.

"It's that fuckwad Bob," says Timothy McVeigh, "and I am gonna saw that fucker's legs off."

Why would anyone want to do a thing like that? you think to yourself. *That's really gross. Not to mention barbaric.*

Your partner sees an old rope ladder lying in a heap in the corner. "We could hang 'im right now with that!" he says with unrestrained enthusiasm.

But before your partner can begin lynching Bob—can begin executing him for his crimes against humanity, *for his crimes against Timothy McVeigh*—you hear a strange commotion outside the trailer, where Elohim City's finest have begun congregating, weapons at the ready.

You slowly emerge from the trailer, Timothy McVeigh with his Glock, loaded and aching to be discharged. And you with your Air-Lite—the fated revolver that set your destiny into motion.

"Well, if it's not our own little A.T.F. contingent," says Pappy, brandishing his shotgun. You'd wager that he means business—that both barrels are loaded.

"We can neutralize these motherfuckers right now," says Dennis the Menace through gritted teeth. Carol lingers off to the rear in a combat stance. Tightly gripping her Luger with both hands. Waiting to be deployed.

Roger Moore is resting on his cane in the extreme background, standing inside the entryway to one of the Airstream trailers.

"You can shut your freakin' piehole," says Timothy McVeigh to an enraged Pappy. "If anybody's A.T.F., it's you guys—*or Bob*. We're driving outta here right now," your partner announces to Elohim City's bewildered patriarch. "Carol can come with us, but the rest of you can all go to hell!"

"I'm staying right here," she says, discreetly flashing an A.T.F. badge behind her back as you make your way to the Pontiac. Pappy and Dennis the Menace follow closely behind, with Roger Moore still standing by the trailer, a knowing smile growing across his face.

It was Bob, you chuckle to yourself. It was Roger Moore who sent us the anonymous warning. *Just had to be.*

As Timothy McVeigh revs up the station wagon, you climb into the passenger's seat, still training the AirLite on your pursuers. If you had to open fire on the Elohimians, you wonder to yourself, would you be able to hit the broad side of a barn? Or would you and your partner expire in a bloody shoot-out, Bonnie and Clyde–style, on a dusty country road?

"IT'S FEDS, FEDS, FEDS—wherever we turn," says Timothy McVeigh, motoring the Pontiac along the interstate as he speeds away from Adair County. "I still can't believe that Carol's a dirty A.T.F. agent," he continues. "If it's Carol, then it's damned near everyone we know. And if it's nearly everyone we know, then—*well, then we're dead. It's sayonara, and that's all there is to it.*"

It's not *sayonara* by a long shot. You still have your wits about you, you think to yourself, and as long as you have your wits about you, then you can do darned near anything on God's green earth.

And ministering to Timothy McVeigh will be a breeze. As safe and easy as milk and cookies. *And just about as satisfying.*

24 Roughing It

Timothy McVeigh is piloting the station wagon across the hills and dales of Junction City, Kansas, pop. 20,604. You are traveling from your seedy room at the Dreamland Motel to a Firestone auto-care center—and you are on an honest-to-goodness, balls-to-the-wall emergency mission. The Pontiac has been overheating and leaking coolant all the livelong day, and you are beside yourselves with fear and desperation. "This thing is on life support," says your partner hesitantly. "I think we've blown a gasket."

Is that serious? you ask.

"It might as well be a death sentence," he answers, consternation growing audibly in his voice.

As Timothy McVeigh wheels the wheezing vehicle into the Firestone parking lot, the engine turns over for the last time. Sputtering and dying on the spot.

"This is really gonna cut into our negotiating power," your partner laments.

You follow Timothy McVeigh into the repair shop, where you meet a clean-shaven attendant wearing greasy blue overalls and scruffy black boots. His name tag identifies him as Tom.

Your partner carefully removes his camouflage wallet from his back pocket.

"I got three hundred bucks," your blood brother announces. "You tell me if it's cheaper to fix this old piece of shit or if I need to go buy a car at some junkyard."

"You're in luck, friend," says Tom. "I may have just what you're lookin' for out back."

Tom leads you behind the Firestone complex to a faded yellow 1977 Ford Mercury Marquis resting in a field of weeds. It's a genuinely sorry sight to behold.

"It may not be pretty," says Tom, "but it runs."

Timothy McVeigh exhales loudly as he begins sizing up the automobile.

"I won't lie to you," Tom continues. "It has a few problems. There's the broken gas gauge, for one thing. And then there's the transmission, which slips like crazy. The engine burns a lot of oil, of course, and the tailpipe tends to spew raw gasoline. And then there's the small matter of the odometer. It clocks in at 97,000 miles, but I gotta figure it's double that number, given the age of the vehicle."

That's some sales pitch, you think to yourself. *Who could possibly resist?*

"Normally, I wouldn't part with it for less than three bills, but I remember seeing you at Fort Riley 'round the time of Desert Storm," he says to Timothy McVeigh. "Let's call it a service discount," Tom adds, "and settle up for $250. I'll even throw in some transmission fluid and a spare tire."

"Beggars can't be choosers," says your partner, smiling to himself as he hands over the cash, seemingly without a care in the world. If you didn't know any better, you'd think he was a tourist, innocently trekking his way across the country.

TIMOTHY McVEIGH IS DRIVING the Ford Mercury Marquis out of the Dreamland Motel's gravelly parking lot. The car hiccups and coughs as your driver steers it, gingerly, onto the freeway. One big rig after another passes your ancient vehicle, leaving you and your partner in its dusty, unruly wake.

The Marquis is a truly ugly and unimpressive car, you think to yourself.

Oh, what the heck. *The Marquis is a truly ugly and unimpressive car,* you say out loud to Timothy McVeigh.

"Shut the fuck up, JD," he replies curtly. "We're on a budget here—a no-frills budget." His face is still pink and blotchy from your barrage of fisticuffs back in the motel room.

Timothy McVeigh brings the vehicle to a stop next to a historical marker just south of Herington on U.S. Highway 56. The seal of the great state of Kansas is welded above the sign, depicting the sun rising as a steamboat chugs downriver, transporting wealth and prosperity to a grateful nation. The historical marker itself commemorates the 1825 treaty between the federal government and the Osage nation that afforded settlers safe passage along the Santa Fe Trail. *And we've been wreaking havoc all over the place ever since,* you think to yourself sarcastically.

As you gaze at the sign, Terry Nichols pulls up in a battered old pickup truck. His decrepit Honda has joined the Road Warrior and the Pontiac, it seems, in the great junkyard in the sky.

Did you just drive in from the Thumb? you ask Terry.

"Marife and I live in Herington now," your kidnapper replies, quietly as always. "Been living there since I got back from the Philippines."

Why would he visit the Philippines? you wonder to yourself. He already has a mail-order bride. *Perhaps he's about to become the world's first mail-order bigamist?*

"See you at the rendezvous point," your partner announces.

Sweet Jesus, another secret rendezvous, you think to yourself, recalling Grandpa Walton and his veritable Roman legion of feds back in Cairo, gripping their assault rifles in the bushes and waiting, *just waiting,* to deal out a lethal dose of Judgment Day for you and your boon companion.

AS TIMOTHY McVEIGH SPEEDS along the interstate toward your mysterious destination—toward Oklahoma City (*you're not a dolt, you can read a map*)—you wonder how long you will be able to keep up the charade.

You've gone plenty far already, you think to yourself. You've been to Kingman, and you've cleaned out the Candy Store. You've even been to Elohim City and back. How far will you be able to go—*how far will you be willing to go?*—before you make your final, calculated move? The final, calculated move that, in a moment of great heroism and unassailable virtue, saves the day? Not to mention Timothy McVeigh's life and the lives of countless others. Perhaps even the life of Dakota Fish.

And maybe even your own.

Before you know it, your partner is guiding the Marquis along the familiar streets of downtown Oklahoma City. But instead of making the expected left turn onto North Robinson, he suddenly cuts down the alleyway behind the Y.M.C.A. building. As your blood brother predicted during your previous visit, Santa Claus is long gone by now, working his tail off, you can only imagine, for yet another Christmas season in the not-so-distant future.

Moments later, your partner brings the Marquis to a stop in a corner of the weed-ridden city parking lot that he selected back in December. As always, Timothy McVeigh is thinking several moves ahead, producing a hand-lettered sign from the glove compartment for your inspection. It reads "Not abandoned. Please do not tow. Will move by April 23. (Needs battery & cable.)"

While your partner places a blue, gas-station tissue wipe over the vehicle's fuel cap, you carefully affix the sign inside the musty, driver's side window of the Ford Mercury Marquis.

"If the tissue's been tampered with when we get back here on Wednesday," Timothy McVeigh explains, "then we'll know that the feds have been sniffing around. That we're under surveillance and that we have to initiate Plan B."

What, in the name of all that is holy, is Plan B?

As your partner begins walking back toward the alley, you take one last, lingering glance at the ugly and unimpressive Marquis. *At your faded yellow getaway car.*

As you stroll across the pavement in front of the Y.M.C.A. building onto Northwest Fifth Street, Oklahoma City is beginning to surrender to dusk. And Terry Nichols is nowhere to be found.

"I will personally kill that son of a bitch if he's left us in the lurch!" your partner exclaims to the empty streetscape. Ahead of you towers the glossy front of the Murrah Building, its massive windowpanes transforming from a baleful black to a brownish tint as the evening sun fades on the horizon.

"Where could that Michigan schmuck possibly be?" he bellows, glaring up and down the street—past the Greek restaurant and toward some industrial-looking apartment buildings to the west.

Westward ho, you think to yourself automatically.

And then you see him—your former kidnapper. Terry Nichols tooling along Northwest Fifth Street in his ramshackle blue pickup truck.

THE FOUR-HOUR RIDE BACK to Kansas makes for one of the longest journeys of your life, with Timothy McVeigh refusing to speak to— *much less look at*—Terry as he wheels the cramped pickup truck back to Herington. And beyond that, to the Dreamland Motel.

Along the way, Madonna's "Take a Bow" crackles into life on the radio. Dear God, when will it stop—you wonder to yourself—*this Madonna-mania?*

This masquerade is getting older, you sing along automatically.

It sure is, you think to yourself.

Older. Old. So very old.

TIMOTHY McVEIGH IS LUMBERING into Elliott's Body Shop, Junction City's Ryder truck rental franchise. And you, as always, are lagging behind. The sky is turning a soft, yellowish color after the torrential rainstorm that only just ended—and that is now wafting its way off to the east. Toward the Missouri border.

"I'm Robert Kling," your partner remarks to Eldon Elliott, the stocky, fair-haired attendant, "and I'm here for the twenty-footer that I reserved on Saturday."

Will this be the final, shadowy appearance of the elusive Bob Kling? you wonder to yourself. The same Bob Kling who's been burning up the telephone lines from Arizona and Michigan to Texas and Oklahoma? All across the continental United States and then back again.

Wearing your trusty Carolina Panthers cap, you glance around the establishment at the other patrons. A tall, dark-haired man is waiting in line behind you. He is staring intently at the tattoo on your upper arm. Meanwhile, a heavyset woman behind the counter is looking in your direction. Smiling as she eyes you from head to toe. *As if she were storing your image in her memory banks.*

"The vehicle is ready and waitin' out back," announces Eldon Elliott helpfully. "I see that you've prepaid the balance in full. The only thing left is the small matter of the optional hazard insurance," he adds, "but that's entirely up to you, sir."

Smiling quietly to himself, Timothy McVeigh shoots a quick look in your direction—as if to say, *They want me to buy insurance on this thing? On a truck I'm gonna blow to fuckin' smithereens?*

Having declined the option, your partner signs the rental agreement. Eldon Elliott dutifully time-stamps the Ryder documents and sends you on your way.

"Have a safe trip," says the attendant convivially. "Ya'll come back and see us!"

The time is 4:19 p.m.

YOU WAKE UP, early the next morning, to the gut-wrenching sounds of Timothy McVeigh screaming into the telephone.

"Get in your fuckin' truck!" your partner barks into the receiver. "*Now!* This is for keeps!"

You gaze in the direction of the paper-thin wall that separates your room from the manager's office next door. You can't help but wonder how much longer you can stay at the Dreamland Motel without wearing out your welcome. *Without attracting undue attention.*

"That sorry bastard is gonna blow this whole thing wide open," your partner tells you, slamming the telephone onto its cradle. "Leave it up to Terry to bring this action to a grinding halt."

WITHIN A MATTER OF HOURS, you are standing on the bluffs overlooking Herington. Standing in front of your old familiar haunt—storage unit number two.

Together you and Timothy McVeigh begin unwrapping the faded Christmas packages, which have been languishing inside the storage unit since you returned from Elohim City. Much to your partner's relief, the Tovex and the blasting caps remain intact. The Winchester repeating rifle is there as well, leaning against a nearby wall—not far from the bags of ammonium nitrate fertilizer, which seem to have tripled in number since you last visited the storage facility. In addition to the barrels of liquid nitromethane, there are stacks of empty, 55-gallon translucent drums. And there are hundreds of feet of green cannon fuse, wrapped together neatly in coiled strands.

After Timothy McVeigh backs the Ryder truck into the storage area, you begin loading the materials into the cargo bay. As you carefully maneuver the heavy barrels of highly flammable nitromethane into the vehicle, Terry finally makes the scene, bringing his pickup truck to an abrupt stop beside the storage unit.

"Dude, the rental truck is already halfway loaded," says your partner, chiding Terry for his habitual lateness. "We're damned near ready to drive out to the lake."

YOUR DRIVER IS BESIDE HIMSELF as he pilots the Ryder truck some twenty-one miles outside of Herington, with Terry following closely behind in the blue pickup.

"Terry freakin' Nichols isn't a patriot—he's a goddamned saboteur," says Timothy McVeigh. "Our friend from Michigan is attempting, single-handedly, to derail this mission. *And I won't have it.* He'll be lucky, I tell you, if he doesn't end the day with a bullet in his head."

As your partner gently steers the truck off of the highway, you find yourself on the fringes of a tranquil state park. Timothy McVeigh wheels the vehicle through a wooded preserve and, beyond that, to the edge of a modest lake. As he brings the Ryder truck to a halt, your partner gestures, ominously, toward a nearby sign that reads "Geary State Fishing Lake. Obey All Signs as Posted. Ranger on Duty."

"Ranger Rick better not do any snooping around," cautions Timothy McVeigh, fingering the Glock in his shoulder holster. "It's go time—and we're not going down for the count in the backwaters of Kansas. Not by a long shot. *No sirree.*"

As you and Terry start arranging the materials inside the cargo bay, your partner begins his maneuvers, walking a regular beat outside the rental truck. You observe Timothy McVeigh as he gazes across the lake with his Thousand-Yard Stare. His battle-weary soul is in full force, you think to yourself, and it's going to take everything you have—*and then some*—to derail his last, most desperate mission.

At one critical juncture, a man and his young son troll nearby in a fishing boat, putting Timothy McVeigh on high alert. Glaring at the fishermen from the side of the Ryder truck, your partner begins plotting their demise.

"If they come any closer," he tells you, "I'm gonna shoot the father right between the eyes to minimize the amount of gunfire. Meanwhile, I want you to grab the kid," he continues, "and we'll restrain him in the cab with some duct tape and a blindfold that I've stowed away in the glove compartment. We can let him go in the morning— he'll be no worse for wear, and the action will go ahead as planned."

Except that he'll be an orphan, you think to yourself.

"But how would you dispose of the body?" asks Terry inquisitively.

Without uttering a word, Timothy McVeigh gestures toward the cargo bay, already brimming with explosives. As usual, your partner has thought of everything—plotting out every contingency well in advance. But before you can act, the father powers the fishing boat to another part of the lake, and the threat passes without incident. *At least for now.*

And then Timothy McVeigh takes charge with a vengeance, supervising Terry Nichols and yourself like you were a couple of green recruits. Which in your case is entirely true.

As the afternoon sun pours down upon the yellow rental truck, your partner begins arranging the 55-gallon drums in the shape of a capital *T,* with the top of the letter sitting flush against the cab. With you and Terry operating a bucket brigade of sorts, you distribute the liquid nitromethane and the fertilizer among the giant plastic drums.

At times, Timothy McVeigh's bizarre crew of bombardiers seems more like the Keystone Kops than a gang of cold-blooded conspirators.

"Hand me the—the whatchamacallit," says Terry as you attempt to deploy the Tovex and the blasting caps.

"The what?" answers Timothy McVeigh tersely.

"The—*you know,*" says Terry, fumbling for words.

"*The what?*" barks your partner.

"The sausage," says Terry.

Sausage—but not sausage! you think to yourself automatically.

With his massive weapon's shock charge finally in place, Timothy McVeigh begins drilling holes in the cab of the Ryder truck in order to facilitate the dispersal of the cannon fuse.

"This is the perfect redundancy," says your partner. "Two fuses completely independent of each other and wired into completely independent caps." It's as if he were talking, nonchalantly, about a science project. *As if he were looking for your approval.*

"We'll be able to light a two-minute fuse and a five-minute fuse from inside the cab," he continues. "Failing that, I'll stand outside the truck and begin shooting it with my sidearm. One way or another," he concludes, "it'll be *mission accomplished.*"

Standing behind the truck, you exchange knowing glances with Terry, who seems to be on the verge of experiencing new levels of stress and catatonia. Fraught in his anxiety, he can do nothing but stare, blankly, at the sodden ground beside the lake bed. For your part, you realize that your awful work is nearly over. *That a new phase of your journey with your blood brother is only just beginning.*

Walking around to the rear of the vehicle, Timothy McVeigh gently tosses the Winchester into the back of the Ryder truck, laying it to rest among the 55-gallon drums of liquid death.

"Now *that's* how the West was won," he exclaims as he carefully lowers then latches the truck's massive rear door.

Plunging his terrible payload into darkness.

25 Lighting Out for the Territory

As daylight gives way to the dark of night, Timothy McVeigh wheels the Ryder truck into Ponca City, Oklahoma, pop. 26,359. Steering the heavy-laden vehicle off of the interstate, he brings it to a rest in a vacant parking lot behind a McDonald's.

Across the highway, the neon lights of Amazing Ray's American Steakhouse are all lit up, blinking and winking in the nighttime sky.

As Timothy McVeigh secures the truck for the evening, you gingerly make your way across the interstate to Amazing Ray's. Using the light from the neon sign as your desk lamp, you hastily scrawl a letter to your mother.

You would love to have told her that she was right about the nausea-inducing bedspreads in sleazy motels and that her advice about the green-eyed monster of jealousy was right on the money. That firecrackers really aren't a toy—that they have no place going off near a person's eyes and ears. And that you can never—*never*—overestimate the value of good manners.

But you don't tell her any of these things, of course.

Instead, you take out a postcard and inscribe it with the only thing that keeps you going—*the selfsame mantra that has kept you alive and kicking lo these many months.* Besides, you figure that your chances of surviving tomorrow are virtually nil, so why get too long-winded about much of anything?

"Don't worry," you write. "I am heeding the call." And then, as a hasty afterthought, you add, "Won't be back forever."

AS YOU AWAKEN from another deep, dreamless sleep, you are stunned by the sight of Timothy McVeigh thrusting an MRE in your direction.

"Eat up," he instructs. "You're gonna need your strength today." Lucky for you, it's beef Stroganoff. *Your favorite.*

Timothy McVeigh is wearing his battle gear—a black baseball cap, black sunglasses, black jeans, and his favorite T-shirt—the one depicting the Liberty Tree shedding the blood of freedom and democracy. Spurting plasma in equal, deadly doses all over the patriots and tyrants of the world.

Amen, blood brother, you think to yourself derisively.

You are already wearing your own battle gear, having slept in it last night in the cab of the rental truck. Meanwhile, your partner is pacing back and forth, checking the fluid levels under the hood, staring vacantly off into the distance. He's clearly nervous, you think to yourself. Anxious to get the day underway.

"Fuck it," Timothy McVeigh suddenly exclaims. "It's go time."

But what about the lunchtime traffic? you ask. The body count?

"We're ready. We're waiting. We're in the trim. Let's do it now," your partner instructs.

You shrug your shoulders in response.

"Let's roll," he announces confidently—with nary a care in the world.

PULLING DOWN THE VISOR in order to deflect the bright morning sun, Timothy McVeigh eases the yellow Ryder truck into traffic.

A light blue minivan coasts in front of you with a bumper sticker that reads "We are making enemies faster than we can kill them."

Your partner switches on the radio, and the hip-hop thump of R. Kelly's "Bump n' Grind" explodes into being.

My mind's telling me no, you think to yourself automatically. *But my body, my body's telling me yes.*

The Ryder truck screams across the silty gray surface of the interstate, its gaudy yellow skin beaming in the morning sunlight.

Southbound, coasting safely below the speed limit, the truck rattles onward, with its quartet of winking hubcaps encircled by their muddy, road-worn tires held earthbound on their spinning axles.

The truck's cargo door bounces and shakes, its canvas handle whipping in its unruly wake. The truck's curt, unsmiling bumper passes no judgment, revealing no emotion, no prejudice. *Nothing.*

There is purpose in the vehicle's forward momentum, in its blind ambition, in its frenetic journey across the plains. The time is rapidly—almost effortlessly, in spite of itself—becoming nigh.

FOR SEVERAL MILES, a police car coasts along behind you, even though your partner is being absurdly careful to stay within the speed limit. To avoid arousing attention.

"Maybe I'm going *too* slow?" says Timothy McVeigh as the police cruiser pulls alongside the Ryder truck.

This is one way of thwarting disaster, you think to yourself. For a moment, you consider leaning forward and signaling the police officer—alerting him that you've been kidnapped by a madman or something to that spine-chilling effect. He'd have to pull Timothy McVeigh over, and the nightmare would abruptly end. Would end in sudden death—*but at least it would end.*

The worst thing that could happen is that you and Timothy McVeigh could die in some preposterous, balls-to-the-wall shootout—or be blown sky-high. Either way, this rig would never make it downtown. Would never make it to Northwest Fifth Street.

But before you can act, the police car zooms ahead, losing itself in the morning traffic. Heading southbound—toward the city.

TIMOTHY McVEIGH PULLS the Ryder truck into a rest stop at mile marker 225, not too far from Lake Perry on I-35. "Let's get out and stretch our legs for a bit," he announces.

Good idea, you think to yourself. You desperately need to relieve the tension. From the stress that is coming. *The tension and stress from what you know you must do.*

You climb out of the truck and look around the rest stop. Timothy McVeigh lingers behind, fidgeting with something—a map perhaps?—in the cab.

You glance just beyond the Ryder truck at a hunter green station wagon, its doors open slightly, the radio softly playing in the background. In the parking lot, a young mother pushes an inflatable beach ball back and forth with her toddler, a quirky smile on his face as the ball bounces above the pavement. His eyes darting up and down as the beach ball's *mélange* of colors—*red, white, yellow, and blue*—spins like a pinwheel over his head.

Timothy McVeigh is still sitting in the Ryder truck, staring at you as you gaze, blithely, at the toddler. Your partner rolls down the passenger's seat window. You turn to answer his call.

"I'm sorry, JD. I know you didn't want for this to happen," he says, gently depressing the lock on the passenger's side of the Ryder truck.

For what to happen? you think to yourself confoundedly.

The look on his face tells you everything you need to know. Everything that it was possible—*ever*—to know about your partner. *About Timothy McVeigh.*

You thought that you could change this. Could stop it from happening.

"You could never stop it," says your partner. "It was always happening. Always gonna happen. You can never stop the Day of the Rope."

This was always a military mission, wasn't it? you ask him. Long before we went to Waco—*before we met, even?*

"This was always a military mission," Timothy McVeigh repeats, almost in a whisper—seemingly without emotion. "It was always gonna be this way," he continues. "Gonna end just like this."

You stand quietly by the roadside. Next to the yellow Ryder truck. *Thunderstruck.*

"You're still my best and only friend," he adds.

You wipe back tears, sudden and unexpected. Tears that, for the life of you, you cannot possibly begin to understand.

"I'll see you in the skies," he says with the first hint of sadness you've heard in his voice. Looking at you with a warmth in his eyes that you have scarcely seen before—or since.

Timothy McVeigh puts the Ryder truck in gear. He takes one last, lingering glance in your direction. His face is expressionless. His eyes wide open. *Unblinking.*

He is gone.

26 Phoenix Unbound

You are standing alone on the roadside, and you are dumbstruck in your predicament. You are absolutely dumbfounded by this sudden and unexpected turn of events.

In the distance, Timothy McVeigh pilots the Ryder truck onto the interstate. You watch, mouth agape, as the vehicle's bright yellow cargo bay vanishes beyond the tree line. The truck's bumper gleams briefly in the morning sun. As if it were winking at you. *As if it were saying farewell.*

And you are alone. Abruptly and mind-numbingly alone. Flummoxed in your disbelief—in your helplessness—as your partner steers his homemade bomb toward its unimpeded oblivion. *Where is God in here?* you wonder to yourself.

You glance rearward—toward the parking lot of the rest stop, where the young mother still busies herself with her toddler as he grasps at the beach ball with his tiny, outstretched hands.

And you know exactly what you must do. You have no choice, really, as you make a break for the hunter green station wagon.

As you slam the driver's side door shut behind you, the mother turns with a shriek. Locking the door, you fumble with the ignition. The toddler begins crying loudly as the beach ball rolls toward the dusty roadway. And his mother—*God help her*—begins pounding on the window glass with her balled-up fists.

And then it occurs to you—belatedly as usual—that you have never driven a car before. And that your driver—*the only driver you have ever really known*—is making his escape somewhere, southbound, along I-35.

The mother continues banging away at the driver's side window, punching it with all of her might and spewing a fusillade of expletives in your direction.

"What the fuck are you doing?" she screams.

She should really mind her language in front of the baby, you think to yourself as you throw the car into gear. The station wagon bolts into reverse, slamming backward, violently, as it comes to a rest at the base of a nearby pine tree. The sound of crunching metal is overwhelmed by the vehicle's engine, which whizzes and whirs in frustration against the brittle, swollen bark.

Shaken by the collision—*but undeterred in your resolve*—you thrust the station wagon into drive. You realize—as the vehicle leaps forward, rocketing beyond the bawling toddler and his angry mother—that your foot has never left the accelerator since you turned over the ignition.

AND LIKE A FLASH, you are on the interstate, bobbing and weaving among the morning traffic. Thundering your way toward the city in a mad dash to thwart your partner. To remake your destiny before it's too late.

You are terrified beyond belief as you make your way along the highway. You grip the wheel of the station wagon with all of your might, your hands slick with sweat as you hang on for dear life.

At one point, you glimpse a yellow box truck up ahead in the distance. Cruising along beside the vehicle, you are startled to see a family—father, mother, and wee baby daughter—ensconced across the front seat. In the act of moving, you can only guess, to their new life in Oklahoma City. You can only hope that they're not planning to live downtown.

As the skyline looms ahead, the station wagon is slowed by the growing throng of rush-hour traffic merging onto the spur to I-235. For a moment, you consider taking your chances and driving along the highway's gravelly shoulder. But just as suddenly, the traffic opens up, and you coast the vehicle onto the Centennial Expressway off-ramp.

But there is still no Timothy McVeigh in evidence—only one carload after another filled with road-weary, unknowing commuters. Anxious to start the day.

As the city comes into view, you bank the station wagon onto Harrison Avenue, clipping the curb, somewhat forcefully, as you weave your way onto Northwest Fourth Street, where the traffic grinds to a halt yet again. Just ahead, beyond the rail yards and the vacant lots, waits the Murrah Federal Building, its elevator shaft towering aloft in solemn, concrete triumph.

Scanning your eyes across the horizon, you catch sight of a break in the traffic at Gaylord Boulevard. With nothing to lose—and with Northwest Fourth Street caught in a virtual standstill—you gun the station wagon across the boulevard. *It may not be the Road Warrior,* you think to yourself, *but it will have to do.*

Cutting across the twin lanes of Northwest Sixth Street, you glide the station wagon, southbound, along Robinson Avenue before coming to a stop—*finally*—among the throng of traffic purring alongside the old Y.M.C.A. building. Up ahead, on the extreme right, looms the glossy beige exterior of the Murrah Building, the sun glancing off of its massive tinted windowpanes.

And there, parked in the loading zone in front of the building, is the yellow Ryder truck. As you crane your neck forward, you can just make out your partner, his black baseball cap and ceremonial T-shirt in full view, as he steps out of the cab, tosses the keys into the compartment, and gently closes the door.

Climbing out of the station wagon, you catch a glimpse of Timothy McVeigh as he walks away from the Ryder truck, briskly, before disappearing into the alleyway that you know so well. The very same alleyway that you hurtled along inside of the Road Warrior lo those many months ago.

But as sure as you're standing there on Robinson Avenue, Timothy McVeigh ceases to matter. He has transformed from star to bit player in a matter of seconds.

And there is nothing left to see. Only the sight of the yellow Ryder truck, resting in the shadows of the Murrah Building. Waiting for the zero hour that only you, seemingly, can preempt.

Running, you lunge your way forward, hurling your body mindlessly in the direction of the loading zone. Desperately making your way toward the engine of Timothy McVeigh's despair.

But then you feel it.

The massive onrush of the explosion's powerful vacuum lifts you clean off of the ground, dropping you several yards behind in its awful wake. You land squarely on your back on the warm, unforgiving pavement of Robinson Avenue. As you writhe in sudden pain, your Carolina Panthers cap topples gently off of your scalp.

You are overwhelmed by the detonation's thunderclap, the sky transforming from its vivid, azure blue into the bright light of a firestorm before plunging the streetscape into an odd, unexpected midmorning darkness. The air is filled with the milky haze of soot and smoke, the sound of flash fires crackling in the foreground, the unruly noise of nearby buildings as they crumble upon their foundations. And the wispy, dreadful spitter-spatter of glass raining downward upon the avenue. Pocking and slashing its victims with sinister precision.

And you—all you can do is lie there, prostrate on the roadway. Gasping—the wind knocked out of you—as you struggle for oxygen. For a breath of fresh air among the chaos and the mayhem.

As you gather your wits, you are struck by the random brutality of it all. Fingering the AirLite that still fits, snuggly, in your waistband, you realize that Timothy McVeigh's violence is simultaneously much more profound—*and even more unthinking*—than the simple demolition of a French grammar book. Or the gnawing, indiscriminate hate nursed by a backwoods militiaman. Or the furtive, revolutionary buzz of a gun show in full subversive swing.

You recognize, pointedly, that you've never really witnessed violence before. That you've never actually stood in the shadows of cruelty.

Until now.

Nonchalantly gathering up your Carolina Panthers cap—an inexplicably normal act in a day that increasingly defies explanation—you lift yourself up, standing in front of the darkness and the flame that linger before you in the gaping chasm of the Murrah Building. As you gaze at the destruction, the deafening, ringing sound in your ears begins to give way to the siren song of car alarms, literally thousands of them, chirping and erupting in their terrible dirge.

Loping along the wreckage of Northwest Fifth Street—the mangled automobiles, the scattered steel beams, and the broken brickwork hindering your path—you stagger to a halt in front of what used to be a thriving Greek restaurant, a coffee shop for the workaday world that sat across the street from the federal building. What was a bustling eatery only moments earlier has become transformed into a smoldering, fire-addled vision of its former self.

And there, slouching against the shattered lunch counter, lies a torn and tousled businessman, blood streaming from his forehead, shards of glass poking from the skin on his soot-covered face. His eyes glazed over in horror and shock. For an instant, you stare at each other—one casualty to another—before your better angels wrest hold of you.

Lifting him up by the shoulders, you lead him—*slowly, gingerly*—away from the blistering rubble of the Murrah Building. Away from the conflagration behind you and toward the morning light still glowing ahead in the distance. Toward the clear light of day that calls from the north.

As you amble along the avenue, you are met by a pair of stunned paramedics as they climb out of their red emergency vehicle.

"What the fuck was that?" says the younger, mustached paramedic as he gestures toward the city's burning, central core. Taking the wounded man from your arms, they go about the business of rescuing their first victim of the day—one of the lucky ones in a day that would be remembered for the numerous, less fortunate who would never walk away. *Who would never know what hit them.*

As the streets begin to overflow with police cruisers and satellite vehicles, with fire trucks and ambulances on high alert, you continue walking ever northward, back toward the interstate that delivered you into Oklahoma City. And as the news helicopters begin circling overhead, you hitch a ride out of town with a trio of suburban carpoolers eager to flee their city in ruins. Settling into the backseat of a Range Rover next to a dazed, bespectacled C.P.A.—"Who would do such a thing?" she mutters over and over in disbelief—you brush your fingers across your forehead, feeling, for the first time, the lumpy, coagulated texture of the dried blood that coats your naked skin like a shell.

"You look like hell, friend," announces the driver, arching his eyebrows as he glances at you in the rearview mirror. "I'd hate to see that ice-cream parlor of yours now," he adds, shaking his head back and forth with concern.

"Where can we take you?" he asks, pulling the vehicle into the traffic streaming away from downtown.

Don't worry, you think to yourself as you stare out of the window at the vehicles departing in droves beyond the city limits. At the citizenry who became refugees in the blink of an eye.

"Where can we drop you off, pal?" he asks again, his voice brimming over with compassion. With the milk of human kindness.

Don't worry, you repeat to yourself. You know exactly where to go. You know just the place.

27 Lazy Circles in the Sky

You are standing on the dusty off-ramp at mile marker 225, with the tractor-trailers whipping by on the interstate just beyond the rest stop. You still have $11 nestled away in your wallet, along with the AirLite revolver tucked safely into your waistband. You are carrying your dorm-room key and your "Jot It Down" pad in your trouser pockets, and your trusty Carolina Panthers cap—*your battle gear*—rests securely on the top of your head.

You have nothing else in the entire world to call your own. Nothing but your name. Your personal inventory, as always, is remarkably static.

You are alone.

YOU ARE STILL WEARING your Good Humor outfit. And according to your smock, you are still Daryl.

You realize, with a tiny *frisson* of fear, that your identity crises never cease. You are a Quaker, first and foremost, but you are also a fornicator, an attempted murderer, an armed robber, and a gunrunner. And for some fifteen months on the highways and byways of the lower 48, you rode with Timothy McVeigh.

Mostly in silence, but you rode with him nonetheless.

You realize that you no longer know who you are. That you have lost your sense of self—your identity. In your days at Friends University, you pursued a degree—as of yet unfinished, *probably won't be finished*—in English literature. But you have always had the heart of a mathematician.

You decide to begin your identity reconstruction by inscribing a mathematical proof on your "Jot It Down" pad. Only a proof, you think to yourself, can assist you in logically deducing the component parts of your existence, in disentangling the unruly threads of your irreverent Quaker soul:

> You are Daryl—Daryl Bridges.
> If you are going to be Daryl, then you can no longer be JD.
> And if you are no longer JD, then you are no longer you.
> And if you are no longer you, then you will have to become, irrevocably, somebody else.
> Q.E.D.

And if you are to become somebody else—to effect real and abiding change in your life—then you have no choice but to destroy the past. To learn from it—*to be certain*—but to destroy its awful remnants in order, finally, to move forward into the arms of your new, inalienable self. *Into the arms of the future.*

You are inspired by your new sense of personhood. Not to mention your new name—*which must remain a mystery for obvious legal reasons*. You commemorate the precise moment of your rebirth—right here on the rest-stop bench, no less—by composing a haiku. By committing your soul to the poetry of the ancients:

> shadow
> what the tree gives the ground
> and the cloud takes away

Fearing that you will lose sight of your creation, that you will misplace it within the recesses of a less-than-perfect memory, you hastily inscribe the haiku on your "Jot It Down" pad. *But you are loath to discover that there is only a single page left.*

You will have to make the most of it, you think to yourself. The most of your final page. You have waded into the river of no return, and you have lived—remarkable as it may seem—to tell about it.

You remember the Widow Watson's parting words. *What the caterpillar thinks is the end, the butterfly thinks is the beginning.*

It is high time, indeed, that you started thinking like a butterfly.

AS YOU STAND ALONE at mile marker 225, you recognize, intuitively, that you need to lighten your load. To ease the burden that you carry on your back. You have a long and uncertain journey ahead, and there is no time like the present—as your mother used to say—to rid yourself of the earthly possessions that are weighing you down.

You hike to a clearing that lies a few hundred yards behind the rest stop. Kneeling on the ground, you begin digging a shallow grave with your bare, uncalloused hands. Removing the AirLite from your waistband, you bury the revolver in the freshly riven dirt. Where it can no longer hurt anyone. *Where you can no longer hurt anyone.*

You know, in your heart, that you will never see Timothy McVeigh again. He has become lost, irretrievably, among the shadows of the tree. And he has been taken away—*just as all of the lost souls of the world have been taken away*—on the wings of the clouds. You know that you will never understand the evil that exists deep within his heart, and how it manages, time and time again, to outwit the beauty and intelligence—the kindness, even—that lingers in his soul. If only you could help him tame those demons. To wrestle them to the death. If only—

But that door is closed. Finally and ineffably closed. And you will have to learn to live—*somehow, someway*—with that reality.

YOU ARE RIDING on a Greyhound bus, drifting along Highway 50 just outside of Emporia, Kansas, pop. 25,512. The day begins to give way to dusk as acres and acres of farmland—dairy farms morphing into cattle ranches and the occasional wheat field—stream beside your window. An elderly Hispanic woman leans on your shoulder, snoring softly to herself with a copy of *People* magazine clutched in one hand and an empty bag of Fritos in the other. She is wearing your Carolina Panthers cap, which you traded for the balance of your bus fare. As luck would have it, she adores American football.

That night, you dream about a great storm—*a tornado*—that tears across the plains, decimating everything as it makes its brutal progress across the Heartland. It is accompanied by a terrible conflagration, and it heralds no wisdom nor hope of reconciliation. Only suffering and pain. Bitterness and confusion.

You wake up in a cold sweat, shivering from the awful reality of your vision, before falling back to sleep once more—into a deep and restful sleep in which you experience yet another dream. It is a profound reverie about love and redemption. A dream of a new future among the living. It is a dream about Gina. And you. And a new life together somewhere far away. *Somewhere else.*

Quakers were our country's first pioneers, you think to yourself. Perhaps you will rise again—enjoying a new spiritual renaissance just in time for a new millennium? A renewed sense of freedom for a brave new world.

You resolve to be like Dakota Fish and go back to the reservation. Tipping over Plymouth Rock and erasing and rewriting the American charter in the process. In your fondest dreams, you imagine that you and Gina will be like the Quaker Adam and Eve. Repopulating the world in a splendid veil of pacifism, quietude, and light. *Everlasting eternal light.*

You will triple your efforts, you decide. Come morning, you will be in Hannibal, where you will seek out your lost Quaker love. Your platonic sweetheart. You will give it another go—the old college try. You will forgive Gina for her failings, as she forgives you for your trespasses against her. You will revel in the silence—the silence of a new day and of a new nation *in potentia.*

God speaks by silence and can be heard in silence, you think to yourself. You will embrace God's silence and drape yourself in His light. You will try your darnedest—really and truly this time—to heed the call of concern.

As the Heartland greets the dawn outside the bus, you slide the window open. Stretching your arms toward the heavens, you gently release your "Jot It Down" pad to the morning breeze, its pages dancing and flittering in the air before coming to rest among the seedlings that pock the Missouri farmland. Settling back into your seat, you avert your eyes as the sun's glare fills up the faded interior of the bus. As the Greyhound hurtles ever eastward, you are trying not to think about Oklahoma City anymore.

You have cast your lot to the wind.

Afterword

As history well knows, Timothy James McVeigh was executed by lethal injection on June 11, 2001, in Terre Haute, Indiana, pop. 59,614. Exactly three months later, 19 Middle Eastern hijackers brought his dubious record for domestic terrorism to a sudden, cataclysmic end with the deaths of nearly 3,000 innocent civilians. But the devastation wrought by McVeigh still resounds—not merely regarding the 168 lives that he ended on that fateful day in April 1995, but also in terms of the misery experienced by the untold number of survivors and the families forever torn asunder by his act of inhuman brutality.

Attempting to understand this uncharacteristic moment of evil in McVeigh's otherwise law-abiding, ethically centered life is the stuff of futility. While McVeigh later claimed that the Oklahoma City bombing was in direct retaliation for the federal government's role in bringing the Branch Davidians to their ruin in Waco, others saw his actions as the result of a larger complex of issues—namely, personal disappointment over his failed effort to join the Special Forces, his inability to find stable and fulfilling employment in the aftermath of his life in the armed forces, and his subsequent, lonely trek across the United States as a renegade gun dealer. This latter aspect of his pre–Oklahoma City life brought him into the orbit of a number of personally influential figures, including the Nichols brothers, whom he had known from his days back in Operation Desert Storm, gun collector Roger Moore, and eminently more radical characters such as Andreas "Andy the German" Strassmeir and the denizens of Elohim City.

Yet it was McVeigh's most notorious fellow prisoner in the Florence, Colorado, supermax penitentiary who gave rise to our understanding of the Oklahoma City bomber's displaced status in twentieth-century American life. As McVeigh's prison-mate and onetime confidante, the Unabomber, Ted Kaczynski, later wrote, "I suspect that he is an adventurer by nature, and America since the closing of the frontier has had little room for adventurers." Could it be that McVeigh's act of tyranny was more the result of a wayward, lonely adventurer executing a misguided "science project," in the words of Gore Vidal, as opposed to a raging gun nut determined to rain down evil in order to release his venom? Was the Oklahoma City bombing an act of political terrorism or the by-product of a troubled soul—lost, as he was, in the detritus of his ineffectual late twenties?

Equally beguiling are the identities of the "others unknown"—in the parlance of McVeigh's defense attorney, Stephen Jones—who may or may not have assisted the accused in the destruction of the Alfred P. Murrah Federal Building. Although the roles of Terry Nichols and Michael Fortier in the loose conspiracy of the bombing are well known, the guilt of additional confederates has been lost to the fog of history. Nichols narrowly escaped death and was sentenced to life without parole, while Fortier served some eight years in prison before joining his wife, Lori, in the Witness Protection Program in the new century.

As for John Doe No. 2, there is no convincing evidence that he ever existed, only rumor and hearsay during the onset of the largest manhunt in American history. Aside from the mysterious appearance of a man in a body shop wearing a Carolina Panthers cap and sporting a conspicuous tattoo on his arm, the ghostly figure of John Doe No. 2 has never materialized. Beyond the F.B.I. wanted posters and the whispers and shadows of an increasingly paranoid American culture, he remains the epitome of "others unknown."

Acknowledgments

Special thanks are due to Lou Michel and Dan Herbeck for their indispensable volume *American Terrorist: Timothy McVeigh and the Oklahoma City Bombing* (2001), as well as to Jon Hersley, Larry Tongate, and Bob Burke for *Simple Truths: The Real Story of the Oklahoma City Bombing Investigation* (2004). Without these vital works of investigative scholarship, tracing McVeigh's final trek across the United States would have been virtually impossible. I owe a similar debt to Dick J. Reavis for *The Ashes of Waco: An Investigation* (1998) and Jack L. Willcuts for *Why Friends Are Friends: Some Quaker Core Convictions* (1984).

I would especially like to thank Ian Marshall, who graciously lent me his haiku for my novel's final chapter, "Lazy Circles in the Sky." I am also indebted to a host of friends for their encouragement and support, including Lori J. Bechtel-Wherry, Dick Caram, James Decker, Bill Engelbret, George Gardner, Ranjan Ghosh, Michele Kennedy, Carl Larsen, Colleen Lumadue, Gerty MacDowell, Amy Mallory-Kani, Heather McCoy, Nick Miskovsky, Dinty W. Moore, Joe Petrulionis, Steve Sherrill, Rebecca Strzelec, Bob Trumpbour, Nancy Vogel, Tim Wherry, L.A. Wilson, and Fred Womack.

I am thankful, moreover, for the enthusiasm and advice of Alex

Schwartz and Josh Getzler, whose recommendations made formative differences in the direction of my narrative, and particularly to Todd Davis, whose generosity and insight left an indelible mark on nearly every page. I am also indebted to the staff of Switchgrass Books, especially to Tracy Schoenle for her skillful editorial vision, Linda Manning for her French acumen, and Shaun Allshouse for his inspired cover design. I am grateful, finally, to my wife, Jeanine, whose unquenchable reservoirs of love and friendship made all the difference.

Lightning Source UK Ltd.
Milton Keynes UK
UKHW010824300919
350630UK00012B/139/P

9 780875 806402